PHILLIPA ASHLEY writes warm, funny romantic fiction for a variety of world-famous international publishers.

After studying English at Oxford, she worked as a copywriter and journalist. Her first novel, *Decent Exposure*, won the RNA New Writers Award and was made into a TV movie *12 Men of Christmas* starring Kristin Chenoweth and Josh Hopkins. As Pippa Croft, she also wrote the Oxford Blue series – *The First Time W* — *The Second Time I Saw You* a — *Third Time L* —

Phillipa lives i an engineer husband and so — e her arty whims. She runs — ke District, but a big part of her heart belongs to Cornwall. She visits the country several times a year for 'research purposes', an arduous task that involves sampling cream teas, swimming wild Cornish coves and following actors around film shoots in her campervan. Her hobbies include watching *Poldark*, Earl Grey tea, Prosecco-tasting and falling off surf boards in front of RNLI lifeguards.

 @PhillipaAshley

Also By Phillipa Ashley

Penwith Trilogy
Summer at the Cornish Cafe
Christmas at the Cornish Cafe
Confetti at the Cornish Cafe

Little Cornish Isles
Christmas on the Little Cornish Isles
Spring on the Little Cornish Isles
Summer on the Little Cornish Isles

Porthmellow Harbour
A Perfect Cornish Summer
A Perfect Cornish Christmas
A Perfect Cornish Escape

Return to Cornish Bay
(previously published as *Miranda's Mount*
and *Return to Castle Bay*)

Return to Cornish Bay

Phillipa Ashley

Previously published as
Miranda's Mount and *Return to Castle Bay*

PIATKUS

PIATKUS

First published in Great Britain in 2012 by Piatkus as *Miranda's Mount*
This paperback edition published in 2023 by Piatkus

A CIP catalogue record for this book
is available from the British Library.

ISBN 978-0-7499-5983-8

Typeset in Bembo by M Rules
Printed and bound in Great Britain by
Clays Ltd, Elcograf S.p.A

Papers used by Piatkus are from well-managed forests
and other responsible sources.

Piatkus
An imprint of
Little, Brown Book Group
Carmelite House
50 Victoria Embankment
London EC4Y 0DZ

An Hachette UK Company
www.hachette.co.uk

www.littlebrown.co.uk

For John. ILY

This novel was published as
Miranda's Mount and *Return to Castle Bay*

Acknowledgements

Miranda's Mount was one of those books that was a total joy to write but I couldn't have finished it without the writers and friends who helped me with research tips, encouragement and cakes including Nell Dixon, Elizabeth Hanbury, Rosy Thornton, Moira Briggs and Hilary Ely. I'd also like to give a huge thank you to Donna Condon, Piatkus Entice and the Little Brown team for making me welcome. Finally, to my agent Broo Doherty, my husband John and daughter Charlotte – thank you for your support and faith in me.

Chapter One

Miranda Marshall leaned her elbows on the stone battlements and took a deep breath. This was her favourite spot on the whole of St Merryn's Mount and even though she'd seen the view thousands of times before, she still felt a thrill when she looked at it.

Above her, white clouds chased across the sky and the wind tugged at her hair, making her scalp tingle. More than a hundred feet below, Atlantic breakers crashed onto the rocks, their white foam spraying so high Miranda could almost taste it. The tide was in and the causeway that connected the island to civilisation shimmered beneath the sea like a mermaid's road. When the waters receded, the causeway would be uncovered so visitors could invade the island again.

Which would be good otherwise she'd be out of a job.

But until morning, the pubs and shops, roads and pylons of the Cornish mainland, might as well be a whole world away.

'*Holy crap, Miranda, are you in la-la land again?*'

Even above the waves and the wind, Miranda heard her colleague's voice squawk down the radio fixed to her belt. She snatched it up and called back. 'I'm up on the battlements, Ronnie.'

'That's a relief. I've been trying to call you for the past ten minutes. Can you please get down to this quayside? The last boat's about to leave.'

'What? Already? Are you sure?'

Miranda glanced at her watch and her mouth opened. It really was almost five o'clock. Today had whizzed by faster than Usain Bolt after a super-strength vindaloo.

'The boatman wants to load the last few stragglers. Are you coming down to see them off?'

As property manager of St Merryn's Mount, Miranda had made it a tradition that she always saw the visitors off on the last boat of the day, no matter how tired or busy she was. There were days when she didn't get out of her office, and she thought it was important to get some direct feedback from the punters, even if some of it was a little too 'direct' at times.

'Just give me one minute, Ronnie. Don't let the boat sail without me.'

'One minute to get from the top of the castle to the harbour? Have you grown wings, then?' Ronnie was unable to keep the grin from her voice.

'Of course, didn't you know I sprouted them at the same time I had the broom fixed to my bottom?' Without waiting for a reply, Miranda clipped the radio back on her belt, allowed herself a last glance at the view and dashed down the steps. She staggered onto the quayside just as the castle clock struck five, hoping she'd have the breath to wish the day's last visitors goodbye. Around a dozen of them stood in the queue for the boat that would carry them to the mainland. As usual, this early in the season, it was a mixed bunch. There were a couple of middle-aged heritage buffs clutching their Mount St Merryn carriers, several German backpackers, a bloke wearing ill-advised combat shorts and a towering, hawk-faced woman whose tight-lipped expression threatened trouble. Miranda steeled herself, but still felt confident. After almost a decade working on the island in various roles, she'd been there, done that and got the T-shirt, bra and knickers.

As she walked towards the queue, trying to catch her breath, her attention was drawn to another more intriguing visitor. At the very end of the line was a teenager, which Miranda thought was unusual enough in itself. Only geeks like herself loved places like the Mount, at that age, in Miranda's experience. It was also out of the school holidays and the girl looked too young for a student, though she supposed it was always possible. But the girl's age wasn't the thing that made Miranda curious. It was something else.

Miranda always knew when a person had something to hide. She recognised the signs: the Guilty Shuffle, the Casual Saunter, the Toothy Smile. The teenage girl had gone for the Shuffle. She'd pulled her hood over her head, shoved her hands in the pocket at the front of her sweatshirt and joined the end of the queue, dragging her feet reluctantly.

The queue moved forwards and the teenage girl shrank

even deeper into her hoodie. Miranda helped the hawk-faced woman climb down into the boat. 'Have you had a good visit, madam?'

The visitor glared at Miranda, her moustache on her top lip bristling like a walrus. 'It was quite interesting I suppose,' said the woman, 'but the scones in your café are rather dry. You should use best butter. I'll be writing to your chef with a recipe.'

'Thank you, I'll tell him to watch out for it,' said Miranda, knowing the scones that day had been shipped in from the local superstore because the island baker was off work with shingles.

A middle-aged man with a bushy beard and binoculars dangling from his neck was next to get onto the boat. It was, decided Miranda, turning into a bumper day for impressive facial hair.

The man glanced around him then he lowered his voice. 'Did you know you've got choughs, love?'

Miranda gave a startled gasp. 'Really, sir? Choughs you say?'

'Yes, but for goodness' sake, keep it quiet, or the place will be swarming with twitchers.'

Miranda winked. 'I won't tell a soul, sir.'

The birdwatcher climbed on board, smiling at his secret. He wasn't to know that Miranda was well aware of the rare choughs nesting on the island and had shown around six parties from the RSPB that week alone. The girl in the hoodie was only a few feet away now. Miranda smiled at her, feeling like the crocodile in Peter Pan. Any moment now she was going to open up her jaws and swallow the teenager whole. The girl shuffled forwards, hands in her pockets, desperate to avoid being spoken to.

'Have you enjoyed your visit, madam?'

The teenager grunted.

'I'm so glad to hear it. Is there anything you think we could do to improve it?'

'Wha'?'

'I just wondered if you had any suggestions for making your visit here even better.'

The girl glanced up, nose wrinkling in surprise. 'No.'

She stepped forwards but Miranda was even quicker, slipping between the girl and the gangway to the boat. 'Even so, maybe you can still help us. Is there anything you want to tell me?'

The girl shook her head, her sharp little chin bobbing from side to side. 'I said not, didn't I?'

The girl closed her eyes and seemed to sway as if she might faint. Perhaps it was cruel to torment her, but Miranda had to know what she was hiding in the pocket of her hoodie, even if it was only a spoon nicked from the café.

Miranda went for silky yet menacing, part Bond villain, part Clinique counter assistant. 'Are you absolutely certain I can't help you with anything else, madam? Before it's too late?'

The girl opened her mouth, snapped it shut and gave a long, drawn-out sigh which morphed into a weary, 'Oh, fuck it.' She dragged her hands out of the pocket and withdrew a small parcel, wrapped in a serviette from the café. Miranda took the parcel from the teenager, feeling ever so slightly sick. 'Thank you.'

'You're gonna call the police, aren't you?' The teenager sounded resigned as if this wasn't the first time this had happened to her.

Miranda opened her mouth to say 'Yes, what else did you expect?' then hesitated. Carefully, she unwrapped the serviette's folds, brushing off crumbs. Inside was a small bound book. She recognised it instantly as a medieval bestiary and she didn't have to open it to know what she'd see inside. The thick vellum pages were decorated with animals and mythical beasts, burnished with gold leaf and jewel-like colours. It was one of the Mount's biggest treasures and it should have been kept under lock and key in the library.

'I haven't damaged it. I only wanted to look at it.' The girl's eyes brightened as if she was about to cry.

Miranda saw the dark shadows under her eyes, the hollow cheeks and the fear under the bone-hard expression. Was the wobbling lip all an act or was the girl genuinely scared of getting caught?

'Why did you take it?' she asked.

The girl shrugged. 'Dunno.'

'Why this particular thing? There are a lot of lovely things on the Mount. Pieces made of gold and silver and beautiful jewellery. Why this book?'

'Dunno. S'pose I like the animals. I've seen these books on the internet, you know? With all the wild beasts and dragons. I like the gold letters and the old writing. I know I shouldn't have taken it but ... it was just there.' She subsided into silence, obviously ashamed of showing any kind of enthusiasm for anything at all.

'You mean it wasn't in its cabinet?'

The girl shook her head. 'It was just lying about on the table. I didn't think it could be that important, just left there like that.'

Miranda just stopped herself from blurting out a four-letter word, even though it would have been Anglo-Saxon.

'There were so many old books in the castle; I thought you wouldn't miss it,' said the girl.

'Wouldn't miss it?'

'Yeah. I know I shouldn't have took it. I'm sorry. I really am. Please don't call the police. I'll try and pay for any damage.'

Miranda now knew the true meaning of being caught between a rock and a hard place. If the book was damaged, they'd have to call in a specialist conservator and the restoration work could cost a fortune. At first glance, it looked unharmed apart from a few cake crumbs on the cover and calling the police would lead to a mountain of trouble for the Mount and the girl.

There'd probably be a court case, the girl would get a criminal record and a stretch in a young offenders' institute because the bestiary wasn't a paperback from Smith's, and it was a treasure of, perhaps, national importance, worth thousands of pounds. The story would be sure to get in the tabloids and they'd act all outraged and publish pictures of the feral girl and her feckless mother flicking the 'V's outside some court. Or her family might get evicted or kick her out, if she had a family at all, if she even had a mother.

The girl sniffed. 'You gonna call them?'

Miranda made a split-second decision. 'Get on the boat.'

The girl's eyes widened. She must think Miranda had gone crazy, which was probably true.

'You what?'

'I said get out of here but hurry up before I change my mind and don't ever let me see you back here again.'

Over by the visitor centre on the quayside, Miranda spotted Ronnie Stapleton, the Mount's head of security watching her through a pair of binoculars, radio poised in her other hand.

The girl wasted no more time, scuttled down the gangway to the boat, slumped into a corner and pulled her hoodie right over her head, just like a monk.

Miranda called to the boatman. 'OK, Steve, that's the last one.'

As she headed back to the Mount's security centre, she heard the boat chugging out of the tiny harbour on its way back to the mainland. She didn't look back. Her head was filled with the image of another teenage girl, hiding in her bunk in a caravan, fifteen years before. She heard her mother shouting at her to 'stop reading them bleedin' books and get her arse out into the bleedin' fresh air' and her mother's latest boyfriend screaming obscenities at the football and bawling at Miranda to fetch him another can of lager. She felt her tiny bunk room grow dark as she pulled the covers over her head and disappeared into her fantasy world of knights and battles and dragons.

A large and imposing figure waited by the door to the security centre, her arms crossed. Oh God. What would she tell Ronnie? She held up her palms.

'Don't say it. I'm a soft touch and I should be sacked.'

Ronnie shook her head. 'All of those things but I only have one question. Why?'

'Because she seemed genuinely interested in the bestiary. Because she handed it back when I asked. Because she said she was sorry and ... I guess I just wanted to give her a second chance.'

'Do you know many chances she's probably already had?'

'I know you think I'm being soft.'

'Soft? Nah. Stupidly naive and barking mad would be more accurate. If she'd got away with it, you do realise she'd probably have flogged it on eBay and bought a load of crack with it.'

'I don't think there's much of a market on eBay for medieval bestiaries.'

Ronnie raised her eyebrows. 'You'd be surprised. A mate of mine sold his soul on there last year. He got eighty quid for it.' Ronnie tutted. 'Well, it's too late now. What really bothers me is how the hell she got hold of it?'

'She says it was out of the cabinet which is possible but I don't understand why we didn't see her take it. Wasn't one of the team monitoring the armoury CCTV system?'

'I just checked the footage, the CCTV up in the library is on the blink again and we've had some problems with the cameras in the armoury and Great Hall,' said Ronnie. 'I sent you a memo about them a few days ago. You do know we need a new security system throughout the site?'

'I do know but we can't afford it. We'll have to get the service engineers in this time and hope they can repair or replace the cameras. I'll ask them to quote for a new system but I know we don't have the cash. A couple of those Cambridge research students were working on the bestiary in the library this afternoon so I wonder if one of them left it out.'

'They may claim to be the nation's brightest but none of them has any common sense,' said Ronnie with satisfaction. 'I'll call in all the students for a security seminar tomorrow and try to find out which of them did it.'

Miranda winced inwardly, picturing the students blinking nervously under Ronnie's interrogation. But she didn't feel sorry for them; she was in enough trouble herself. Shit. She steeled herself to ask Ronnie a question she didn't really want answered. 'Will you have to report me for letting the girl go?'

Ronnie gave a long sigh and rubbed her chin. 'We–lll. As the head of security, I should report you. As your best friend, I don't want to. If you've got the book back, I could look the other way, but if I see her here again, I'll call the police. Is the book damaged?'

'I don't think so.' A small surge of panic rose again. She wished she'd kept the girl back now while she'd examined the bestiary properly, but the book wouldn't stand too much handling without gloves. 'I'll put it back and ask the conservator to take a look tomorrow. If there are any problems, I'll cross that bridge when I come to it. Now, I'd better go and make sure nothing else is missing.'

'Don't worry, hun, I'm almost sure you haven't just made the worst mistake of your life and ruined your career.' Ronnie grinned reassuringly.

'I hope not. I don't think I could stand any more disasters today. Did you hear about the woman who wanted to exorcise the demons from the castle tower this morning? And the water was cut off to both ladies' toilet blocks for a whole hour at lunchtime. I had to let the visitors use the staff changing rooms for a while.'

'You love the drama, darling,' said Ronnie and Miranda finally laughed.

'I'll take the bestiary back to the library for now. Can you get the CCTV company over, please? Tell them it's urgent.'

Ronnie saluted. 'Aye, aye, cap'n. And by the way, I've booked some tickets to see the latest Hunger Games movie in Penzance for Saturday and reserved a table at the tapas bar next door. I'll drive the Land Rover so you can have a sangria or four.'

Miranda heaved a sigh of relief. 'Excellent. I need to get out of here, especially after a day like this.'

After carefully wrapping the bestiary in tissue paper from the filing cabinet in her office drawer, Miranda hauled herself up the steep pathways that led from the quay, with its cottages, café and visitor centre and offices, right to the castle itself.

Ronnie had been right; despite the scare with the book, she did love the drama that came with the job. She loved almost every aspect of her role, apart from not being able to beam herself up to the top of the castle, Star Trek style. A thousand years before, St Merryn's Mount had been colonised by monks who'd chosen the islet a mile off the coast of Cornwall because it kept them away from the temptations of the wicked world. Since then, the isle had been occupied and the castle gradually developed by generations of St Merryns, the local Cornish aristocrats who still owned it today.

Miranda had done the climb up to the castle half a dozen times that day already and thousands of time during her years working on the Mount. Normally, she scooted up like a mountain goat but today, she felt, frankly, knackered. It was only May and meant to be low season but a pile of paperwork waited for her, teetering in the in–tray in her office. She'd hoped to start planning the Mount's annual Festival of Fools and rejig the staff rota ready for the busier days ahead, yet she hadn't sat down at her desk for more than ten minutes that day.

Still, thanks to Ronnie, there was a night out to look forward to, when she could unwind and let her hair down.

She replaced the bestiary in its display case, locked the cabinet behind her and pocketed the key. As she suspected, it had still been in the lock. One of the students must have got distracted and left the bestiary out on the table with the other less valuable books. She hoped Ronnie's pep talk would, frankly, scare the shit out of them and prevent any more lapses of memory.

She still couldn't shake off her own misgivings at letting the girl go; but then again the urge to give her another chance had been so strong. Or maybe she was indulging herself; trying to turn back the clock, in some strange way, through the girl. But she didn't want to put things right, she reasoned, she hadn't done anything wrong in running away from home, so why did it suddenly feel as if she had? She'd never felt guilty before, not this guilty anyway ... this was silly, she must be tired. She'd had a long busy day, and it wasn't like her to brood.

After locking the door to the archive room, she decided

to make a check on the other public rooms of the castle. As expected, all was quiet in the Great Hall, the panelled dining room and the corridors. The only sounds were her own echoing footsteps and the waves battering the rocks far below the castle walls.

Miranda pushed open the door of the armoury, the final stop on her tour of the castle. With its centuries of weaponry, it was a favourite attraction, particularly with the fathers and boys. The fusty tang of the stone-walled room filled her nostrils. The suits of armour, chain mail and helmets lined its thick walls, all silent and empty.

But not all the visitors had gone. There was a man at the far end of the room. As the door clicked shut behind her, he turned round and looked at her. If she'd been nervous at confronting a teen thief, that now seemed like a walk in the park. Her heart thudded as loudly as the castle's antiquated boiler system.

The man held a cutlass in his hand and it was pointed at her.

Chapter Two

'I'm sorry, sir, but if you don't put down that cutlass, I'm going to have to call Security.' Miranda forced herself to speak calmly and clearly, as if addressing a group of school-children on a tour of the Mount. Even in a highly stressful situation, especially in a highly stressful situation, it was best to be polite to the visitors, even if this one was brandishing a lethal weapon.

The man smiled. He didn't look like a psychopath; in fact he looked startlingly handsome in a rakish way as if he'd just swung down from the crow's nest of a galleon. His thick black hair was trying to escape from a ponytail and he had a tiny goatee beard and a thin gold hoop through his ear. His face was tanned and, while Miranda didn't think he was much above thirty, he had the world-weary look of someone who'd seen and done, and possibly smoked or inhaled, a lot of stuff. Oh bloody hell, she hoped he wasn't on something now.

'And you are?' he asked, lowering the cutlass and glaring at her as if she were the intruder, not him.

'I'm the property manager, sir. The castle closed some time ago and,' she added as goosebumps danced the flamenco along her bare arm, 'I'm afraid we can't allow visitors to handle the artefacts.'

Her mouth was dry, her fingers were slick around the leather case of the radio but she was determined to stay calm. She'd opened the emergency channel to the island's security team as soon as she'd entered the armoury and spotted him so she hoped Ronnie and her deputy could hear her. Sadly, because the CCTV camera wasn't working, they couldn't actually see her. This is where ignoring memos would come back to bite her on the bum, thought Miranda as she fought to stay calm. By her calculations, it would only take a few minutes for Ronnie and Reggie to run up the steps and into the armoury, less if one of them was nearby. That was time enough for her to have the situation under control.

The man gave the air an experimental slash.

She swallowed hard. It was also more than enough time for him to turn her into a doner kebab.

She spoke into the radio, battling to keep the tremor from her voice. 'Hello, Ronnie? Can we have a mop and bucket in the armoury, please? There's been a spillage.'

A smile spread over the man's face. 'A mop and bucket? I suppose that's some kind of code for an incident? Well, there's no need, I'm really not dangerous.'

He took a step forwards, still holding the sword. The arm that held the cutlass was lean but muscular, his shoulders broad and strong. He definitely looked like a man who could handle himself in a skirmish and he was definitely in full control of his faculties. Maybe that 'been there, done that, killed it' look was because he'd been in the Forces or a mercenary. Miranda took two paces back on legs that had turned very wobbly. She prayed that her mop and bucket alert would have the security team racing to her rescue. 'Sir, please calm down.'

'I am calm. I'm only messing about. Have at ye, varlet. Or some shit like that.' He slashed a 'Z' in the air.

'I think you'll find that was Zorro and that he used a rapier. You're holding a cutlass. A very rare cutlass.'

'Really?' He ran a finger over the tip of the sword. 'Ow! Bugger, it's still sharp.'

She scooted backwards, her back now scraping the stone wall. 'Just put down the sword. My team's on its way and I wouldn't want anyone to get hurt.'

'OK, OK. Miss Whiplash.'

He laid down the cutlass on a wooden trestle and Miranda exhaled discreetly as tension ebbed from her body. Thank goodness for that, he was probably just a bit of a prat rather than a serial killer. She hadn't really thought he was dangerous or a thief, not that he'd have got very far with the cutlass unless he planned on swimming.

He raised his palms and smiled. 'You got me bang to rights, guv'nor.'

'This isn't funny you know,' said Miranda, torn between relief at his relinquishing the sword and annoyance at his cheek. He stared at her for a moment then gave a shrug and a sigh, as if he'd suddenly become bored with the game. 'No. You're right. This isn't funny at all but it is abso-fuckinglutely farcical. It is, in fact, the biggest joke on the planet that I'm even here now ... Christ on a bike!'

Miranda let out a tiny squeal as a small studded door behind him flew back on its hinges. In seconds, two burly figures had burst in and pinned the man to the flagstones.

'Get off me, you idiots!'

Oh you shouldn't have said that, thought Miranda. You really shouldn't have said it, not to Reggie, and especially not to Ronnie.

There was a low growl in Ronnie's throat as she sat astride his legs. 'Shut up, tosser.'

Reggie was more polite. 'Now, sir, don't struggle. We don't want to hurt you,' he said, twisting the man's arms behind his back.

'Miss Whiplash over there said that. Now, look what's happened. Fuck it! You're breaking my bloody arm!'

'We advise you to calm down, sir, or we'll have to take further action that you might find uncomfortable.' Ronnie sounded like a Bond villainess before she pulls the lever that plunges her victim into the shark tank. 'Are you all right, Miranda?'

Realising she'd backed into a corner, Miranda stood up straight and brushed dust from the back of her shorts with shaky hands. 'Yes thanks, I'm fine.'

'Hey, there's no need to tie my hands. Ooof.'

Miranda winced as Ronnie pressed the man's face into the flagstones while Reggie secured his wrists with cable tie. Ronnie had been a prison officer at Holloway and Reggie was ex-SAS and Miranda worried momentarily that the intruder might sue them for assault but then, as he uttered a stream of curses into the floor, she decided she didn't care.

A middle-aged woman in a Barbour jacket, leaning on a stick, appeared under the archway leading into the armoury.

'What the blazes is going on here?'

Miranda's heart sank into her trainers. 'Lady St Merryn! I'm so sorry this has disturbed you. An intruder broke into the armoury.'

'Intruder?' The man snorted.

'Shut your mouth,' growled Reggie

'As you can see, we have the incident under control now,' said Miranda.

Reggie hauled the man to his feet. 'He's probably on drugs.'

The man glared at Ronnie. 'I'm not on drugs. Not these days anyway.'

'I advise you to keep quiet, mate,' said Reggie.

'I'm not your *mate*.'

Lady St Merryn shot the intruder a look normally reserved for the castle cat when it dropped a half-eaten mouse on her drawing room Axminster.

'I really don't know how he managed to stay in the armoury after the castle had closed,' Miranda said, tucking a rogue strand of hair behind her ear as if that made everything OK again. 'We did a thorough sweep of the site as usual but this man appears to have been missed. I can assure you it won't happen again, Lady St Merryn.'

It definitely wouldn't happen again; never mind the CCTV system, Miranda was already planning a root and branch review of the Mount's security procedures. Several staff clearly needed to go on refresher courses, including herself.

Lady St Merryn waved a hand dismissively and frowned at her. 'Never mind me, Miranda. How are you? I do hope this miscreant hasn't hurt you. If he has I'll take it out on his hide myself.'

Miranda was astonished. Lady St Merryn was known for her fiery character but Miranda hadn't thought she'd resort to violence. Mind you, it was a very rare cutlass. It had belonged to the fifth Lord, Jasper St Merryn, who was rumoured to have captured it from a pirate ship off Tortuga in 1721.

'There's no need for that, Lady St Merryn. The team will deal with him now.'

They hauled the man to his feet. 'We'll press charges,' said Ronnie.

'What for? I wasn't stealing the cutlass.'

Reggie snorted. 'Only because Miss Marshall caught you. We can do you for threatening behaviour, assault, tres-pass . . . '

'Nothing I haven't faced before.'

Miranda was speechless. She didn't know how he could be so arrogant knowing he was about to be arrested and pos-sibly sent to prison. With a face and body like his, she thought he'd have a very hard time there. She tried to feel sorry for him and failed.

Ronnie's face was grim. 'I'll call the police,' she said.

Lady St Merryn gave a sigh. 'Untie him.'

Reggie tightened his grip on the man's bicep until the skin turned white. 'We can't do that. He could be a nutter, madam.'

'Oh, he's definitely a nutter, Reggie, but please untie him.'

Miranda stepped forwards, astonished. 'Lady St Merryn ...'

Lady St Merryn tapped her way to Miranda and patted her arm. 'Don't worry, my dear. It's fine. I won't say you're perfectly safe with this idiot but I don't think he's about to run you through with a cutlass. I, however, may be taking a horsewhip to him.'

Miranda was speechless. She'd expected Lady St Merryn to be outraged at some oik trying to make off with her heritage, but as for simply letting him go? Yes. She'd let the teenager off but this was different.

Grumbling, Reggie undid the cable ties and, scowling, the man rubbed at his wrists.

'Hurts a bit, does it?' said Reggie with undisguised relish.

'Well, normally, I rather enjoy a little light bondage but not usually at the hands of a man.'

Miranda tried desperately to remain composed, which was difficult considering she'd gone all hot and cold as the man turned his eyes right on her. Suddenly, he gave a little bow in her direction before stepping forwards and planting a kiss on Lady St Merryn's cheek.

Lady St Merryn kissed him back then scowled. 'It will take a damn sight more than that to get round me, Jago.'

He shook his head and gave a weary sigh. 'Delighted to see you too, Mother, you haven't changed a bit.'

Chapter Three

Miranda replaced the cutlass on its stand, frowning at the fingerprints marking the blade. The sword would need cleaning too now, but that could wait until tomorrow when the conservator arrived. She stepped back and looked around the armoury. Her heart rate had slowed and the throbbing pulse in her head had subsided.

Miranda hadn't been able to take her eyes off Jago St Merryn as he'd kissed his mother, her frail figure seeming childlike in his embrace. Despite her harsh words and sarcasm, Miranda knew Lady St Merryn well enough to tell that she was happy, relieved – grateful – to have her son back home. Even if he was a son she never talked about and hadn't even seen – if all the rumours were to be believed – since he'd left university ten years before.

On a day-to-day basis, Lady St Merryn was in charge of the Mount but it was her son, Jago, who had inherited the property and the title from his father, Patrick. He was the heir and it should have been his duty to be in charge of it now. Instead Jago St Merryn had considered it his duty to scarper and leave the castle to be run by his mother and a handful of underpaid, and almost stupidly loyal, residents and staff.

Miranda made her way back down to the harbour where the offices were housed in converted buildings on the quayside. The cottages, strung along the harbour, were home for the thirty staff and their families who lived on the island. Most of the buildings had been there for at least three hundred years, providing accommodation for the ferrymen, servants and trades people and their families, who had once served the Mount or still did.

She walked into her office and opened the filing cabinet. In the bottom drawer, she found a half-bottle of 'medicinal' Ardbeg hidden behind a copy of *Debrett's*. She checked her watch. It was one minute past six and she was officially off duty. She unscrewed the cap, sloshed a generous measure in her Mount St Merryn mug and sank back into her office chair.

'How are you?'

She smiled as Ronnie appeared in the doorway. 'I think I've got over it. Whisky?'

'Unfortunately, I'm still on duty. My shift doesn't end until ten. But if I wasn't, I'd join you in a flash. Hell of a shock, wasn't it?'

'I didn't actually think Jago St Merryn would run me through with the cutlass.'

'I didn't mean the cutlass. I meant it's a shock that bloody Jago's deigned to come back to the Mount, at all.'

'I suppose we should have guessed he'd be back one day, no matter what's gone on between him and his mother. He does own the place after all, but just turning up like that, I admit, it was unconventional.' Miranda clamped her lips together. It wasn't her place to speculate on the private lives of her employers; she left that to the rest of the staff when they thought she was out of earshot. She still enjoyed eaves-dropping.

The look that Jago had given her as Reggie had set him free was also burned into her brain. She gulped down a slug of whisky and wished she had a fan in the office. The May evening was unseasonably warm.

'Handsome bastard, isn't he?' said Ronnie, as if reading her thoughts. 'Bit of the gypsy in there if you ask me.'

With his earring and bravado, Jago had reminded Miranda more of the Corsairs, the pirates who attacked enemy ships for the French kings.

'You know he left for university and never came back?' asked Ronnie.

'I'd heard rumours but Lady St Merryn never talks about him.'

That was an understatement. In fact, Jago might as well have *not* existed. While there were dozens of portraits of the St Merryn ancestors displayed throughout the castle, Jago's handsome face was nowhere to be found. Even in Lady St Merryn's private chambers, Miranda could only recall one photo of him, and that was a print of a sullen little boy, standing by the harbour, holding a fishing net.

'No wonder her ladyship won't speak his name. After the last lord passed away, Jago went straight up to Cambridge from boarding school. He hardly ever came home, from what I can work out and, after that, he disappeared off round the world. Reggie reckons he was banged up in some South American jail for a while.'

Disappeared off round the world. Miranda thought that sounded about right for the man she'd just met. In past times, the sons of great families were often despatched abroad, either to do the Grand Tour and broaden their minds or because they'd done something unspeakable and had to get away until the heat died down. In Jago's case, the unspeakable option seemed more likely. But what could you do these days that was truly 'unspeakable'? The possibilities shot through Miranda's mind. She pictured Jago in a Hogarthian scene of debauchery, lolling on a couch with an opium pipe in one hand, a gin bottle in the other and bare-breasted wenches lifting their skirts in his face.

Yikes. She downed the rest of her whisky. 'I thought you said he'd been working in Australia?'

'He has been for the past couple of years. The landlady of the pub in the village has a cousin who runs a bar in Bells Beach in Victoria. She reckons Jago used to hang out in his bar for a while. But I don't think he's been actually working, unless you call surfing "work" and I think there was some trouble with women but I don't know the details.'

Trouble with women, plural? That seemed feasible. Jago probably only had to flutter an eyelash to have girls queuing up to see his enormous inheritance.

She sipped her whisky, feigning indifference to Jago's alleged charms. 'And he's never been back to see his mother?'

'Not while you've been around, no, and I can't recall ever seeing him since I've started. I think his graduation ceremony was pretty much the last Lady St Merryn saw of him.'

Now he was back, Miranda had hoped he might have changed his ways but her first impressions weren't very promising.

Ronnie carried on. 'God knows why he's crawled out of whatever stone he was hiding under and come back to the Mount.'

'Yes, I'm wondering why I bothered myself.' Jago loomed in the doorway to the office. His T-shirt, dusty from the armoury floor, had seen better days but clung to a torso in its prime. His hair, freed from the ponytail, was tousled from sun, surf and a scuffle with two sarcastic security guards. 'Veronica isn't it?'

Ronnie glared at him. 'Everybody calls me Ronnie.'

'I'm not everybody.'

The hostility crackled through the air and yet Miranda simply couldn't take her eyes off him. He glared back at her from dark eyes fringed by lashes that had no need of the mascara wand. She knew then, how D'Artagnan might have looked if Levis had been invented.

He loomed over above the desk. 'OK, Veronica, do you mind leaving us alone? Ms Marshall will be quite safe. As you can see, I am unarmed.'

Acting as if Jago didn't exist, Ronnie patted Miranda's arm. 'Are you OK, hun?'

'Of course.'

'And you're fine with me leaving you alone with *him*?'

'She is,' Jago cut in.

'I'm fine and, anyway, I'm sure Lord St Merryn doesn't plan on staying down here in the office for long.'

Jago grinned. 'There you are then, Veronica. Miranda isn't afraid of me.'

Ronnie banged down her mug. 'Well, you know where the panic button is if you need me.' She marched out, slamming the door to the office behind her.

Jago raised his eyebrows as the partition wall vibrated. 'What charming staff. Pray, tell me what people skills course do you send them on?'

Miranda didn't tell him that people skills courses were beyond the Mount's budget too but she still winced at the war raging between her best friend and her new boss. Jago obviously wasn't here on a charm offensive but then again, Ronnie *had* sat on him.

'I'm sorry if you find us all a little off guard,' said Miranda, heating up at the thought of being astride Jago, 'but your arrival was rather unexpected.'

'So I've gathered. It was rather unexpected to me too.'

'I think Ronnie's secretly rather embarrassed at having pinned you to the floor.'

'And you're embarrassed at having called security on me?' His dark-brown eyes crinkled at the corners and his mouth twitched in a half-smile. Miranda decided he'd seemed less threatening while he'd waved a sword at her.

'Actually, no. You might have been dangerous for all I knew. I followed the correct procedures and if you'd said who you were from the start, I wouldn't have had you restrained.'

'Come on, would you have believed me if I had said who I was? Do I look like a lord?'

'No. You're far too scruffy, but you could have tried to convince me.'

He rested a jeaned buttock on the edge of the desk. 'I'm genuinely sorry for frightening you. Once you'd found me, I had an inkling of what would happen and I knew I had no means of proving who I was. Alas, I have no royal birthmark on my backside that I could whip out to show you.'

'Or a passport? Driving licence?' she managed, trying not to envisage Jago whipping out anything in front of her.

'I have both, as a matter of fact, but they're in my ruck-sack up in the tower. When I got off the boat, I came up the back route to the living quarters, dropped my stuff in my old room then went straight to the armoury once the castle had closed.'

'But why choose the armoury?'

'Perhaps because I'm a closet serial killer? I really have no idea.'

'And you didn't think to introduce yourself to anyone?' Miranda went on, feeling more and more like a headmistress telling off a naughty student. She didn't care; Jago deserved all he got.

He shrugged. 'Actually, I didn't see anyone. The place was as deserted as the *Mary Celeste*.'

'That's because we were doing a property sweep to check there was no one left behind.' Miranda thought it better not to mention the almost-stolen bestiary to her new boss. 'Fortunately, the team spotted us on the CCTV system.'

'Yes, and I was almost having fun until the Kray twins arrived.'

'They were only doing their job.'

He shifted his other cheek onto the desk, obscuring a memo from the Health & Safety Executive. Miranda pushed her mug away from his bottom, a little uncomfortable at being found drinking, even if it was off duty. She didn't want Jago to think he'd unsettled her for a moment but inside, her stomach was churning and not only because she fancied the aristocratic pants off him. After hardly setting foot in the place for ten years, he must have a very good reason to return now, and she had a feeling that it couldn't be anything pleasant.

She stood up, refusing to be intimidated. 'Setting aside our earlier meeting, what can I do for your lordship?'

He shook his head. 'You can stop all of that lord shit for a start. Call me Jago or I'll have to have you thrown in the castle dungeon.'

'We don't have a dungeon, your lordship.'

He scowled at her. 'If you really want to play this game, you know perfectly well that I'm an earl, and that the correct form of address to me is "my lord".'

Miranda smiled sweetly. 'Of course. How silly of me! So what can I do for you, my lord?'

'Oh, for God's sake, Miranda!'

'I'd really prefer Miss Marshall.'

Outside, the evening sun broke through a cloud and filled the tiny office in warm light. Finally he gave a rueful smile and Miranda's stomach flipped, not once but twice.

'You know, it would be better if we downed weapons now and spoke to each other like grown-ups.'

'I think that would be a very good idea.'

'At least we agree on something, but let's go outside to

talk. I'd like to see what I've missed over the past ten years. Take me on a tour and I'll introduce myself properly. What's the matter? You seem surprised?'

'I'm just a little taken aback that you want a tour of your own home.'

She half-expected him to deny the place was his home but he didn't, starting a flutter of unease in her stomach.

'It's been a long time. Things have probably changed quite a bit.'

As he followed Miranda out of her office and onto the quayside, Jago knew that things wouldn't have changed because St Merryn's Mount could never really change. Every flagstone, every beam and family heirloom resonated with the past and expectations of a dozen Lord St Merryns before him. His father, Patrick, had died of a heart attack some years before, leaving Jago and his mother alone and mistresses wailing throughout London and the West Country. The mistresses were probably wailing because his mother and Jago had inherited all his money. His father had been a stickler for tradition in that respect.

Even before he'd been packed off to boarding school, Jago had picked up on the signals that his parents' marriage was more horror story than fairy tale. In his vacation visits home, he'd spent most of his time down on the quay trying to avoid the rows and silences up at the castle. His mother had thrown all her youth and energy into running the castle. His father liked to handle the financial elements of the business but it was his mother who was the heart of the place. It was she whom the staff respected and liked and put in the hours of work. When his father collapsed outside his mistress's flat in Mayfair, everyone at the Mount kept up the pretence that Lady St Merryn was his one true love.

At the funeral, Jago followed the coffin to the family tomb in the parish church, his mother on his arm. He couldn't remember her shedding a single tear. Perversely, he'd sobbed his heart out for the old bastard despite the fact that his father had been a strict disciplinarian, who thought showing affection for his son was almost a crime. Perhaps Jago had been crying for what he'd never had, rather than what he had lost.

He was sure his father's death had come almost as a relief to his mother. He'd told himself that when he'd left for university. At eighteen, he'd found it easy to crush any guilt he felt at leaving her to run the Mount because all those years ago his mother had been strong-willed, still in good health and relatively young. She hadn't needed him, she'd convinced him of that so he'd gone away and he'd stayed away.

He suspected that Miranda had already formed an opinion of him, fuelled by the gossip and rumours that would already be spreading through the castle like wildfire. He hadn't helped his cause by behaving like a total wanker in the armoury. He still wasn't sure what had possessed him to scare the woman like that, God knows she'd done nothing to him. It was this bloody place that had made him stupid and reckless, or maybe he'd felt some perverse need to live up to the reputation that had surely preceded him. Perhaps, he told himself, acting the idiot was easier than revealing the true Jago, not that he was sure who his real self was any more.

'Lord St Merryn?'

Miranda's voice, hesitant and unsure, snapped him out of his thoughts. She'd stopped outside a row of old fisherman's net lofts on the quayside.

'As you can see, we've upgraded the Visitor Centre, added a new café and shop since you left,' she said.

'Sorry?'

She was a bit pissed off that he'd gone AWOL while she was talking and he didn't blame her.

'These buildings were expanded last year. We won an eco-award for them. Look, they have a green roof and we recycle the grey water in the washrooms.'

He flashed her a brief smile. 'Well done. Very smart.'

He knew he should be impressed but he'd hardly even glanced at them. His eyes were drawn to the harbour, with its boats bobbing. When the tide was out, you could walk from the mainland to the castle but a boat was the only means of escape when the sea closed in. To visitors, the place seemed the ultimate in romantic isolation but Jago had always found it no more than a luxurious prison.

'We invested in extra visitor boats last season to meet up with demand,' Miranda explained in her 'professional voice'. He feigned an interest in the new fleet as she went on. 'You'll be pleased to know that visitor numbers are up thirty per cent on three years ago.'

'And our turnover is up fifteen point five per cent and you've won South West Tourist Attraction of the year three years running and been nominated for a tourism marketing award.'

Her mouth opened in a small 'o' of surprise, her eyes full

of confusion. She clearly didn't know how to take his remarks.

'I did have access to the internet on my travels and I've read the report on how well the Mount is doing,' he said. 'And my mother has been singing your praises.'

Her cheeks coloured and Jago had a sudden, unbidden urge to know what lay beneath the buttoned-up exterior of Ms Miranda Marshall. He wondered what she looked like with her hair loose and out of the tailored shorts and polo shirt that were far too prissy for her. That uptight act must hide a wilder side. She surely couldn't maintain the facade twenty-four seven?

'Would you care to see the new security centre, my lord?' Her pretty face tilted up to his, her eyes innocent, not a trace of irony in her voice. Yet Jago knew he was being slapped down, and found himself at a loss for a flippant reply. Perhaps she really was every bit as uptight as she seemed. No matter, he hadn't come here to delve into the desires and motivations of the Mount's staff, no matter who they might be. In Miranda's case, it was better if he knew as little about their personal lives as possible, considering what he had planned for them. He was already regretting his arrogance in the armoury, he'd behaved like a grade A shit and genuinely scared her for a little while. From now on, he'd try to conduct himself in a businesslike manner, even if it killed him.

'Not now,' he said, his throat suddenly dry as he realised just how difficult his job was going to be and how hard he'd have to try to avoid getting closer to anyone affected by his decision. 'But I'd appreciate seeing the grounds.'

'Really? I hadn't thought of you as a gardener.'

'I'm not, but I'd like to look round *my* property.'

It was excruciating to place that slight emphasis on the 'my', but he'd had to do it. He really had to place some distance between himself and Miranda, even it meant she thought him brusque and cold.

She led the way, reeling off facts about the grounds, pointing out the subtle but well-thought-out improvements that had been made while she'd been there. As she spoke, her eyes sparkled with life and enthusiasm. Her cheeks coloured and her delicate, almost prim features, seemed to open like a flower. She waited by a wall overlooking the terraced gardens that hung above the sea. The sun was slipping towards the horizon where the Atlantic Ocean beckoned.

'And this must be the most beautiful view in England.' She turned to him and suddenly seemed hesitant. 'At least, I think it is.'

Jago smiled and was rewarded with her glancing away from him, slightly embarrassed by her own enthusiasm. Perhaps she sensed his discomfort. It would certainly make it easier for him to carry out his plans if she'd been incompetent or uninterested in her job. What he had to do would be tough and unpleasant but he'd faced harder decisions before . . . much harder.

Miranda cleared her throat and started off up the steps that led to the main castle gatehouse. 'We haven't done any major rearrangement of the gardens. Much of it was laid out in these terraces during the fifth lord's time – but, of course, you'll know all about that.'

'I had my heritage drummed into me by my father.'

'Yes. I expect you did.' Miranda laughed.

She obviously thought he was joking and why wouldn't she? His mother clearly hadn't decided to go all confessional with Miranda Marshall, but then again, Jago knew she would rather die than share the family's dirty laundry with a member of staff. In truth, the 'drumming in' of his heritage had been literal at times. He'd grown used to the back of his father's hand, but he'd never accepted his father's emotional abuse of his mother.

He realised his hands had tightened to fists at his sides. God, *why* had he come back? The answer flew back instantly as it had every time since his mother had called, begging him to return: because the alternative would cause far more damage.

Chapter Four

'Come in.'

Lady St Merryn turned from the window where she'd been gazing out to sea.

'Hello, my dear.'

Miranda smiled but her heart sank. Since Jago had arrived, his mother seemed even more bowed down. Her shoulders slumped and she leaned more heavily on her stick. Miranda guessed that years of running the castle, of never showing any weakness despite her arthritis, had taken their toll more than she'd ever noticed before.

'I have some good news. The visitor figures so far this season,' she said, deciding to act as if all was normal.

'What?'

'The visitor numbers for the castle are up by ten per cent and it's only mid-May. We could consider opening longer once June starts.'

Lady St Merryn leaned on her stick. 'Yes, good idea. Well done.'

'Shall I get the website updated and rearrange the staff rota?'

'If you think so.'

Taken aback, Miranda hesitated. Lady St Merryn usually wanted detailed justification for even the slightest change to opening hours or staffing. But she'd already turned back to the window, one hand on her stick, the other grasping the stone ledge for support.

'Are you feeling well?'

There was a pause then she said: 'Quite well. That will be all, Miranda. Thank you.'

Dismissed? Just like that? Like a child? Miranda picked up her document wallet, puzzled and disturbed.

There was a quiet knock at the door and Jago walked in. Her stomach swirled as his eyes lingered on her. Hmm. That wolfish look was probably him deciding to make her redundant when he took over the reins of the Mount. She was convinced now that Lady St Merryn had decided to retire and summoned Jago back to rule the place with a rod of iron.

'Hello, Miranda.'

'Jago.' She resisted the urge to curtsey and a smile tilted the corner of his lips as she used his name. After some sleepless nights, she'd decided that new tactics were required if she were to keep her job. Antagonising him more than was necessary was probably not the best policy.

Lady St Merryn's back was still turned, as if Miranda and Jago weren't even there.

'I'll be going then, if that's all?'

A small sigh and a wave of the hand told Miranda she was dismissed. She tried to avoid Jago's eyes but could hardly back out of the room without speaking to him.

'Is there anything you want to discuss, Jago?'

His eyes rested on her before he answered. Her heart pitter-pattered. Was now the time they would tell her what was going on? Surely they wouldn't keep her in suspense any longer.

'Not at the moment, thank you,' Jago said, glancing over at his mother.

'In that case, I'm going to go back to the office and will start planning the new opening hours, but if you need me you can reach me on the radio.'

'Thanks.'

And with that she was firmly put in her place.

Back in the office, Ronnie greeted Miranda like a dog who'd retrieved a very big stick from the sea. If she had a tail, it would have wagged, thought Miranda, unable to suppress a smile.

Miranda laughed. No matter what was in store for the Mount, she had great colleagues to entertain and infuriate her. Their night out on the mainland had left Miranda with a king-sized hangover but they'd had a great time meeting up with a couple of friends from Nanjizal rowing gig club after the cinema. Getting off the island wasn't a matter of just jumping in a taxi on a whim, you had to plan it around the tides but that was part of the fun and her fondness of the people who lived there, like Ronnie, were a major reason she'd stayed so long on the island.

'Guess what? I found out *exactly* who left the bestiary out.'

'Really?' said Miranda, throwing her fleece over the back of her chair.

'Don't sound so interested, will you?'

'I'm winding you up. Of course I want to know. Which one of the students was it?'

Ronnie was almost panting with excitement. 'None of them. It was their tutor. I called the whole group in for a routine update on security procedures and said you'd found the book lying outside the cabinet when you checked the library after closing. Apparently, Professor Smartarse thought one of her students had locked it away and didn't bother to check. She confessed straightaway and I didn't even need the thumbscrews.' Ronnie gave a sigh. 'Pity. I like torturing academics, they're so bloody smug.'

'Good work, Poirot. You won't be surprised to hear that I left the theft out of my report to her ladyship,' said Miranda.

'Wise move. How is she? She doesn't look too good lately if you want my opinion.'

'I don't think she's feeling too well either.'

'I bet she's called Jago back to take over. I just know it.'

Miranda couldn't deny she thought the same way. 'It looks like it. I hope he's not going to make big changes.'

Ronnie's face was grim. 'Or bankrupt the place.'

'I'm sure that won't happen.'

'Bollocks.'

'OK, then I *hope* he won't bankrupt the place.' Miranda spotted the day's post on her desk, secured with an elastic band, the top being from the Health and Safety Executive.

Her heart sank a little. 'Is there anything else I should know about while I've been in my meeting?'

'Nothing life-threatening for once. But you have had a call.'

'Who from?'

'Theo Martin.' Ronnie said the words with relish, as if Theo was a cream doughnut or a giant block of chocolate.

'And?'

'He said he wants to review the Mount's emergency evacuation procedures with you but I think he just wants an excuse to talk to you. He promised to try to drop by over the next few days.'

'Right.'

Ronnie tutted loudly. 'Miranda. Don't.'

Miranda fingered the letters. 'Don't what?'

'Play the Ice Maiden. Theo's just about the best-looking guy in south-west Cornwall, if you like short men that is.'

At well over six feet herself, Ronnie had trouble finding a man who could look her in the eye or had an even chance of beating her in a fight. Theo, at a five ten-ish was considered almost a Munchkin by her standards. However he *was* a gorgeous Munchkin, Miranda was well aware of that, as were half of the girls within a fifty-mile radius. 'Thanks for passing on the message,' she said. 'Now, I'd better make a start on the Health and Safety paperwork.'

'Coward. I'll be sure to show Theo right up if I see him before you.' She hesitated before adding mischievously, 'I wonder if he knows that Jago's back yet.'

After Ronnie had left, Miranda picked up the desk calendar perched atop a pile of old *Country House* magazines.

The current month featured a shot of the Nanjizal lifeboat vessel racing to a shout. She couldn't see Theo in the photo but she knew he would have been at the helm. He was the coxswain of the lifeboat, the only salaried member of a crew which comprised volunteers from the local area. He was a proud man; devoted to his job and, if you cracked him open, Miranda reckoned he'd have Cornwall running through him like the letters in a stick of rock. He also had a fan club that ranged from teenagers to great grannies; the combination of rugged good looks and regularly risking his life for the community had made Theo the equivalent of royalty in Nanjizal.

Miranda liked him too, he was sexy, he made her laugh and she admired his commitment to the village. But why had Ronnie been interested in his reaction to Jago? Theo wasn't a fan of the St Merryns, that was true. As well as Cornwall running through his veins, he also had a chip on his shoulder about the family and their power and influence over the local community. Fair enough, Miranda acknowledged that he was entitled to voice his opinion and he'd certainly never mentioned Jago specifically to her face. Why would he? Ronnie was imagining things or, more likely, winding her up again.

Miranda heard her laptop ping as email messages started to pile up in her inbox. She put down the desk calendar, slipped the elastic band off the letters and reached for the paper knife. She smiled to herself. If only she'd had it when she'd found Jago in the armoury, she could have fought a duel with him.

Chapter Five

Miranda was a little surprised when Theo didn't turn up as expected that week. He usually kept his promises, but the timing of his visit had been vague and, anyway, Miranda had other things to occupy her. For the past few days, Jago had kept out of the offices, but not out of her way. She'd bumped into him a dozen times or more, mostly on the back routes to the castle that were closed to visitors and once, after the property had closed, in the armoury. She wondered if he'd been trying to keep an eye on her or how hard she worked. That kind of pettiness didn't seem his style, but you never knew.

She'd gone into the armoury one morning before opening time to find him examining the sword again. He'd laughed at her expression, which, she had to admit, had probably been a mixture of dismay and naked lust.

'You're quite safe this time,' he said, replacing the sword on the display

'If you wanted another tour, you only had to call me,' she said, crossing to the cutlass and peering at it as if checking for damage. 'Are you aware, my lord, that this is a rare early eighteenth-century cutlass captured by the fifth Lord St Merryn from a buccaneer in the West Indies?'

He scratched his chin. 'And here was me thinking my great-grandfather acquired it from a market stall in the Portobello Road.'

'There is, I suppose, some element of doubt about its provenance but I prefer the more picturesque version.'

Jago shook his head. 'Oh God, a romantic. That's all I need.'

'Not really, the visitors prefer the pirate story too. It's good for business.'

He seemed about to say something more but just said, 'I'd better leave you to your work,' and marched off.

She watched him jog down the stone steps of the armoury and across the now deserted castle courtyard until, finally, he disappeared down a narrow path that wound its way to the harbour. The way he'd dashed off made her think he was planning to run away from the Mount again. She wasn't sure if that was a good thing or not.

On balance, she thought with a shiver, she rather hoped Jago would stay.

When she finally got back to her cottage that evening, it was gone nine o'clock. She listened to a message from Theo saying he'd call in the next day and then fell asleep on the bed in her uniform.

When she awoke, the bedside clock said 1 am, Miranda's heavy limbs said 6 am would come round all too soon, yet her thoughts tossed about like a skiff on a stormy sea. The curtains stirred in the breeze and the scent of salt and ozone wafted over her. She'd left the casement window open, hoping the air would circulate as she lay awake, and that she'd be lulled asleep by the halyards clanking on the yachts in the harbour. Instead, she tossed and turned in her bed. Grit prickled her eyelids and her legs ached. Years of walking up and down the steep slopes had kept her fit but she was exhausted by the events of the past few days. She thumped her pillow and flopped back against it with a sigh. The window creaked open as the wind from the Atlantic freshened and changed direction. Out here on the island, even though it was barely a mile from shore, the weather could change from mild to angry in minutes. She started to slide into that half-asleep state where fantasy and the real world mesh and the subconscious reigns.

A shadowy figure climbed through the window.

'My lord?'

Miranda gasped as Jago appeared at the foot of her bed, silhouetted against the moonlight streaming through the window. He wore a billowing white shirt and dark breeches tucked into leather top boots but she didn't find his outfit at all strange.

'Lord St Merryn. Wh–what are you doing here?'

He smiled in a way that made the tiny hairs on the back of her neck prickle. 'Come now, you must know, Miranda.'

She pulled the sheet up to her neck; despite the fact that in her fantasy, she wore a full–length nightgown like her great-grandmother used to own.

'Don't do that.' He crossed the room, his boots thudding on the floorboards.

She twisted the sheet tightly in her fists. 'You shouldn't be here!'

He sat on the bed next to her, a wolfish smile on his lips. 'I can do anything I want. This is my land, my home.'

'But it's my room.'

'No, Miranda, it's *my* room. Everything here is mine.' He reached out and touched her cheek. 'Including you.'

In a flash, Jago tore the sheet from her hands and flung it back, revealing Miranda's nightgown. She tried to let out a shriek but her vocal cords were paralysed in contrast to every nerve which zinged and tingled.

'You've heard about *droit de seigneur*. Well, I'm here to claim mine.'

He pulled off his boots and climbed onto the bed, making the mattress creak alarmingly. She tried to move her arms to fend him off but they seemed to be paralysed too. He sat astride her and lowered his head close to hers. His hair was loose. She made a monumental effort and found her voice but it sounded far away.

'But I'm not getting married, my lord, and I'm um ... actually not a virgin.'

Jago started to unbutton his breeches. 'If you're already a strumpet then I'm definitely going to take you.'

'Um ... no,' she whispered, aware that she didn't sound very convincing. 'You really shouldn't, my lord.'

'Shouldn't? Who are you to tell me what I should and shouldn't do, wench?'

Jago grabbed the hem of her nightgown and ripped it

apart, from bottom to top, exposing her naked body. She cried out and sank back onto the pillows, helpless to resist as he closed his mouth around her exposed nipple. As he sucked, she let out a groan as all her senses sprang into life. She felt his calloused hands parting her thighs and heard his ragged breathing. She didn't mean to touch him back but found her hands tugging down his breeches anyway. Being an eighteenth-century brigand, of course, he wore no undergarments so she could clutch his muscular cheeks and squeeze them rather hard.

Lifting himself off her, he kicked off his breeches, his cock standing proud and hard. Miranda screwed her eyes tight in shame. *Cock?* What a rude word to think, even in a fantasy.

'I mustn't,' she said, 'I mustn't do you, I mean, do *this*. Or even think this!'

'Lie back and think of England,' he snarled.

'If I must. Ohh . . . oh my God!'

She was vaguely aware that she was still crying 'No, my lord!' as Jago thrust into her hard.

'Oh, Jago!'

Just as 'Jago' was having his very wicked way in her imagination, the window slammed back against the wall, instantly pulling her out of her fantasy. The breeze had whipped up into a squall and the window was banging away for dear life.

'Miranda!'

Miranda snatched at the sheet to cover her shameful nakedness before realising she was actually still wearing her uniform. She stumbled to the window where the blast of chilly Atlantic air felt like a bucket of icy water had been sloshed over her flushed skin. The moon had disappeared behind a cloud but she could make out a tall figure on the quay beneath, staring up at her. She blinked as Ronnie shone a torch up at the window.

'I heard you scream and the banging. I thought you'd got burglars.'

'Burglars? How would they get over to the island? It's high tide.'

'You can't be too careful. Are you all right?'

'F-fine. I must have left the window open and it blew back in the squall.'

The beam wavered as if Ronnie was trying to get a better look at her guilty face. 'I thought I heard you call out Jago's name.'

Miranda laughed. 'Jago? Why would I call for him? He's probably in bed.'

'Yes, and not his own. I saw him head off to the mainland on the last boat. Bet you he's with some village tart now.'

Miranda squinted at the torchlight. 'I'm fine, as you can see.'

The beam of light dropped to the quayside, leaving her temporarily blinded. 'Right then, if you're OK, I'll see you in the morning. Sweet dreams.'

'Goodnight, Ronnie.'

Miranda picked her way through the darkness and back into bed, pulling the duvet over her. So Jago wasn't even on the island and Ronnie might well be right; he could well be romping with some village girl – or girls or girls *and* boys right now. Outside, the rain pattered against the window and the distant thunder rumbled over the sea. As for sweet dreams, she had a feeling she wasn't going to sleep well on the Mount ever again.

Chapter Six

The next morning, Miranda stood in the old library at the top of the Mount, unable to believe what Jago had just said. When he'd called her there, she'd braced herself for unwelcome news but not this.

He'd opened the door to her when she'd knocked and indicated the chaise longue under the window. 'Thank you for coming. You'd better sit down.'

'I'm fine, thanks.'

'OK. Have it your way, but my news is going to come as a blow, I'm afraid. My mother says you should be the first to know and, more importantly, I think you should be too.'

He'd stopped as there was a loud shriek from outside in the courtyard. It was children messing about and enjoying their visit but Jago frowned and seemed disturbed. Then he'd turned to face her.

'I'm selling the Mount.'

Until that moment, she hadn't thought it possible that anyone's jaw could drop to the floor but hers felt like it had plunged through the stone flagstones and ended up far below on the quayside. It wasn't possible, either, that she heard those four words. Jago must be joking; that's what he did. Threatened women with cutlasses and wound up security guards. Well, she wouldn't be taken in.

She winked at him. 'Selling the Mount? Oh, that's a good one. However, I'm sorry, my lord, but I'm not falling for it this time.'

Jago's expression didn't waver. It was still serious with, she thought, a convincing touch of regret and even sadness. He really was very good at playing the game.

'Miranda . . . '

Her stomach lurched again at the change in tone from almost brusque to gentle. 'You are joking? You must be.'

'I'm afraid not.'

'Say you are. Please, stop this.'

'I can't stop it. It's true.'

Miranda had always laughed at the way Victorian ladies sank back onto sofas in shock in novels but that is exactly what she did now. She collapsed onto the chaise longue with a thud. 'Ow!'

Jago stepped forwards, his face creased in concern. 'What's the matter?'

Reaching under her, Miranda retrieved a spiky teasel head, placed there precisely to stop visitors parking their patrician bottoms on the family furniture.

'I'm sorry, that was a nasty shock, like my news, I see,' he added gently, taking the teasel from Miranda's hand and dropping it into a Chinese bowl.

'But why are you selling? I thought you'd come back to take over the running of the Mount from Lady St Merryn?'

'It's true that my mother does want to give up her responsibilities for the running of the castle.'

'I . . . I wondered. Yesterday when I met her to discuss the new opening hours, she didn't seem like herself but she never complains. I never dreamed she might want to give up the Mount entirely.'

'Things change. I think you're aware that we've been apart for some time now, but we have been in contact intermittently. She emailed me a few months ago and asked me to come home so I knew that something was wrong.'

Miranda clasped her hands together, trying to get some kind of control as one piece of horrible news after another rolled over her. Lady St Merryn ill? The Mount being sold? 'I should have noticed. I've been so busy running the place, but I should have seen she was ill.'

His voice softened. 'Not ill, exactly . . .' He paused as if he was about elaborate but then carried on briskly. 'Her arthritis has become very painful, I think, and running the Mount on top of her health problems has become too much. Being responsible for this place is like carrying the world on your shoulders and I have no intention of being Atlas. This place is a burden I'm not prepared to bear.'

'But your father did!'

Miranda had blurted out the words without thinking. Annoyance crossed Jago's face but it was too late to take her criticism back and she was hardly in the mood to be reasonable. He sat in the chair opposite her and pushed a hand back through his hair. A guilty gesture in Miranda's opinion and, oh, how she wanted him to feel guilty, she wanted him to feel so bad that he'd change his mind right now. 'I appreciate the work you do here, Miranda; God knows the place would probably be bankrupt without you. I can assure you that your position here will not change when the St Merryns leave.'

'*The St Merryns leave.*' She couldn't believe she'd actually heard him say that. It was ... obscene, the family leaving the Mount, after so long.

'I don't understand why you have to sell it at all?'

His mouth set in a hard line. 'Because I can and I want to. More importantly, the time is right. I've received a very good offer for the place from Southcastle Estates and I've decided to accept it.'

Miranda's mouth gaped. 'Southcastle? The leisure corporation that owns Ye Olde Warbeck Towers and the Rockholme Medieval Experience?'

'And Thornley Pleasure Beach, several pub chains, a bingo empire and a substantial portion of Kensington.'

'But they'll turn it into a tacky theme park!'

His voice was sharp. 'That's an exaggeration. They've assured me they won't make major changes.'

It couldn't be real. Surely this was a fantasy like last night and she'd wake up in her bedroom with the window banging and Ronnie shouting.

In that moment, she came as close to telling him to stuff the Mount up his aristocratic arse as she had ever come. And yes, there had been a few times when she'd felt that way about her job. Never mind that the Mount was regarded as a jewel of Britain's heritage, it would now be turned it into Disneyland.

She jumped to her feet, knowing that she had to put some distance between them or she might do something she'd regret.

'I know you need time to take this in but, please, hear me out first.'

She shook her head, the tears stinging the back of her eyes. She would *not* cry in front of Jago. 'Not now. I have to go. I've got a lot to do.'

She walked out, ignoring the fact that an iron ball seemed to have settled in her chest. Never mind her silly fantasies, Jago was a real brigand who'd come in the night intent on stealing the future of everyone who worked on the Mount. She dashed around a sharp turn in the path but Reggie blocked her route down to the quayside.

'Miranda! I'm glad I've found you. We have a fracas down at the café.'

She waved him away. 'Not now, Reggie.'

'But . . . '

'Can't you deal with it yourself? You were in the Special Forces.'

Reggie folded his arms, his bulk almost blocking her way. 'Yeah I was, but dealing with a coach party of WI ladies whingeing about the quality of the catering is not what I'm trained to do. Unless you want me to abseil through the roof and take them all out?'

'No, of course not . . . Oh, can't you just get the café

manager to sort them out?' She squeezed past him and scuttled off down the path. Oh, shit, shit, *shit*.

Reggie didn't deserve that from her. He'd worked for the St Merryns for years, even longer than Miranda. Despite Jago's 'assurances', she knew that Reggie's livelihood and his very reason for being were now in jeopardy. Jago might genuinely believe that Southcastle Estates would keep the status quo and look after the Mount's staff, but Miranda was a realist. She knew their aim would be to capitalise on their investment – which must run to tens of millions of pounds. Profit and growth would drive every decision they made; making enough to keep the Mount ticking over would not be enough. Anyone considered not to be pulling their weight would have to go.

She stopped to catch her breath on her 'favourite' terrace. Across the sea, the windows of Nanjizal glittered in the morning sun and the masts of the yachts pointed skywards in the small marina. The bright orange lifeboat bobbed alongside the harbour wall, probably recently returned from a 'shout'.

'You know your trouble,' her mother used to say, when justifying yet another disruption to Miranda's young life. 'Your trouble is that you get too attached to people and they only let you down. Take it from me; don't wear your heart on your sleeve.'

The Mount wasn't even a person, it was just a job but it was too late to unattach herself now. After a childhood spent moving from one school, caravan and 'stepfather' to another, this place had represented stability and continuity. That was why she'd studied history at university in the first place. It was why she'd volunteered at historic properties, working in the cafés and cleaning the toilets until she finally got her degree and a job as a junior in the Mount's ticket office. She knew she'd been looking for a place she could connect with the past and future and the fact that it was someone else's past didn't matter. She'd made it her own now, in so many ways.

A stray ice cream wrapper flapped around her ankles. It must have been tossed over the wall of the keep far above her. A brief snatch of young laughter reached her on the wind. Children, playing, not thinking. It happened . . . She really must have a word with the maintenance department about providing more litter bins . . . She stepped forwards to pick it up but it whirled away from her. She dashed after it. 'Bugger!'

It flew off, tantalisingly out of reach.

'Bloody rubbish!'

A large boot stamped on the wrapper, trapping it.

Miranda stared at Jago as he screwed up the wrapper and shoved it in his jeans pocket. Why had he followed her? She hadn't wanted to see him again, whilst she felt so raw.

'There's no use asking you not to hate me, I know you must,' he said.

'Of course I don't hate you. It's your property. You can do what you like with it,' she said, unable to keep the sarcasm from her voice.

'If only it were that simple.'

'Why isn't it?'

His eyes flashed angrily. 'It's personal. I don't have to explain myself. I know it's going to be a challenge but I need you to work with me and with Southcastle during the handover. The staff are going to look to you to guide them through this. I'm selling, I won't change my mind, and so we're all just going to have to make the best of it.'

It sounded as if Jago was already infected with Southcastle's corporate speak and seduced by their promises. She was surprised in one way, but not in another. It was clear he wanted as easy a way out of his responsibilities as possible. He was no Lady St Merryn.

'This will be a massive change for them; some won't survive it,' she said.

'Maybe not. There'll be generous redundancy for those that want it.'

'Working here isn't just a job. It's their lives and their homes, in some cases.'

'No one will lose their job or home. I'll make sure of it.' He shifted awkwardly. 'I must also ask you not to share this news with anyone else yet. I know that will be difficult but the deal is at a delicate stage. I want time to have everything legally settled, so I can protect everyone.'

Miranda was furious that he'd shifted the burden to her; it added insult to injury. 'You won't be able to protect them. Only as lord can you do that. It's your duty.'

'This isn't the thirteenth bloody century. I don't have a duty, beyond to my mother and, I might add, to myself.'

Miranda's mouth opened in shock. His tone was so hard and laced with bitterness.

'Look, I promise you I'll do my utmost to take care of the staff. And you.'

His voice softened but she was in no mood to cut him

an inch of slack. 'I don't care about me. I can get another job.'

He raised his eyebrows then shrugged. 'I know you can but, as for the Mount, you must accept my decision. I'm selling to Southcastle and my mother agrees with me. I suggest you talk to her. Now, please, our conversation is confidential; I can't force you not to tell the staff, but I do expect you not to. Let's make this as painless as we can for all concerned.'

They faced each other, the sea crashing onto the rocks below, children laughing above them on the courtyard. Jago turned away, leaning on the wall. She knew he was guilty and ashamed but she hardened her heart and steeled herself to ask what she'd been dreading to know.

'When's . . . *it* happening?

His voice was barely audible, snatched away by the wind. 'The end of the season.'

She gasped. 'That soon?'

'It's five months. November is a long time away.'

Miranda closed her eyes.

Five months in eight hundred years? It was just a heartbeat.

Chapter Seven

'I'm sorry, my dear. I know the news has come as an awful shock. Perhaps I should have warned you first but I needed to speak to Jago. I wanted to tell you but he insisted on telling you himself.'

Lady St Merryn handed Miranda a cup of tea. The best day china service was out so Miranda knew things were serious. Her gnarled hand trembled as Miranda took the cup. How could she not have noticed how tired she'd become? Maybe, her heart whispered, because she'd been so completely wrapped up in her work. What other things were passing her by as she devoted her life to the Mount?

'Thank you.'

Lady St Merryn inched her body down onto the seat of the armchair.

'I hadn't realised . . .' Miranda began.

'Why should you?' Lady St Merryn winced. 'It's not

just the arthritis though, I must admit, it's getting me down.'

That meant it must be excruciating, Miranda thought.

'What do they say? It's not just the years, it's the mileage? My dear, I've given most of my life to this place. I was barely nineteen when I married Patrick and I've managed for fifteen years since he died. I love every stone of the Mount and everyone who works here, even the visitors.'

Miranda noticed she didn't say anything about loving her husband.'I know.'

'But lately, I've begun to doubt myself. I may not have very long.'

'I'm sorry.'

Lady St Merryn waved a hand. 'It's nothing terminal, please don't worry about that. Apart from the usual things heading south and seizing up, I can't complain.' She pointed to her head. 'It's up here, my dear, that the problem lies. I need to see what's beyond these shores before it's too late. For so long, my world has literally revolved around this tiny island and you might not believe me but I have plans. I want to see what's out there. You may think I'm a batty old thing but I want to see the world. The great big world.'

'Of course not. I don't blame you.' Miranda gave a tight smile. No matter how much she'd tried to see Lady St Merryn's point of view, she still felt horribly let down. Surely there was some way that his mother could change Jago's mind?

'I called Jago back to try to persuade him to take over the reins. It was a vain hope, of course. He absolutely refuses.' Miranda realised that Lady St Merryn wanted her to defend

Jago but she couldn't bring herself to do it. 'By your silence, I can see you don't approve but, please, don't judge my son too harshly. You don't know what he's been through.'

Been through? Miranda wanted to understand Jago's decision-making and waited for Lady St Merryn to elaborate but she just sighed. 'There's nothing to be done but to try to make the best of it, I'm afraid. You've done a marvellous job here and Jago assures me the new owners will respect the staff. I'm sure you have nothing to worry about.'

What could she say? She felt angry with Jago and betrayed by his mother, and angry with herself for being so disappointed. Lady St Merryn's words about the big wide world also played on her mind. Was she confining herself too tightly? Wasting her own life working for these people who clearly felt they owed her nothing? Maybe she should start looking outside this cosy islet. She'd been here since she'd left university and perhaps now was the time for her to branch out too and the sale of the Mount was her opportunity. Maybe, the sale was fate.

She replaced her cup carefully in its saucer, feeling nauseous and unconvinced by her own reasoning. Her radio crackled. 'Excuse me.' She listened for a minute as one of the security team spoke to her.

'Trouble?' asked Lady St Merryn as Miranda replaced the radio in her belt.

'One of the birdwatchers has slipped and hurt his ankle trying to get a picture of the choughs.'

Lady St Merryn rolled her eyes. 'I really have no idea what the fascination with birds is. All the damn things look the same to me and they make a mess everywhere. Still, you'd better go and see how this twitcher person is. Soon, these things will be no concern of mine, which, perhaps, may turn out to be a good thing in the end. This place probably needs fresh blood, it's just a pity it won't be a St Merryn's.'

Miranda stood up, determined to fight her corner whatever the consequences. 'Lady St Merryn, this isn't my place to say but can't you . . .'

'Persuade Jago to change his mind?'

'Yes.'

'I have tried, my dear, but there's no hope, I'm afraid. I've never seen my son so set on anything as getting rid of this place.'

Chapter Eight

Miranda had gone back to the cottage after speaking to Lady St Merryn. She'd denied herself any tears, simply splashed her face with cool water and tried to compose herself before heading back to the office.

It was a midweek day in May, so not horrendously busy, although there were plenty of people milling about on the quayside. While the visitors at this time of year were still mainly younger families and older couples, there was a school party sitting at the picnic tables outside the visitor centre, tucking into their packed lunches. The kids were huddled in their jumpers and waterproofs and Miranda didn't blame them. The Mount's position left it exposed at the best of times and it was now a dull, cool day; the sky seemed to be painted entirely from a palette of grey. She zipped up her fleece to her chin and tried not to romanticize the place; she'd done far too much of that already and it seemed pointless now.

She walked around the harbour and saw a familiar figure in the process of manoeuvring a small RIB alongside the harbour wall.

'Hi there!'

Catching sight of her, the man shouted and Miranda flapped a hand in his direction. Tears started to spring to her eyes again at the sight of his broad grin, as if he was a friendly face among people who had let her down so unexpectedly and were no longer what she'd thought they were.

'Miranda! Here, grab this!' He threw her the mooring rope, and she held on while he leaped up the stone steps and onto the quayside. 'Thanks.'

Miranda admired the taut muscles in his forearms as he secured the RIB's ropes to the mooring post on the harbourside. Theo was ruggedly handsome in the way of men who battled the elements for a living and loved it. She thought of the contrast between Jago, selling the Mount and his soul, and Theo, who would have given his soul for the community. She dug her nails in her palm, wondering if it had really been such a great idea to meet Theo now when she felt so raw. The news she'd just heard weighed on her like a great slab of stone.

Theo turned his eyes on her. Miranda always laughed when she heard anyone's eyes described as 'blue as the sea' but that's just what Theo's were like: deep blue-green like the shallow waters of the bay when viewed from the heights of the Mount. He must have known she was watching him. Tiny lines fanned out from the corners of his eyes as he smiled at her. 'I'm sorry I couldn't call in sooner but I ended up covering for another coxswain in St Ives on my day off and then I had to get the engine repaired on the RIB.'

'That's all right,' said Miranda, feeling both cheered and a little discomfited as she always did in Theo's presence. She was never sure if he took her seriously as manager of the Mount and suspected he was faintly amused by her passionate commitment to someone else's property. Yet Miranda wasn't turned on by the St Merryns' position like some royal hanger-on, she just loved the chance to be in charge of almost a thousand years of heritage, even if it was borrowed.

Theo climbed up onto the quay. 'How's things?'

Crap, she wanted to say, crapper than the crappiest thing in the whole world. Instead, she managed a non-committal shrug.

'Oh dear. Are you OK? You look a bit pale.'

'I'm fine. Late night.'

Theo folded his arms, his biceps bulging. 'You work too bloody hard. Don't let them run you into the ground. The St Merryns will take advantage if you let them. Especially *him*.' He flipped a thumb in the direction of the castle.

'News travels fast,' said Miranda, realising at once who Theo meant.

'His lordship's been spotted in the village already. Not on his own, of course.'

Did Theo mean he'd seen Jago with a woman, or women, Miranda wondered, more mortified than ever about her stupid pirate fantasies. The note of sarcasm in Theo's voice was also ringing alarm bells. So there had been something in Ronnie's comments about Jago and Theo.

They were a similar age, was there some history between them?

'Why's the git back here anyway? Run out of money, and wants a sub from Lady St Merryn?' Theo gave a rueful smile. 'It's OK, I'll shut up about Jago. I'm sure he's not likely to run out of cash but I hope he's not here to make trouble for you and the people at the Mount.'

Trouble was exactly what Jago had caused and recent news was just the start of it. But she couldn't possibly tell Theo that. 'I don't really know. I've kept out of his way as much as I can.'

He frowned. 'You look about as comfortable as a fish on a hook. I was joking but if Jago is here to make life difficult, it wouldn't surprise me. The landlady of the Pilchard almost dropped a glass when he strolled in a few days ago.'

'So he was in there before he came back to the Mount?'

Theo nodded. 'Apparently there were women swarming round him. Likes to make an impact, does his lordship.'

The image of Jago surrounded by fawning girls fitted in so well with Miranda's actual and imaginary idea of Jago that she longed to believe it. Too much, in fact. She decided to take Theo's report of the prodigal's return with a small but healthy pinch of salt and yet Jago had been in the pub, there was no denying that, and her own experience in the armoury had proved he liked to make an impact. She itched to ask Theo for the juicy details but didn't want to betray more than casual curiosity.

'Let's forget him for now,' said Theo, delivering a double whammy of relief and frustration. 'I know you're always busy but do you have time for a coffee? I wanted to talk to you about the Mount's evacuation procedures. I doubt you'll ever need them but there's always the outside chance of a tidal wave or crazed gunman running amok through the castle.'

'That's not funny,' said Miranda, a shiver running down her spine.

Theo assumed a deadly serious expression. 'I know, my jokes are terrible. Black humour goes with the job, I'm afraid. Now come on, I'll pay for the coffee and I'll try to make the experience as painless as possible.'

Miranda smiled. 'The coffee will be free.'

He patted her on the shoulder and his touch felt comforting and tingly. Perhaps Theo *did* understand how she felt, more than she'd been willing to acknowledge.

'And so is my advice,' he said, as Miranda decided her day had just gone up several notches.

An hour later, Miranda left the café with pages of notes which needed to be typed up into a risk assessment. Procedures in the event of waterspouts, fire, flood and mad axemen had all been covered, and only the possibility of aliens invading had been left out.

As she watched Theo's RIB power towards the mainland, the emptiness inside her returned at the thought that she might have to leave the Mount – and worse, leave Cornwall – and never see Theo and her friends again. Or was it disappointment that Theo had gone? Several times back in the café, as they'd chatted and laughed, he'd touched her hand briefly and she'd been almost sure that he was going to ask her out. He hadn't but maybe Ronnie was right. Perhaps Theo did like her as more than a friend. She'd known him a few years, she'd begun to think of him as a friend but she'd never got any vibes that he thought of her as more. He was surely out of her league for a start . . . and why had he seemed to show more of an interest in her now after she'd found out the Mount was being sold and she might have to leave? Did he sense some kind of change in her, a willingness to move on or do something different with her life? Or was that her imagination?

A few days after breaking the news about the sale to Miranda, Jago sat in his study in the tower of the Mount. Reading through the latest proposals from Southcastle was driving him mad. Wearily, he shoved the folder of papers away from him. No matter how resolved he was on the sale, seeing the details set out in black and white was not a pleasant experience.

He'd gone through Southcastle's proposals with his mother, not wanting to leave her out of the proceedings. Lady St Merryn had questioned many of the points in the draft contract, as Jago had expected, but, ultimately, she'd said the final details were up to him; it was his decision to sell and he must take responsibility.

He knew she didn't really agree with the sale and hoped he would change his mind, and he wouldn't have expected anything less from her. At the end of the day, he was alone in this one.

What was new about that? The previous decision he'd had to take had been the most lonely of his life, and he still wasn't sure he'd done the right thing. His stomach knotted even now at the memory of the dilemma he'd had to face. He would never forget what he'd done, or rather what he hadn't had the courage to do.

A sudden squall rattled the window, wafting the sound of the ocean and the smell of ozone into the study. He could almost feel the salt tightening on his skin. He should be on the sea now – he smiled to himself – or more likely, in the sea. He hadn't surfed a break in Cornwall for years and he'd probably get wiped out within thirty seconds.

He crossed to the window and squinted at the beach. A calm sea licked the shore as the tide crept in and out each day. Waves battered the Mount in winter, but it was bucket and spade land. For surf, he'd need to head for Godrevy or Porthmeor.

Not that he'd ever surf again.

He saw someone enter the courtyard from the staff pathway and walk across the terrace. That rear view was unmistakable. Miranda, tight arsed in every way. She strode across the courtyard, carrying a clipboard – God, did anyone need a clipboard nowadays? He edged a little closer to the leaded panes.

She'd stopped, apparently to inspect a litter bin and seemed to be marking the flapping sheet of paper on her clipboard. Surely she could have got one of the staff to do that. Hadn't she heard of delegating responsibility?

He inched open the leaded window, careful not to make a sound with the iron catch, and leaned out. She had her back to him, trying to tug her shorts and knickers out of her bottom. Oh dear, she *was* having trouble with those shorts. It was sweet, really, and strangely sexy, not that he was interested. Smiling in spite of himself, he nudged the window open wider.

'Shit!'

His head bumped the window, the catch slipped and the window crashed back against the masonry. Miranda flashed round, eyes instantly riveted on his guilty face. He wondered if he could detect a blush on her cheeks.

Jago lifted a hand and nodded politely like he'd just met her walking the dog. He desperately wanted to laugh but Miranda's expression was stormy. She marched off and disappeared down the steps that led to the dining hall.

No more box-ticking for her today, he'd put a stop to that.

He closed the window and trooped back to his desk, sat down in the leather chair and tried to read through some paperwork but no matter how many times he saw words on pages, none of them were making any sense to him. His mind seemed to seethe and boil with conflicting emotions like the currents around the Mount. He couldn't shake off the image of Miranda, gazing up at him, in contempt and embarrassment and . . . Had there been something else in her expression other than hostility towards him? Was she in some bizarre way attracted to him? No matter how hard he tried to deny it, he was attracted to her physically and if, in spite of her attitude towards him, she felt the same way . . . what then?

It would be bloody inconvenient, that's what. And disturbing. He couldn't let it happen, but what if it was already too late? A weird tingling had begun inside his cheek; a bizarre buzzing that spread through his whole body, right to the heart and lower. He hadn't felt anything like it since Rhianna . . .

The memory slammed into him, like a freak wave, dragging him under and spinning him out of control. He remembered the last time he'd made love with Rhianna before their world had imploded. They'd slipped away into the dunes on a remote beach, the grass shading them from the fierce heat of the Southern afternoon. The sex had been glorious, heart pounding, sweet and tender and then it had happened. When he opened his eyes, four stone walls confronted him – and Miranda.

He hadn't heard the door open. She stood in front of the desk, clutching the clipboard to her chest defensively. He thought of getting to his feet, like a gentleman would have done when a lady walked into the room.

His bum stayed firmly in the chair. 'Hello.'

'I saw you were in. I hope I'm not interrupting you.'

'As a matter of fact, you are, but it doesn't follow that the interruption is unwelcome.'

She pursed her lips at him, unsure how to take his remark. 'I'd like to discuss the Festival of Fools,' she said primly.

'The Festival of Fools?'

'Yes.' Her voice grew higher. Maybe she was nervous or maybe her knickers were bothering her again. 'The Festival of Fools,' she repeated, enunciating each word as if he was an idiot, 'is the Mount's main event of the year. We have entertainers, stalls and attractions and all the proceeds go to good causes. I'm sure you must remember it.'

He felt angry and knew it was because her barbs had begun to land too close to home and his heart whispered, because he'd been thinking of her in the same place in his mind as Rhianna and that was wrong. It *had* to be.

He tried to keep his voice gruff. 'I do remember. It's been going on for years, even before my grandfather's time when, as I'm sure you know, the proceeds went to the local poor fund. But why do you need to ask me about it?'

'Because,' she said patiently, 'the choice of charity each year lies with the owner of the Mount. In the past, I've asked your mother's opinion, of course, but she said that this year it should be your decision. She did, however, suggest the local lifeboat fund as one option. It's been fourteen years since they last benefited.'

Clever Mummy, adding another tiny weight to his burden of guilt by reminding him of how many people depended on his role as landowner. No matter what his mother said, Jago was sure she hadn't accepted his decision to sell. His mother would certainly hold out hope until the ink was dry on the contract. 'The lifeboat sounds like a good idea,' he said, glancing down at the papers on his desk.

He heard Miranda click the top on her pen. 'So that's definite? I need to know so I can start the publicity campaign for the Festival. We need to let the lifeboat fundraisers know too, so they can promote it.'

'Yes.'

Miranda made an exaggerated mark halfway down her form. Clearly, that was him ticked off the list.

'Right. Thank you. I'll leave you to get on with your work.'

He took in her tanned legs, her slight figure swamped by

shorts and polo shirt like an urchin growing into a big sister's clothes. She was the kind of woman who didn't want to be noticed. She raised the clipboard. She definitely didn't want to be noticed by him.

Too late.

'If you could spare a few minutes, I'd like to discuss something with you,' he heard himself say.

The clipboard shot up in front of her chest like a shield. Was she that scared of him? He only wanted to talk to her. Hadn't known how much he wanted to talk to her until this moment. He stood up. 'Do you fancy an ice cream?'

'What?'

'An ice cream. Cold stuff, comes in lots of flavours.' He smiled. 'It's such a lovely day and I think I should make another inspection of the property.'

'I really should be doing a risk assessment of the visitor facilities.'

He felt reckless, and not quite in control, like the man who is terrified of heights yet is drawn to the edge of the cliff. 'You can do a risk assessment of me if you like.'

Christ, what was he saying?

Miranda ignored him, her eyes telegraphing 'twat'. 'I thought you were busy with the Southcastle plans.'

'How do you know that's what I'm doing?'

'An educated guess? Plus I saw the letterhead on your desk when I came in. You had your eyes closed so I realised it must be something riveting.'

Ignoring her sarcasm, Jago flipped a thumb at the door. 'Please?'

Her eyes widened in surprise then she glanced at her

watch although he suspected she was fully aware of the time. 'I suppose I can spare ten minutes but that's my limit.'

'Don't worry. I wouldn't dream of taking you beyond your limit.'

Her lips twisted, but she led the way down the path that led from the library to the quayside.

He followed her, fascinated as she skipped down the steps, a little too fast, in his opinion, obviously uncomfortable with being followed. Fascinated too by his own boldness and stupidity. Jesus, he was almost flirting with her back there and, worse, he'd been enjoying himself. It was wrong but he didn't want to stop, not yet, not just yet . . .

He quickened his step as Miranda speeded up. She took the steps two by two and he did the same, his longer stride bringing him closer to her. He knew she could hear him close behind. In fact, she almost had to jog to keep the distance between them. He lengthened his stride. If he reached out with his hand, he could touch her arm. He heard her breathing hard and felt guilty at taunting her. He slowed but she kept up her pace.

His reaction to Miranda had shocked him, not only because he was attracted to her but because he reacted to her. She made him feel again – if only annoyance, amusement, frustration, a desire to provoke her. He hadn't felt that way about another human being, of any sex, for a long long time.

Since Rhianna had gone, he'd been numb for months, seeing the people around him, like figures who lived on the other side of a thick grey veil that separated him from the rest of the world. He'd certainly not been interested in women in any serious way and, God knows, there had been enough of them in Australia – sometimes literally throwing themselves at him. One, an ex-model, had broken into his bedroom at the surf centre and lain on his bed, stark naked.

He'd ordered her out and thrown her clothes after her, earning himself a reputation as a bastard in the process. Sadly, his reputation had only served to attract even more women and, eventually, he'd given in to quite a few of them, for the touch of another human being, for the relief of uncomplicated, emotionless sex.

It had certainly been emotionless on his part and, as for the girls, he knew he was sorry if they'd been hurt but, being brutally honest, he hadn't truly *felt* sorry. All of his guilt had been used up on Rhianna. He'd had none left for any other woman.

Soon, he found himself tarred with the image of the playboy aristocrat, and perhaps he deserved it. It was what was expected of him, and there was some comfort in that: doing what everyone expected.

He guessed that word of his exploits had reached the Mount, probably distorted and enhanced by gossip and speculation and sheer boredom. Not a lot happened in Nanjizal. Before he'd arrived back at the castle, via his lawyers in London, he'd called into the local pub for a drink. He wasn't sure quite why he'd gone in there. He didn't need a pint, but did want to delay the moment when he finally set foot on the island again.

In the short time he'd spent in the bar, he'd realised that he was still hot property in the village. He'd had phone numbers scrawled on his arm and shoved into his jeans pocket, not to mention being felt up while he'd been washing his hands in the Gents. Some bloke had asked him to a gay night in Penzance and three girls had invited him for a ménage à quatre in their tent.

The village had changed a bit since he'd left for university.

Maybe that was why he was so intrigued by Miranda, because she was one woman who clearly hated his patrician guts. Because he couldn't have her and so was safe from hurting her or himself.

'Oh dear, just look at the roof on the toilets! There's a slate missing.' As they reached the quayside, Jago landed back on planet Earth with a thud. Miranda stood with her hands on her hips, tutting at the lavatory block opposite the ice-cream kiosk. 'I must go and phone the roofers right away.'

She started to walk away from him but he took her arm. 'No you don't.'

'But ...'

'Later. Compulsory ice cream first.' He steered her in the direction of the kiosk.

'There's a queue,' she protested, looking panicky at the trail of people waiting at the open window in front of the kiosk.

'Then we'd better wait our turn.'

Miranda was in dire need of cooling off by the time they reached the front of the queue. This might be crazy but Jago had seemed almost to be ... *hunting* her. She'd tried to get out of their ice cream date by spotting the damaged loo roof but he'd had none of it and now here they were. Daisy, the woman who managed the ice-cream shop, raised her eyebrows when she saw them together. She cultivated a local wench image, which went down brilliantly with the visitors, particularly the male ones. It was an unorthodox business strategy but Miranda approved wholeheartedly. Ice-cream sales had increased by a third since Daisy had taken over the kiosk.

She scooped a generous dollop of strawberry ice cream into a cone for Miranda. 'There you go, my lover.'

'Thanks, Daisy. Business good?'

'As ever. Be even better when the schools break up proper and the dads and grandads are on holiday.' She winked at Jago. 'And what can I do for you, Lord St Merryn?'

Jago seemed amused, his mouth twisted in a smile. 'A double mint choc chip cornet, please.'

'Coming up.' Daisy crammed the double cone with ice cream. 'You want clotted cream on top of that? And choco-late sprinkles?'

She made the offer sound positively obscene. Miranda tried hard to keep a straight face.

'Yes, please. To both.'

Leaning forward out of the kiosk window, Daisy's ample bosom squashed together as tightly as Jago's twin scoops of mint choc chip. 'That'll be four pounds twenty please, my lord.'

Jago fumbled in his jeans pocket, while holding the cone in one hand. He pulled an apologetic face. 'Bugger.'

'What's up?' asked Miranda.

'I don't appear to have brought any cash with me.'

'Like the Queen?' she said, relishing his sheepish face. 'I'll get these.' She handed over the cash. 'Thanks, Daisy.'

'A pleasure, my dears. Now, who's next?'

Jago walked with Miranda to the sea wall. 'Look, I think we need to make a fresh start. You must think I'm a bit of a prat,' he said.

Miranda took a long lick of her ice cream before replying. 'Not a bit of one.'

He laughed then rescued the trail of minty cream about to drip onto his T-shirt. 'Shall we?' he said, waving his cone in the direction of the harbour. The gulls squawked overhead as they strolled along by the water, licking their ice creams. Miranda had the urge to avoid stepping on the mortared cracks in the great slabs of stone that had been dragged from the mainland to make the harbour. If you didn't step on them, then you could become invisible.

As a child, she'd tried that trick a lot, especially when her mum's boyfriends had been around. They'd thought she was an alien for wanting to read in the stuffy caravan when it was sunny outside. One of them had threatened to throw her books on a bonfire.

'Amazing that they managed to build this place,' said Jago, watching her.

'What place?'

'The castle. What's the matter? You seem miles away.'

'Brain freeze,' she said, pointing at the ice cream 'What did you say about the castle?'

'That it was incredible, how it was built in medieval times, considering they had no mechanical tools.'

She stared at the turrets and towers, rising up in a Gothic

fantasy. Except it wasn't a fantasy. It was a living and breathing community where people had lived and loved and which they'd died to defend. 'They had faith, I suppose,' she said.

'And I don't?'

'I didn't say that, Jago.'

'You don't have to.'

Miranda pushed her tongue deep into the cone, caught Jago staring at her and quickly removed it. 'What did you really want to talk to me about?' she asked.

'A few things.'

'Ah, Jago! Idling as usual.'

At the shout from the harbour, they turned to find Lady St Merryn being helped from a boat that had just arrived. She waved a hand as the boatman helped her up the gangway and onto the quayside.

'Mummy needs me,' he said. 'We'd better go and meet her and save her the walk.'

Lady St Merryn's arrival was a welcome distraction. Miranda wasn't sure she wanted to hear what Jago had been about to say; it couldn't be anything she wanted to hear. His mother shook her head in mock disbelief when Jago arrived. 'Good grief. You've actually let down your hair and come down from the tower.'

Miranda felt wicked. 'He wanted an ice cream.'

'I needed to inspect the café,' said Jago, licking a drip of ice cream from his finger.

'Hmm. I hope you're not wasting my property manager's time.'

Miranda dumped the end of her cone in a litter bin as Jago swallowed his whole.

'How was Penzance, Mother?'

'As exotic as ever. There's talk of John Lewis opening but I can't see it myself . . . not that it matters to me any more.' She held up a carrier bag of brochures. 'I've been to the travel agency.'

Jago shook his head. 'You could have booked a trip online. I would have helped you.'

'You're right. I could have wasted a day of my time, getting precisely nowhere and probably spending half of it watching videos of skateboarding dogs. I'm quite capable of finding my way around a website, thank you, but I prefer to deal with human beings and it's all sorted now. I've got my flight booked.'

Miranda itched to ask more. She didn't believe that Lady St Merryn simply wanted to 'see the world' and was convinced there was some other motive. Was she going abroad for treatment for her arthritis or for something more serious? Or was she emigrating permanently, or, Miranda felt a shiver run up her spine, going abroad to die?

Whatever her employer's reasons for leaving, it was one more nail in the coffin of the Mount. Miranda didn't want to ask directly and her ladyship obviously wasn't going to volunteer any information out here in public.

Lady St Merryn thrust the carrier at Jago. 'If you've finished your ice cream, I'd appreciate you carrying these up to the castle for me and don't you dare offer me your arm or a wheelchair. I'll get up there myself. I'm not decrepit yet.'

'I wouldn't dare.'

She glared at him. 'I know that you'd dare do a lot of things. Don't forget I gave birth to you. Miranda, goodbye.

Don't allow my son to distract you from your work and, Jago, I want to talk to you later.'

Leaving Jago with the carrier bag, she walked along the quayside, nodding as she went to the staff.

'Are you sure her ladyship is all right?' Miranda cast out her line, hoping Jago would bite.

'She's fine.' He hesitated, and then said, 'I wanted to tell you something.'

No bite then and worse, he was going to deliver some new blow. She could tell from the way he ran his hand through his hair. A nervous gesture, maybe a guilty one?

'Southcastle Estates are coming to visit the Mount next week. I'd really like you to help me show them around.'

Out of the corner of her eye, Miranda spied Ronnie on the harbour side, eyeing them suspiciously. Despite the ice cream, she suddenly developed a nasty taste in her mouth. 'Can't you do without me?'

'I could but I don't want to. You're my property manager and it's going to look odd if you're not on board with this as well. I want to present a united front.'

'So Southcastle know you haven't said anything to the staff yet?'

'Of course they do. They've already been here informally of course.'

'I wasn't aware of that.'

He had the grace to look uncomfortable. 'No. They just arrived as ordinary visitors. I arranged it before I arrived but my mother knew about it.'

Miranda had to take herself in hand very firmly. The news that the potential new owners had already checked out their territory shouldn't have come as a shock. What did hurt was the fact that Jago and Lady St Merryn had arranged the visit behind her back. But, she kept on reminding herself, it wasn't her property, it wasn't her decision, and she had to focus on that fact.

'Until everything is signed and ready to announce to the press, there's no need for the staff to know.' He spoke more gently but she wasn't soothed one bit.

'I just . . . hate deceiving them like this. It's not fair.'

He threw up his hands in exasperation. 'For God's sake, grow up.'

She snorted. '*Me* grow up? That's rich coming from you.'

Bugger. He opened his mouth, clearly on the verge of lashing out at her. She'd gone too far, she knew that. It was just . . . she so much wanted to respect Jago, wanted the man inside to live up to the strong and handsome exterior. But you couldn't always have what you wanted.

'You're my senior member of staff and I've asked you to take part in a confidential meeting. I expect you to do as I say.'

It was Miranda's turn to be shocked now. Do as he said? Who did he think he was?

Briefly, he covered his mouth with his hand, if he wished his words unsaid. 'That was unworthy of me. I apologise.'

So now he wanted absolution from her or perhaps her approval. She'd set her expectations of Jago too high. People always let you down. How could they live up to what she wanted? Her mother couldn't. Jago wouldn't. She suspected that the problem lay within, in her own idealised view of what life should be, of what people should be.

Was it her own fault that she was so devastated by the news that the Mount was being sold? People lost their homes and livelihoods every day and they had to get on with life. She glanced at the castle towering overhead and briefly saw it as a Hammer House of Horror. 'There's really no need,' she said, desperately trying to sound neutral and calm.

'Of course, I'll help you show them round. Now, I have a ton of things to do. Thanks for the ice cream,' she said sarcastically.

'I'll pay you for it!' he called after her but she'd already begun to walk away before she made things any worse between them. She was getting everything out of proportion and caring far too much about what Jago thought of her – and, far more disturbingly, what she thought of him.

Chapter Nine

Miranda had hoped for rain, mist, even the tail end of a North Atlantic hurricane for Southcastle's visit. Anything to show the Mount at its worst, with all its problems. Anything to put the bastards off.

Instead, the weather gods delivered pristine blue skies and unseasonal warmth. The scents of the gardens wafted right to the water's edge; blown on a breeze as soft as a baby's breath – some said you could smell it on the mainland. She didn't really believe that myth, but the Mount *was* definitely at its most alluring. It seemed determined to pull out all the stops to seduce its new buyers.

Jago waited with her, looking killingly cool and sexy in a white collarless shirt and jeans. Briefly, she tried the old trick, when feeling intimidated, of imagining your enemy naked. In Jago's case, that was not a good idea. Though it was barely eleven o'clock, her short-sleeved top was already sticking to the small of her back. She'd chosen a smarter top for the visit, with a cotton skirt just above the knee, and her best ballet pumps. Her uniform would have been just as comfortable but she'd wanted to smarten up, differentiate herself somehow. Maybe she was trying to distance herself from the establishment.

As the first boat of the day pulled alongside the harbour wall, Miranda spotted the Southcastle party. Wasn't hard to do. Of the dozen or so visitors aboard only two wore suits and ties. Waving away the helping hand of Jake the boatman, they climbed up the steps onto the gangway and made their way along the quayside.

Jago leaned in close to Miranda, his warm breath making her cheek tingle. She could almost forget he was selling the Mount. For a nanosecond. 'That's the main man, in the pale-blue shirt and black shades.'

Miranda lowered her sunglasses briefly then pushed them back up her nose. 'Really?'

'He's called Pierre Jumeau and he's the CEO of Southcastle Estates. The bigger guy with the laptop case is Andrew Devlin, their marketing man. I've met Devlin before in London, but not Jumeau.'

Met him in *London*? So Jago had been planning the sale for even longer than she'd thought.

He touched her shoulder briefly. 'I appreciate how difficult this must be for you. And I know you'll be completely professional. Shall we go and get it over with?'

She wasn't sure how to feel about his comment and there was no time. They were almost here, Devlin following Jumeau, his boss, along the quay.

Jago cast a glance at her and mumbled. 'You look very . . . smart. Ready to face the enemy?'

But which enemy, thought Miranda. 'They're here,' she said. 'Smile.'

Jago stepped forwards to greet them with a laid-back nonchalance that surprised her. If he was nervous or guilty about showing the visitors round his heritage, he was hiding it very well. Unless, of course, he was genuinely happy to sell or simply indifferent.

'Lord St Merryn, good to meet you at last.'

She bit her lip at Pierre Jumeau's greeting, knowing Jago would cringe inwardly.

He shook hands with Jumeau. 'Jago is fine,' he said briskly. 'This is Miranda Marshall, our property manager.'

She saw her image reflected back in Pierre's mirror lenses. She winced. It was not a good image, part fairground attraction, part Telletubby.

Jumeau took off his glasses and held out a hand. 'Delighted to meet you, Miranda.'

'Good morning, Monsieur Jumeau.'

'Pierre, please. And I apologise for the cliché. It is my real name, not one I use because people expect it.'

She smiled back. 'I apologise for mine too.' She kicked herself. She hadn't meant to engage with him but it was too late. Perhaps he wouldn't understand.

'Ah yes,' he said, deep brown eyes glinting with amusement, fully aware of his effect for bad and good. 'You are named for Miranda from *The Tempest*, the duke's daughter trapped on a magic isle. "Full fathom five, thy father lies . . ."' he quoted then added, 'I studied the play at the Sorbonne.'

Miranda found herself impressed against her better judgement, particularly as her French ran to ordering a glass of wine in the local bistro. 'May I call you Miranda? That won't offend you?' he asked.

She smiled politely. 'It's absolutely fine by me, Pierre.'

Devlin laughed loudly. 'My God, it's a bit early in the morning for Shakespeare, isn't it? Hello, Miranda, I'm Andrew Devlin; it's me you'll be dealing with after the sale.'

He offered a large hand, with fingers so big they seemed almost swollen. A large man, blokey and jokey. Dangerous, thought Miranda, more dangerous than Pierre Jumeau, because she might grow to like him. He grasped her hand firmly but not too hard. Shit. This was no good. She had to keep her distance and things in perspective. This was her future now or the mid-term at least.

'Good morning, you picked a beautiful day for it,' she said.

'A good omen, no?' said Jumeau, glasses back in place

Jago looked at him, his eyes glittering with repressed anger. Or maybe that was what she fancied she saw. It was naive of her. Jago might hate them too but that didn't mean he wouldn't sell to them.

'Shall we take a look round on our way up to the castle? My mother will have coffee waiting but there's no other route up there but by foot.'

'That's part of the charm, although it is a bit of a hike. I should take it easy, if I were you.' She cast a dazzling smile at the red-faced Devlin.

'It's not that bad,' said Jago.

Miranda threw him a smile. 'Well, it is a bit of a pain, you have to admit, Jago. Unless you're used to it, that is. And *very* fit.'

'As you clearly are.' Devlin's gaze lingered a little too long on her for Miranda's liking. She was suddenly very self-conscious of her bare legs.

'How do you get all the supplies – food and materials – up to the top?' asked Jumeau.

'There's an old goods elevator that lifts heavier stuff from the quay up through the rock to the lower terrace,' said Jago.

Miranda cut in. 'But it can't take *everything*, can it? It transports the smaller deliveries but the heavier materials for building work have to be craned in. The contractors have to send them up in small batches.' She winced. 'It costs a fortune every time we need any renovation work done and you so do *not* want to see our repairs bill.'

Jago looked ready to go pop with fury but Jumeau smiled. 'We already have seen it and have accounted for it in the budget.'

'Just so you know. I'm sure Lord St Merryn wouldn't want you to have any nasty surprises when you take over the place.'

'Oh, I don't think there's much that would shock us. Our acquisitions department has been very thorough in its research. There's not much we don't know about the Mount.'

Behind Jumeau's back, Jago shot her a WTF glare. Miranda ignored him. 'After you, Andrew?' she said, with a dazzling show of teeth.

'Oh, I'd never go in front of a lady. After *you*.'

Her skin prickled as Devlin followed her up the steps. She

upped her pace, hearing the big man just behind her, breathing heavily. She heard her own breath coming harder, yet he kept pace nonetheless. At the turn of the steps, she glanced behind and smiled at the sweating Devlin. Jago had stopped a little way down the path, pointing out the view over the Cornish coast to Jumeau. The Frenchman was as unruffled as a freshly pressed shirt and nodding urbanely.

Devlin wiped a hand over his forehead. 'You were right about this path. You really are fit, Miranda.'

'No choice, really. You'd be the same if you lived here.'

'Well, I can tell you I play First XV rugby but I don't think I could ever get into the shape you are.' His leer seemed to wrap around her body like cling film. Her concern that she might get to like him had evaporated and her skin crawled. 'Shall we carry on? It's not far to the castle now.'

Desperate to reach the castle gatehouse, she took the next few steps two at a time. The steps were uneven and one took her by surprise. She caught an uneven edge, stumbled slightly and grabbed the iron handrail to stop herself from falling.

'Hey. Watch out!'

In seconds, Devlin was behind her, his arms were around her waist, steadying her. Her top had untucked from her skirt and his large hands were in contact with her bare flesh. She tried not to flinch as he kept one hand at her back.

'Are you OK? It's a pretty hot day for all this rushing about,' he said, finally releasing her.

His damp palm seemed imprinted on her skin. She left her blouse untucked, not wanting to draw attention to her body again. The next time they were here, she decided she would wear a boiler suit and Doc Martens, no matter what the weather. 'I'm fine. It's usually a bit bracing here at this time of year. It can get very stormy and sometimes completely wild.'

She climbed another step and he did the same until he was eye to eye with her. 'Stormy sounds sound very alluring. In fact, I think a little wildness would add to the charms of this place.'

'Perhaps you wouldn't think that on a winter's night when the storms lash the castle or when we have a spring tide and the causeway's covered for days. You can get trapped here.'

'Being trapped might not be too bad under certain circumstances. And with certain people,' said Devlin.

'But the storms can cause such a lot of damage,' she said blithely. 'And that's *very* expensive to put right.'

He patted her arm. 'I think we know what we're taking on and, believe me, we're more than prepared for it.'

He leaned in a little towards her, so close that she could smell his aftershave and almost gagged. She gritted her teeth. 'I just thought I'd warn you of all the pitfalls of the place.'

Jago and Jumeau had caught them up. Jago watched her, his jaw tight. 'Everything all right here? Miranda, did I see you fall?'

'No. I just tripped. I'm fine.'

'It's OK. I came to the rescue,' said Devlin.

'I'm sure Miranda doesn't need rescuing.'

Devlin winked at her. 'No. Perhaps we need rescuing from her. She's been warning me about the dangers of taking this place on.'

'I've been telling Andrew here about the dry rot and the rising damp and the problem with the roof on the Great Hall,' said Miranda. 'And then there was that time we had an enormous high tide and the lower cottages were flooded. You should have been here then, Lord St Merryn. The damage was *terrible*. We all thought we might be washed away.'

Jago's face was like thunder but Devlin started laughing, followed by Jumeau. Miranda realised they thought she was joking. Which she was, so why was she fighting back tears? 'What do you think of the view?' she threw out in desperation.

Jumeau gave a sigh of pleasure. 'Magnificent. It reminds me of a *village perché* in Provence.'

'Is that where you're from?'

'Yes. I grew up outside a village called Castellane in the Hautes Alpes and still have a home there.'

'There's a chapel on a rocky outcrop at the edge of the village, isn't there?'

'You know it?'

'I spent a few days there on one of my university vacations and I climbed up there with a friend. The view from the chapel over the Alps is amazing.'

'It is but, you know, I think this view surpasses even that. So you can see why I would want the Mount.' He paused and it hit her. She almost believed that this clever, handsome man genuinely loved this place and had a connection to it beyond its investment potential for his company. 'So, you see, in a small way, the Mount feels like home,' he added smoothly.

'It *is* her home,' said Jago, holding out an open hand in the direction of the stone archway through to the keep. 'Would you like to see the castle, now?'

Jago led the way across the courtyard and through to the armoury. Hit them with the big guns first, she thought, knowing the armoury never failed to make an impact on visitors, whether they were awestruck or horrified. The contrast between the warmth outside and the cool corridors made her want to shiver. Jago pushed open the studded oak door to the armoury and the two Southcastle men wrinkled their noses.

Miranda allowed herself a brief smile. She'd long learned to ignore the faintly musty smell but it often took visitors by surprise. The armoury had a decent humidity control system, but the smell of age and ancient walls still lingered. The wrinkled noses were soon replaced by wide eyes and open mouths.

Devlin exhaled. 'Wow.'

Jumeau's lips twitched in a smile. 'Remarkable, Lord St Merryn.'

'It is,' said Jago, 'Please take a look. Handle the weapons, if you want to.'

Devlin and Jumeau needed no further invitation, treading carefully at first then casting aside their politeness and exploring the walls and cabinets, all packed with gruesome treasure captured and looted by Jago's ancestors over the centuries, weapons used to kill, to defend the castle and subdue people far and wide. The armoury was widely thought to have one of the finest collections of weaponry in England, but Miranda had no intention of pointing that fact out. Their visitors probably knew that anyway.

Jago stood with his back to the window with Miranda beside him. The casement was open a little and a hundred feet below the sea crashed against the rocks. She watched the visitors picking up the weapons, Devlin grinned as he rifled through the loot like an overgrown schoolboy. Jumeau coolly assessed each piece, as if weighing up its value.

Miranda risked a sideways glance at Jago. His lips were pressed together tightly as if he wanted to give the visitors space to look at their new acquisition – or found it painful to watch them handling his ancestors' possessions. Her heart sank as Jumeau peered at a shield and frowned. She didn't think she could bear to watch either.

She moved closer to Jago and whispered, 'I think it's going well, my lord.'

Jago said nothing, keeping his eyes on the visitors.

Miranda stifled a gasp as he touched the small of her back, briefly, right on the spot where Devlin's fingers had been. He released her almost immediately but the way he'd touched her seemed as if he wanted to erase the other man's print – or make his own mark on her.

His breath feathered her ear. 'If you address me as "my lord" once more, I won't be responsible for my actions.'

Her reply sounded like her throat had been dragged over glass, her skin still burning deliciously from that brief, confusing contact. 'What actions would they be, my lord?'

There was a clatter as Devlin almost knocked over a breastplate, then a laugh of relief. Jago smiled urbanely at Devlin. Jumeau stared up at the decorated ceiling and Devlin grinned, mouthed 'sorry' and replaced the breastplate. They moved towards the far end of the armoury where the cutlass rested on its stand.

'Jago . . .' she whispered.

His reply was so soft it was barely audible. 'Behave or I'm going to tip you over the castle wall.'

'If you sell to these sharks, I'll gladly jump.'

'Chilling yet still beautiful.' Jumeau's voice echoed round the armoury as he swung round.

Miranda half stumbled forwards as Jago touched her again then withdrew his hand, just in time.

Jumeau stood in a shaft of sunshine in front of the cutlass. 'This piece is exceptionally beautiful. May I touch it?'

'Be my guest.'

The air shimmered with tension as Jumeau took the cutlass reverently from its stand. A myriad of tiny dust motes danced around him in the light. Devlin turned to watch.

'Be careful,' said Jago.

'*Bien sur*.' Jumeau held the cutlass in front of him, transfixed. The steel blade gleamed in the sun, the light glinting on the razor-sharp edge. 'How old is it?'

'Well over three hundred and fifty years. Legend has it that it was captured from a pirate ship called *Jacaranda* off Tortuga in 1721,' said Jago, Miranda allowed herself a tiny smile. She still fizzed from Jago's fingertips, still reeled with confusion and desire.

'Three hundred and fifty years?'

'Yes. The fifth lord took it from the skipper of the *Jacaranda* himself, so they say.' Jago stepped forwards until he faced Jumeau. 'And I'm afraid, he used it to decapitate the captain then threw the head to the sharks.'

Jumeau held the cutlass away from him, momentarily, as if in fear of its power then laughed. 'A fitting end for a thief.'

'It was.'

'If it's true, of course. These old stories have a way of being – how do you say? – *embellished* over the years.'

Jago smiled but Miranda could tell he was angry. Jumeau was no soft touch but how had Jago ever expected him to be?

Jumeau balanced the sword across his hands and held it out to Miranda. 'A magnificent but lethal weapon. I will let you return it to its rightful place.'

Miranda took the hilt and found it cool and smooth. Carefully, she rested it back on its stand. Jago caught her eye; she couldn't read his expression properly. It was a mix of anger, sadness and challenge. Her skin prickled as she realised all three men were focused on her. She had a ridiculous urge to cover her eyes with her hands. I can't see them, so they can't see me. That's what she'd done when her mother had brought home a man she didn't like. She hadn't liked many of them. They'd made her skin crawl as Devlin and Jumeau had done.

As for Jago. He was part little boy, part very grown-up man. She wanted to look after him and guide him in the right direction and also give in and make love with him. His touch on her back had been . . . tender, possessive and tentative. Adventurer or robber? She just wasn't sure which he was and she couldn't afford to find out.

She checked her watch, alarmed to find her fingers trembling. 'You know. I think it's time we went for coffee. Lady St Merryn will be waiting for us in the library.'

Her ladyship was already at the door when they arrived,

clearly having heard their tread on the stone steps. Jago introduced the men to his mother. She smiled briefly but Miranda knew her too well to believe she was even remotely happy to see them. And yet, if she wasn't fully behind the deal, surely she would never have agreed to it?

Jago opened the door for them. 'Please do go in. I need a quick word with Miranda,' he said to Jumeau.

'Won't you be joining us?' asked Jumeau.

'I'm incredibly sorry but I've just had a message to say I'm needed urgently in the visitor centre,' said Miranda, before Jago could speak.

The door shut and he and Miranda were left alone.

'What message?' he said with a glare. It was all she could do not to laugh. Glaring made most people just look barking mad but being pissed off suited Jago. A few frown lines and weariness made him look older and more serious. She could almost believe he had depth to his character; that he'd suffered. Miranda had an insane urge to back him against the wall and push her tongue down his throat. Or was that hysteria taking over? What a bizarre morning. She felt like Red Riding Hood showing the wolf round Granny's cottage.

'I've done my duty for today,' she said.

'You did a bloody good job of trying to put them off, thank you very much!'

'No need for thanks, it was a pleasure.'

'And a lie. We don't have dry rot and rising damp.'

'I only pointed out some of the drawbacks to the place.'

Jago looked her up and down and folded his arms. 'I think they're already aware of those.'

Did he mean her? She didn't care. She remembered the

warmth of his hand on her back again and a shiver of desire rippled through her 'You weren't exactly friendly to them either.'

His eyes lingered on her. Was he going to apologise for touching her? Explain why he did it? Tell her it was inappropriate behaviour and he should be ashamed? She didn't want to hear those words. She wanted to let him know that touching her was highly appropriate and that she wanted more of it. A lot more.

And she hated herself for her weakness.

'I know this is difficult, Miranda. I do understand,' he said with unexpected gentleness.

'You'd better not keep your visitors waiting,' she said and left him alone in the corridor.

Chapter Ten

Ironically, a genuine radio call from the offices had Miranda scuttling down to the quayside where she almost ran into Ronnie.

'Wow, you look hot. Not in that way, of course.' Ronnie grinned. 'You're not my type despite what some of the villagers think.'

'I've guessed that by now.' Miranda smiled. She knew that Ronnie's Amazonian physique had people making assumptions. Living on the Mount wasn't exactly the place to meet a wide variety of single, available people, let alone a man who could measure up to a six feet tall, ex-prison officer with cropped hair and a nose ring. Miranda pushed her hair out of her eyes. A few strands had escaped her ponytail. 'I'd better get changed into my uniform.'

'Why the civvies, anyway?'

'Oh . . . we had visitors.'

Ronnie folded her arms. 'I saw. That exotic-looking suit is hot in every way. Who was it?'

Here we go. 'He's called Pierre.'

'Pierre? You have to be kidding? Frenchmen aren't really called Pierre, are they?'

Miranda laughed, mostly with relief. 'I don't think French mothers quite understand the irony. He's a business acquaintance of Jago's. They came to see the Mount and offer their ... opinions.' At least, that wasn't a fib but guilt swirled through her. She desperately hoped Ronnie wouldn't ask her what the men wanted, she wasn't sure she could lie straight out. And why, she thought with sudden anger, should she even try?

Ronnie blew out a breath. 'Wow. Has Jago decided to grow up and run the place at last?'

'I don't know anything else. I just gave them a tour.' Was it possible to actually die of guilt? thought Miranda.

Ronnie's radio crackled. 'Yes? What? Oh, for God's sake, not again.'

'What's up?'

'Some idiot's tried to smuggle a peacock out in his rucksack and got halfway along the causeway. I'll have to go and deal with it. By the way, Reggie says the drains are blocked by the harbourmaster's office. Can you get the handyman out to them fast or there'll be a right stink in this hot weather.'

Ronnie started to walk out then turned back with a worried face. 'Oh and there's just one more thing.' Miranda's stomach did a flip. Was this going to be a Columbo moment? Was Ronnie going to ask her about the sale? If so, she would have to tell Ronnie. She couldn't go on like this.

'Theo Martin phoned while you were up at the castle. He said he wanted to talk about the arrangement for the Festival of Fools but he'd call back when you were here.' Ronnie grinned. 'If you want my opinion, I definitely think he fancies you.'

'I don't want your opinion,' said Miranda, secretly glad of any distraction that took her mind off the morning's events

'Well, I must go. Peacock smuggler to catch.' Ronnie dashed off to deal with the bird thief.

Peacock smuggling, drains and Fools. Oh the glamour, Miranda thought. Yet it was *her* glamour. The Mount, with all its quirks and problems, might only be a job but she had felt needed here; not an unwanted inconvenience, like she'd felt at home.

She walked back to her cottage, locked the door and leaned against it. Not only had she practically lied to Ronnie about Southcastle but she'd put up completely no resistance when Jago had seemed to start flirting with her in the armoury. If ever he'd had a way of distracting her and making her complicit in his plans to sell the Mount that had been it. She'd melted like a bloody snowflake on a bonfire. She knew there was a connection between them – not so much of a connection but a dangerous spark – but what he wanted to use it for, she didn't know. Maybe he was clever enough to use her animosity towards Southcastle – by playing up to it and pretending he shared it, he'd got her to engage with him and now she was doing his dirty work with the staff, or rather not doing it by not telling them anything.

Wearily, she walked upstairs to the bathroom. Stripping

off her clothes she stood naked in front of the wardrobe mirror. Her skin was flushed, her hair limp in the heat. She twisted round, as if there might be a mark left by Jago's fleeting touch. She imagined his fingers resting at the base of her spine and slipping lower down the back of her skirt to cup her bottom. She closed her eyes.

'Bugger.'

It was crazy to think in this way about Jago, not to mention masochistic. Yes, she fancied him, along with half the population, probably. He was knicker-wettingly sexy and he was going to hurt her badly if she carried on like this. She stepped into the shower cubicle and slid the door back so hard it rattled. She turned on the shower and gasped as chilly water blasted down. It hurt but it focused her mind. She had to get on with the plans for the Festival of Fools and when she got back in the office she'd call Theo.

Chapter Eleven

A few days later, Miranda put down her office phone and punched the air. 'Yes!'

Ronnie glanced up from writing her daily report. 'What's up? Won the lottery?'

'No, but I've just booked the Fishermen's Choir to sing at the Festival of Fools. They had a last-minute cancellation.'

Ronnie rolled her eyes. 'Rock and roll. The grannies will be chucking their thermals at them.'

Miranda giggled. 'Don't laugh. The older visitors will love them; they were on *Strictly* last week.'

'I rest my case. Can't you get Rage Against the Machine? Or Ozzy Osbourne? Then again, Ozzy would probably run off with one of the grannies.'

'Our funds won't run to it; we're getting the choir at a reduced rate as it is. But there's lots of other entertainment.

I've booked jesters, fire–eaters, a storyteller, scrimshaw carvers and a bouncy castle.'

'Great. *If* you're five years old.' Ronnie grinned to let Miranda know she was being wound up. 'Did you call Theo Martin back?'

'I might have.'

'And?'

'He and the crew are bringing the inshore lifeboat over to the island for the Festival. The kids will love that.' In fact, Theo had been very helpful and friendly, obviously delighted that the Lifeboat Station would benefit from the proceeds of the day. He'd promised that his crew and their supporters would turn out in force to support the day.

'Only the kids?' asked Ronnie.

'Ronnie, give me a break. I don't know Theo that well.'

'But you like him.'

'He's nice, yes.'

'Nice?'

'OK. He's probably the best-looking guy in Nanjizal and I love him to bits – along with everyone else, from the tod-dlers to the grannies.'

'And?' Ronnie wasn't going to let her off the hook.

'He said he'd see me around, which is very likely con-sidering we both spend most of our lives within the same five–mile radius.'

'That's it?'

Miranda threw up her hands in exasperation. 'Yes. Is this a full-blown interrogation or can we please talk about some-thing else?'

Ronnie gave a sigh. 'I suppose so, but don't think I've

finished with you and Theo. I'll be watching you closely, Miss Marshall. Now, what other attractions have you arranged for this Festival besides a bunch of hunky men in yellow wellies?'

'We're going to lock people in the old stocks by the visitor centre and charge visitors to throw wet sponges.'

Ronnie's face lit up. 'Now you're talking! The stocks I can relate to. Who's going in there? I can think of a few. That bloke who ran off with the peacock for a start. The gardener says that the poor bugger hasn't been the same since.'

Miranda rested her chin on her hand and sighed. 'Well, *actually*, I was looking for volunteers.'

Ronnie shook her head. 'No. No way, Jose. I'll be on duty anyway.' She reached for a stapler from the desk tidy. 'So forget it.'

'Reggie said he'd do ten minutes in there.'

'Reggie's barking mad.'

'Pretty please?'

Ronnie banged her hand down on the stapler. 'No.'

'Please, Ronnie. I'm doing half an hour myself and a couple of the young gardeners have offered, as have some of the lifeboat crew. The old guy who works part-time in the café said he would too but I'm worried he won't be able to sit that long. It's not a soft option being pelted with those sponges. Some of them hurt and people can be really vicious. I'm still short of volunteers. It needs someone tough.'

'So you thought of big, butch Ronnie?'

'You're not butch but you are brave and fear no one. You keep telling me this.'

'And I'd probably scare the kids off. Sorry, I really am on

duty all day or I would do my stint. No, don't look like that at me. Believe me, there's sure to come a moment when I'm gagging to be locked up. Like when some brat throws up their Mount St Merryn cream tea after their mum's left 'em for three hours in the bouncy castle.' She slotted her report into a manila folder. 'What about his-bloody-lordship? Thought of asking him?'

Miranda snorted. 'Jago? You are joking?'

'Have you tried?'

'No. And I'm not going to. There's no way he'd do it.'

'You'd make a lot of money,' said Ronnie. 'Even if it was you chucking most of the sponges at him.'

'I don't hate him that much.' She pulled the Fishermen's Choir CD towards her and pretended to study it.

She heard Ronnie pick up her radio from the desk. 'I have to go and do my rounds. Do you fancy a drink on Friday night? I'm off duty. Tide's out and we could walk to the Pilchard, if you like. I'll treat you to scampi and chips then we can go on the lash. Maybe we'll even meet some-one nice.'

'OK, thanks. Sounds great.'

Miranda felt her cheeks glow. She hadn't exactly told the whole truth to Ronnie about her conversation with Theo. What he'd actually said was that he might see her around in the Pilchard on Friday night, as he was meeting a few mates. It wasn't exactly an invitation to a date, but going along with Ronnie was a good compromise. A break away from the island, even if only in the local village pub, would do her good and if Theo was there, so much the better.

*

On Friday evening, Ronnie and Miranda climbed the steps from the causeway to the quayside and headed up the short steep lane that led to the Pilchard, the inn that was the heart of the fishing village of Nanjizal. It was an old whitewashed stone pub, squatting above the harbour, almost groaning under the weight of its tiled roof.

The inn sign, with its fading fishy symbol, creaked softly in the breeze as the girls walked through the tables of people drinking pints and devouring bar meals. The food at the Pilchard was hearty and good value, and on a fine light evening, the place was jammed full of locals and early season tourists.

Ronnie put a hand on Miranda's arm. 'Hang on a minute. Shall I get a table while you get the drinks?'

'Good idea.'

While Ronnie set off in search of a free table and, Miranda guessed, a good-looking man who wasn't a tourist or gay, Miranda went into the bar. The buzz of voices, laughter, cheesy background music and glasses clinking hit her ears. She took a long breath in and the tension eased from her body. Wow, had she been that wound up? She hadn't realised how on edge up she'd been until she'd seen and heard what a normal relaxed situation was like again. She couldn't see Theo yet but that didn't matter; it was such a relief to forget about the sale and Jago for a few hours.

The pub landlady folded her arms as Miranda reached the bar. 'Hello, stranger.'

'Sorry, Karen, I've been really busy.'

'I've seen so little of you lately, I thought there was a man involved.'

Miranda gave an 'I-should-be-so-lucky' grimace. 'No, but the season's getting into full swing and I've been planning for the Festival of Fools. Will you be able to come?'

'If I can get away from here for an hour or so.' Karen reached for a glass from above the bar. 'Half a lager?'

'Yes, please and a white wine spritzer for Ronnie.'

Karen raised an eyebrow. 'Not a pint of Tinner's? If she's gone for such a wussy drink, she must be on the pull.'

You could say that again, thought Miranda as she carried the tray drinks back to Ronnie, nodding at locals she knew. She didn't hold out much hope for Ronnie, but you never knew. A miracle might happen and there were certainly plenty of people around. Ronnie had chosen a table in the middle of the Pilchard's beer garden. Unfortunately, it overlooked the Mount, a major attraction for the pub's tourist visitors but rather a busman's holiday for her and Ronnie.

On the other hand, Ronnie's attention was occupied by a far bigger attraction.

She snatched at Miranda's arm after she'd set down the tray of drinks on the table. 'Oh my God. Have you seen that?'

A group of guys were laughing and drinking at a nearby table. They were all hefty and wearing shorts and rugby shirts.

'Who *are* they?'

Miranda tried to make out the faces around the table. 'I'm not sure, but I think I've seen one or two of them before. They're from a rugby team over in Penzance. They were drinking outside the pub by the museum in St Ives when I went to that seminar on maritime history a couple of months ago. You can hardly miss them, can you?'

'No and the big one can do the Haka with me any day.'

All of the men were built like brick outhouses, but the one that had caused Ronnie's jaw to drop stood head and shoulders above them. His laugh rumbled round the garden like an express train. He looked like a Maori to Miranda and reminded her of a modernist sculpture, beautiful yet stark. The arm lifting up his pint was adorned with inky tribal tattoos.

'Don't look, don't look. He's seen us!'

Ronnie pulled the hem of her Lycra skirt down her thighs but it immediately pinged back up again. 'Oh God, you don't think I look too tartish, do you?'

Miranda shook her head. 'I don't think he'll mind. If he's single.'

'Single? If he is, do you think any woman would dare get in my way? And, oh, isn't that Theo with them?'

Miranda did a double take as Theo came into view, having previously been swamped by his crowd of hulking rugby mates. 'Yes, it is but I didn't know he played rugby.'

Theo placed a tray of pints on the rugby players' table.

'Miranda,' Ronnie purred in her ear, 'you don't feel like contributing to community relations, do you?'

Miranda thought her friend sounded like a lioness scenting a helpless gazelle. The Rugby God had no chance, single or not. She sincerely hoped he wasn't gay.

'You mean you want me to talk to Theo?'

'I'll love you forever and have your babies, if you do.' Ronnie leaned in closer to her. 'After I've had *his*.'

The Rugby God laughed and the earth shook again, at least it did for Ronnie who gulped down her spritzer like lemonade. Miranda wondered how subtly she could catch Theo's eye but was saved by him catching hers and immediately heading for her table. Miranda caught several pairs of envious female eyes trained in her direction as he joined her.

'Hello, ladies. Been let out on parole from Mount Alcatraz, have you?'

Miranda laughed. 'Ronnie fancied a night off.'

Theo winked at her. 'I could see you were dressed to kill.'

Miranda glanced down at her strappy dress and dinky ballet pumps, wondering if she'd overdone it and decided Theo was just teasing. She hardly had a chance to wear them at the Mount and tonight was their first outing of the year. Her mother was always telling her to dress up, put on a bit of slap, anything to get her out of the caravan and acting 'normal', she'd supposed. Maybe her mother had been genuinely worried about her turning 'peculiar'. An obsession with Egyptian mummies wasn't that odd for a child, but if you were still fixated on them at sixteen maybe your mother had grounds for anxiety.

'We don't get out much,' she joked.

Theo's gaze drifted from her head to her toes. Miranda felt rather like a marine engine being inspected. 'You should do something about that. You spend far too much time locked away on that thing.' 'That thing', the Mount, loomed on the horizon behind him in the evening sun. Theo's expression hardened and he pressed his lips together as if he wanted to say more but didn't trust himself.

'It's not that bad over there,' joked Miranda, a bit pissed off with Theo for suggesting that she was being held prisoner on the Mount. 'I'm here now, too.'

'I didn't know you played rugby, Theo?' Ronnie cut in, desperation to turn the conversation hitching up her voice an octave. Playing matchmaker to Theo and Miranda had obviously been pushed down the agenda by her eagerness to get to grips with the Rugby God.

He turned round briefly to nod at his friends. Rugby God raised his glass to him and Theo waved his back. 'I don't play the game myself but I've got a few mates in the team. They're organising a tug-of-war to raise money for the lifeboat station and we decided to hold a meeting about it. In the pub, of course.'

'A tug-of-war? What? *All* of you?'

'Yeah and, somehow, I don't think we're going to lose. Not with Neem over there on our side.'

Ronnie heaved a sigh. 'He is absolutely enormous.'

Miranda seized her chance, hoping Ronnie wasn't going to need oxygen. 'That sounds exciting. You don't think your rugby mates would consider doing a tug-of-war at the Festival of Fools, do you? As it's in aid of the lifeboats.'

He scratched his chin. 'I don't know. Never thought of that but it's a bloody good idea. I'll ask.'

'It would be great entertainment for the visitors. The kids would love it. If you could find some opposition, that is,' said Miranda, realising that she was the one who sounded desperate. Theo might think she fancied Neem, or that she was angling for a date with him.

'Oh, they can always find some chancers wanting to take them on. Even with their star player,' he said.

Miranda felt the frustration radiating from Ronnie and blundered on. It was too late to worry about what Theo thought of her. 'Will Neem be able to come along to the Festival too?'

Theo shrugged. 'I dunno. Maybe. He's over here for a couple of years doing a jewellery course at the college in Falmouth so if he's not busy I guess he might be able to do the Festival.'

Ronnie almost choked on her spritzer.

'He *lives* here? He doesn't look like a jewellery designer, I mean,' Miranda said, feeling increasingly like Ronnie's ventriloquist's dummy. All she needed was to sit on Ronnie's lap and have her jaw worked up and down. Theo really would think that she fancied the God herself if she pushed it any further.

Theo pulled a pendant out of his polo shirt. It was a tiny silver dolphin strung on a leather cord. 'We all take the piss out of him but you should see the stuff he turns out. Look, he made this.' He held the pendant between his calloused finger and thumb. 'He's hoping to open his own studio one day. He's got a few pieces in the gallery here in Nanjizal.' He let the dolphin rest back against his tanned chest, and it nestled in a fluff of dark-blond hair. Then he gave Miranda a searching look. 'Perhaps you should drop by and visit him if you're that interested.'

Miranda decided she'd gone beyond the call of duty. 'Oh, *we'd* love to see his pieces in the gallery. Wouldn't *we*, Ronnie?'

Ronnie made a sound somewhere between a squeak and a honk. Theo glanced at her, shook his head slowly and gave a wry smile, as the penny dropped. He put down his pint and bellowed to his mates across the garden. 'Hey, Neem. These ladies want to meet the artist. Come and show the girls your wares, mate!'

Neem detached himself from the group and made his way over. When he stopped in front of their table, his bulk blocked out both the evening sun and the Mount. Ronnie seemed to be melting in a puddle of drool but somehow managed to struggle to her feet. Although she was six inches taller than Miranda, Neem was another eight or nine above that. Miranda felt like a Chihuahua at Crufts, standing next to a borzoi and the Hound of the Baskervilles.

'Neem, this is Miranda,' said Theo.

Neem held out a hand like a digger shovel. It was an old-fashioned gesture but Miranda bravely offered her fingers, expecting to have her bones mashed to a pulp.

'Hello, I'm Neemia Mealamu,' he said, pressing her fingers gently but firmly, like a man who was well aware of his strength and of using it judiciously. His gaze lingered longer on Ronnie and he smiled warmly, showing a set of perfect white teeth. Miranda revised her opinion: the guy was more like a giant golden retriever than a Baskerville.

'And who's this?' he asked in a rich, deep Kiwi accent that sounded as if it had been mined from the depths of the earth.

Ronnie, mesmerised, offered her hand. 'Veronica S-stapleton. But you can call me R-ronnie.'

Faced by a crazed man with a cutlass or a peacock smuggler, Ronnie hadn't batted an eyelid. Confronted by six feet eight of New Zealand's finest beef, she'd been tackled, brought down and would probably need a stretcher and the trainer.

'Your glasses look a bit low, girls. Can I get you a drink?' asked Neem.

'Arf,' squeaked Ronnie, with an uncanny impression of a sea lion.

Miranda rescued her. 'She means yes. Half of Tinner's and a Pimm's for me, please.'

'Coke, Theo?'

''Fraid so, mate. I'm on emergency duty.'

Neem winked at Ronnie. 'Want to give me a hand carrying them back from the bar?'

'Arf arf.'

'After you, then.'

Ronnie didn't exactly skip alongside Neem – Miranda didn't think Ronnie had ever skipped in her life – but the eagerness with which she accompanied Neem to the bar came pretty close.

Theo laughed as Neem stepped back to let Ronnie go into the bar then ducked his head under the beam. 'Well, I never thought I'd see Ronnie lost for words.'

'No. I thought she was going to pass out at one point.'

Theo took a long sip of his drink and smacked his lips. 'What about you? You seemed impressed by the big man, too.'

'Neem's gorgeous but he's not my type and, anyway, I'd have to step over the dead body of Ronnie to get to him first.'

He watched her thoughtfully. 'What is your type then?'

Bugger. Miranda had asked for that one. Theo's eyes

crinkled into lines at the corners, fully aware he'd put her in a corner.

'I don't really have one.' Miranda laughed, a little nervously.

After making her blush, Theo backed off a little but Miranda guessed he was well aware of his effect on women. 'It's good of you to nominate the lifeboats as your charity this year for the Festival,' he said, more seriously.

'That wasn't my idea, I'm afraid, though I did suggest it.'

'Lady St Merryn's choice, was it?'

'Oh, no.'

'What? Not Jago's, surely?' Theo seemed be annoyed that Jago had chosen to support his crew.

'It was Jago's decision, but I suggested you – the lifeboats – as our charity. Jago just had to rubber stamp our decision.' Well, it was true and if Miranda had thought Jago wouldn't agree, she'd have just gone ahead anyway. But she wasn't going to tell Theo that.

'Maybe Jago's not such a total twat as most of us think.' He sounded unconvinced. 'Most of the blokes round here think he's a waster, but, unfortunately, the women seem to like him from what I've heard and seen since he's been back.'

She was taken aback by the bitterness in his voice. 'Theo . . .'

'OK, maybe I shouldn't say that about our noble benefactor but he was never around much when he was young and after his father died, he just left her ladyship to run the place on her own. No man should run away from his responsibilities like that.'

Plenty do, though, thought Miranda. Like her father,

111

whoever he was. Like her mother. Like she had, running away from home at sixteen and never going back. She'd had good reason, though. Hadn't she?

Yet Jago had rattled Theo's cage in some way, though how he'd had time to do that in the short time he'd been back, Miranda didn't know. Theo hadn't immediately struck her as the jealous type; he was such a babe magnet himself, he had no reason to feel insecure where girlfriends were concerned.

He finished his Coke then said quietly, 'Must have been a shock to you all at the Mount, Jago turning up out of the blue? Come to run the place, has he? Or is it just a flying visit?'

Ah. She could finally hazard a guess at where some of Theo's animosity had come from. Understandable envy of the St Merryns combined with a partly justifiable contempt of Jago for abandoning his duties . . . it figured. Sort of. Theo would go down with his ship before he'd give up on the chance to help the community, whereas he probably thought Jago would be first in the queue for the lifeboats.

'I'm not really sure that I can . . . '

'Slag off your employers in public? In that case, I'll change the subject and, anyway, your new lord and master just crawled in.'

Before Miranda had time to protest, he shifted to one side and Jago headed through the gate into the pub garden. He glanced in Miranda's direction, gave a brief nod then disappeared straight into the bar. Neem walked out a few seconds later, a pint in each hand, followed by Ronnie with a Pimm's and a Coke for Theo. Miranda was struck by her friend's face, she seemed to have lit up inside, like a lantern glowing on a dark night. Perhaps love at first sight really existed, thought Miranda. Lust at first sight certainly did. She knew that too well.

Some time later, Ronnie and Miranda sat at the table while Neem and Theo nipped off to the Gents.

Miranda blew out a little breath. 'You know, men don't usually go the loo in twos.'

Ronnie bounced up and down on her seat. 'Not for a slash, they don't. But there's more than bogs in the Gents. Oh my God, I hope the machine has a condom big enough. Oh, bloody hell . . . ' She sat down with a thump. 'I hope I can cope.'

'Ronnie, I love you to bits and I hope you have a great night, but that is way too much information.'

'Yes. Sorry. You don't mind if I go back to the Mount with Neem, do you?'

'Of course not.'

'You can walk over with us, if you like, but I get the feeling you'd rather stay with Theo?'

Miranda wasn't sure yet, but she also wasn't going to make Ronnie feel uncomfortable by playing wallflower. 'I'll follow in a little while. Give you time to get settled into the cottage first.'

If Ronnie could have smiled any wider, her face might have cracked. 'Thanks.'

'Don't do anything I wouldn't do,' she said.

'Bugger. That doesn't leave me much.'

As Neem came back, looking suspiciously happy, Miranda spotted Jago at a table on the edge of the garden, surrounded

113

by what could only be described as a fan club. She recognised three girls from the local beauty salon, the junior
partner from the solicitor's and the man who ran the crys-
tals shop on the seafront. They were gawping, giggling and
touching his arm like he had the power to cure them of the
palsy or the plague. From time to time, Jago deigned to nod
and smile in between puffs of a cigarette.

''Bye then,' said Ronnie. She kissed Miranda on the cheek
and then whispered, 'Wish me luck.' Neem had barely
touched Ronnie but the air crackled with a connection
between her best friend and this giant of a man.

'Enjoy,' she said and truly meant it. In a moment, Ronnie
would leave and she would be left in a crowded garden, surrounded by people and Theo and Jago. She squashed down
a shiver. She suddenly felt as alone as she ever had done and
didn't know why.

'You too,' replied Ronnie with a theatrical wink.

Miranda cringed inwardly then Ronnie was gone, with
Neem's huge arm around her waist. Miranda wondered how
Ronnie's bed would bear the weight.

As soon as they'd gone, Theo turned to her. 'So, now that
we're finally on our own, I wanted to ask you something.
You don't have to say yes, not if you're busy, but I was wondering if you might ... that is ... oh, shit!' The pager clipped
to his belt buzzed. 'We've got a shout. I have to go but I was
going to say —'

A piercing whistle rang out by the gate. A woman waved
frantically at Theo and he shouted back, 'Coming!' He
turned to Miranda. 'I'll phone you. Tomorrow.'

'Take care,' called Miranda.

She had been sure Theo had been going to ask her out and she hadn't known what to say in reply. There was bitter edge to his comments about Jago, yet, on the surface, he seemed a genuinely sweet guy. She didn't know why she was even hesitating. God knows it was time she met someone nice and you couldn't get much nicer than Theo. The rest of the village thought he was a sweetheart, unlike someone else ... someone walking over to her table right now.

Jago was not nice or sweet. In fact, he was a feckless, over-privileged bastard who had so far managed to be a dis-appointment on every level. Yet at the sight of him heading for her like a heat-seeking missile, Miranda needed scraping off the flagstones of the Pilchard's beer garden.

Chapter Twelve

Jago wore ripped jeans, knackered flip-flops and a faded T-shirt. He looked like a mythical god who'd fallen to Earth naked and had to raid a recycling skip.

Maybe, she thought, it was imprinted in the genetic code passed down from her mother. Some people got frizzy ginger hair or wonky teeth. She'd been handed a predisposition to fall for a gorgeous, useless object like Jago. Perhaps she could get some aversion therapy that would make her want nice, steady Theo, pillar of the community and serial hero.

He put his pint down on her table and took a long slow drag on his ciggy before smirking. 'Putting some pennies in Theo Martin's collecting tin, were you?'

'Just supporting a good cause.'

Her throat tightened with anger and confusion. What had Theo done to upset Jago? Determined not to get dragged into a fight, she tried sarcasm. 'You do know your mummy would kill you if she knew you were smoking.'

Jago gave a sigh. 'Well, if I've been such a bad boy, why don't you put me over your knee and spank me?'

A fire kindled beneath her cheeks. Was Jago drunk? He must be to say something like that to her and, worse, spanking Jago was a scenario she dare not even begin to contemplate in a public place. Too bad, the image was now etched on her brain, possibly forever. She hated him for saying it, but at the same time her whole body seemed to glow like a fire had been lit within her. She sought refuge in prissiness. 'Your father died of a heart attack. You know your mother hates smoking.'

'Oh, I shouldn't worry too much. I have many vices but a fag is only one of my occasional ones. But if it offends your delicate sensibilities, I'll happily put it out.'

'Don't bother on my account.'

'I don't do anything on other people's account, you should have realised that by now.' He dropped the fag on the flagstones and stamped on it with his flip-flops. Miranda had hopeful visions of smouldering rubber and Jago hopping about shrieking, but it wasn't to be. He was too cool for that and he had to be a little drunk, which might have accounted for the extra edge to his so-called humour.

He nodded at her glass. 'Can I get you a drink?'

'I've already got one, thanks.'

'Call that a drink? A quarter of a glass?'

'There's no point. I'm going back to the Mount in a minute.'

'The tide's coming in.'

'I've still got time.'

'Possibly, but I wouldn't try crossing over on your own, now Ronnie's gone. Who was that I saw her with?'

'He's called Neem and he's from Christchurch, but he's working as a jewellery designer. When he's not playing rugby. With Theo,' she added mischievously.

'Theo doesn't play rugby. He's too busy with his little boat.'

'He's on a shout,' said Miranda loyally.

'Yes. He's a hero. Unlike me.'

So that was it. Jago was feeling guilty as well as being half-cut. Well, Miranda wasn't going to absolve him. She drained her glass and shouldered her bag. 'You know, I really didn't expect to see you in here at all,' she said.

'You mean you didn't expect I'd dare show my face in the circumstances?'

'No, well, yes, that's what I meant. Everyone must be wondering, asking you questions, wanting to know if you're here to stay?'

His mouth curved in a wry smile. 'Actually, most of the people who've spoken to me tonight seem to want to sleep with me.' Her skin fizzed. Did he mean her too? The arrogant egomaniac git. 'Present company excepted, of course. I know you'd never dream of sleeping with the enemy,' he added.

'You're not the enemy. Please don't flatter yourself that I think so. You're my employer and I work for you. I'm just trying to help you achieve your goals as effectively as I can.'

118

He stared at her then shook his head. 'If I'd known the Mount's finances were being wasted on teaching my staff to talk management crap, I'd have come back years ago.'

'Jago. Has anyone ever told you that you are the most annoying bastard that ever walked the Earth?'

He smiled. 'That's better. I'll fetch you a drink.'

'Suit yourself but I'm leaving.'

'Sit down, Miranda and don't be so stupid.'

His voice was sharp as he flipped a thumb towards the sea. She could see the waves lapping the cobbles at the Mount end of the causeway. She'd have to leave right now if she wanted to walk over. She knew the tides as well as the back of her hand – it was touch and go if she would make it without wading. Never mind, she'd risk it.

He softened his tone. 'Come on, Miss Whiplash. I'll get you a drink.'

'I'll be gone when you get back from the bar.'

'Perhaps. But somehow, I don't think you're that predictable.' It was catch-22. Damned if she walked off. Damned if she didn't. 'I'll be back shortly,' he said. 'And we both know it's already too late to walk away.'

Her heart thumped, in anger and nervousness and pure desire. She put her bag back on the table and closed her eyes. Why couldn't she leave? She'd been so determined to walk away, knowing that Jago was like a bottle of cheap champagne on special offer at the supermarket. You couldn't help buying one, even though you knew it would end up tasting just as underwhelming and nasty as you'd expected.

But he was right. As she waited, she realised she'd been kidding herself that she could see the Mount end of the causeway. It was already shimmering as the water closed over the cobbles and she might have had to wade the last stretch. She shivered a little, that would not have been a good idea; the currents swirling around the island could be fierce, no matter how good a swimmer you were. She'd have to persuade one of the rowing club or fishermen to lend her a boat or stay on the mainland in the pub or a B&B. She didn't think Jago would have trouble finding a bed for the night.

She thought of Ronnie and Neem, breaking the bedsprings in Ronnie's cottage. That's if Neem could even squeeze through the doorframe. She smiled at the thought of Ronnie getting her jollies and felt a stab at the thought of Jago getting his. A stab of jealously and longing and lust.

Jago returned to the table with a glass tumbler, steam rising from the surface in wispy tendrils. Miranda sniffed the air and smelled spices and rum.

'Here, have some grog. You look cold, but, dare I say it, slightly less ready to kill me.'

Miranda kept her eyes ahead. She would not look down at her dress. It really had grown chilly in the garden. She took the glass from him, muttered a 'thanks' and gulped down a glug of punch. 'Oww!'

'Here.' Jago handed her his beer. 'Cool your tongue on that.'

She swilled her scorched mouth with cold beer.

'Better?' he asked.

She swallowed the beer and blew on the punch as the alcoholic steam fill her nostrils. 'Mmm.'

'Good. I'd hate you to have a burnt tongue on my account.'

Miranda ignored him and pretended to take an interest in a woman across the garden who seemed to have just noticed Jago's presence. Dressed in some kind of Roman toga with her hair piled on her head, she smiled coquettishly at Jago and mouthed a 'Hello, darling.' Jago lifted a hand to her, twitched his lips in a half-smile then turned back to Miranda. The toga woman glared at Miranda as if she was something nasty stuck to the sole of her gladiator sandal.

'Is Toga Girl one of your fan club?' Miranda asked, immediately hating herself for sounding as if she cared.

He raised an eyebrow. Bastard. He knew she was jealous. He knew Toga Woman was jealous too. That made Miranda the same as her. Arghh.

'Toga Girl, as you call her, is an old school friend on holiday down here but I'm liable to bump into someone who knows me anywhere. I can't hide away even if my visit here is only going to be a short one.'

'But by appearing in public,' she began, rather pleased with her image of him moving among his people like a monarch, 'you must be dodging questions about your plans all the time.'

He sighed briefly. 'I don't like it but the pain will be of short duration.' He frowned and hesitated then said quietly, 'As short as I can possibly make it. I don't want to make anyone suffer longer than they have to.' He stared at his pint for a few seconds.

'What's the matter?' asked Miranda as the silence lengthened and Jago seemed to be searching for an answer in the bottom of the glass.

'This place brings back too many memories, I suppose.' He gave a short laugh. 'Now drink your grog.'

She sensed she'd touched a nerve. There was something he didn't want to talk about but she wasn't going to let him off the hook. 'Do you miss Australia? People say you were a surf instructor over there.'

He laughed without any real amusement. 'Is that what they call it?'

'Ronnie did.'

'Really? Are you sure she didn't say I was a sponging parasite and a layabout?'

Miranda considered lying then saw his eyes, drilling into her. 'Those too.'

'Both are probably accurate. I left uni and bummed around, picking grapes, working in bars. I ended up at Bells Beach learning to surf, then I got a job as an instructor.'

But ten years, Miranda thought, ten years of bumming around and riding waves. Surely that couldn't cover the whole of his absence from home.

'And?'

He smiled, bitter as acid. 'And nothing.'

Miranda couldn't conceal her surprise at his sudden change of subject but she had reached the stage where it was hard to conceal her feelings at all. After the earlier drinks, the hot rum punch had tipped her over from ever so slightly defensive to ever so slightly pissed. Maybe it wasn't the punch but being with Jago, talking to him and almost empathising with him. Whatever the cause, her inhibitions were melting fast. 'I don't believe you.'

'And nothing I want to talk about. Are there not things that have happened to you that you don't want to rake over?'

She stopped, glass to her lips. Her past? Running away from home. Putting herself through university. Working in the vacations in country house teashops, cleaning loos, as a gardener's labourer. Anywhere quiet and isolated with a sense of history that she didn't have. Then the Mount. 'I suppose so,' she said, refusing to reveal any detail, no matter how pissed she was.

'And do you want to bare your soul to me?'

'No.'

'What about your family?'

'We're estranged.'

'Estranged? Now there's a word.'

'I don't have any contact with them,' she said. How much it hurt to admit even that much. She felt like he'd taken wire wool to a raw graze. Was that how he felt about her questions?

'You never talk about them,' he said.

'How do you know I don't?'

'My mother says you've never been back to see them and you don't mention them. She thought it was unusual but not her place to pry. I, on the other hand, have no manners.'

'I've already worked that out, Jago.'

He smiled. 'So having established I'm a rude bastard, tell me about your family. What happened?'

Should she tell him? That her father left before she was even born and that she hadn't been part of her mum's plans,

123

period? And that, one day, her mother had done something that there was no coming back from. 'I thought it was better if I just left.' The glow from the rum punch had disappeared into the cool night air. She shivered. She'd already said more to Jago about her family than she ever had to anyone and she'd reached her limit. The combination of alcohol and his questions made her feel like crying. Why didn't he leave her alone?

'It was a long time ago and very far away. You must know how it feels, after you left the Mount for Australia.'

'To an extent, but I wouldn't say I was "estranged" from my mother. Contrary to popular belief, we have kept in touch. Not that regularly, but enough for her to know I've been safe and well. She came over to Australia a few years ago, in fact when . . .' He stopped and, to her horror, reached out and touched her hand. She couldn't cope with his sympathy, she might cry. 'Whatever happened must have been pretty bad for you to stay away for all these years and never go back . . .' He hesitated.

She felt the hot sting of tears in her eyes, the moisture on her lashes. His touch had made her question the past thirteen years, the past thirty even. She couldn't face that now, not from him. 'Don't tell me I should try to contact my mother.'

'I didn't say that, Miranda.'

'I know but . . .' That's what he was thinking, Miranda knew, or maybe, a small voice added, that's what she'd wondered herself at times. She crushed the notion immediately, both in his mind and her own. 'Nothing will have changed, even if I did try to go back. You won't change how you feel about selling the Mount will you?' she asked, rubbing her hand across her eyes, ashamed of her tears.

'No. I won't and I'm sorry for upsetting you. You're probably right and I really should mind my own business. Here.'

She caught her breath. He reached out and rubbed a thumb gently under each eye. 'No clean white handkerchief like a gentleman should have,' he said. 'Only a grubby thumb.'

'You're making things worse,' she said, trying to smile but feeling full to the very brim. One more gentle word, one more probe of the wounds, however tentative, and she would tip right over the edge. Be a bastard again, she wanted to say to him. Be an arrogant boy not a complex man she couldn't fathom out and was finding difficult to hate in the way she needed to.

Her relief when Jago changed the subject was like falling onto a giant bank of cotton wool, when you'd expected to crash onto rocks. 'Now, referring to my earlier misdemeanours with the fags,' he said, 'if you're not going to take up my willingness to be chastised, I could suggest another way of me doing penance. I heard that you're looking for really bad people to put in the stocks.'

This was good. Not only the prospect of Jago going in the stocks but the levity and the banter after the emotional stuff she found impossible to deal with. Having escaped with her life, she now felt recklessly happy. Or was it the rum punch? 'I like the sound of that,' she said.

'I knew you'd approve of people throwing rotten veg at me.'

'Only wet sponges. I hope there won't be any tomatoes. But I thought you'd never agree to take a turn in the stocks.'

'I may be selling the place but I'm not devoid of a sense of humour.' His eyes glinted wickedly. 'I might even be persuaded into a costume for the Festival.'

'What sort?'

He laughed, at her not with her, but so gently that she tingled all over.

'Spongebob Squarepants. What do you think? I thought of Blackbeard. A wicked pirate would be appropriate in the circumstances, wouldn't it?'

She shifted her bottom on the bench. 'I really hadn't thought about it.'

'What about you? Who are you going to be?'

'I'll probably just wear my uniform,' she said, staying as far away as possible from her helpless virgin fantasy.

'Over my dead body, you will.' His bare knee brushed hers under the table as he leaned forwards. His dark eyes gleamed wickedly, inviting her in deeper. Miranda wanted him to pull her face against his and snog her, tongues, and all in full view of everyone in the pub. She wanted to hear the gasps of jealous outrage from the Toga Woman and the thuds as Jago's fan club hit the flagstones. She wanted to be dragged off to one of the Pilchard's creaky old bedrooms, clutch the iron bedstead until her knuckles whitened and scream as he thrust inside her.

His voice, sexy and amused, slid into her consciousness. 'More grog?'

'Mm ... yes, please.'

As he disappeared into the bar, Miranda was confronted by the Mount looming ahead of her in the twilight, surrounded by a sea as silver grey and smooth as mercury. She might be physically on dry land, but she had a horrible feeling she was already way out of her depth with Jago.

Chapter Thirteen

Miranda was wrapped in Jago's sweatshirt. Funny, she didn't remember him wearing one at the pub. Even funnier — ha ha ha — she didn't give a toss! She also didn't remember how his arm had crept around her shoulders but she cared about that because it felt warm and strong and very right.

The sky was now inky blue, the lights shining in the village and beyond from the cottages that scrambled up the hillside until they stopped at the edge of the moorland. A few lights also winked on the yachts in the harbour, swinging gently from side to side as the masts rocked in the night breeze. However, the lane from the pub to the water's edge was dark and silent. There was no one about. Why would there be? It was almost midnight.

Miranda vaguely remembered a conversation with Karen about a room for the night and her giggling. She heard the bolts on the door of the Pilchard locking behind her and felt

Jago holding her hand as they walked down the steep lane towards the sea. The Mount seemed to float above her, its battlements and towers silhouetted against the moon, a few lights still strung along the distant quayside like fireflies tangled in a net.

Oh, how romantic. She giggled again now and Jago's arm tightened around her shoulders. 'You can stop laughing, my lady, and start working out where the hell we're going to get a boat from at this time of night?'

She blinked into the darkness at the myriad boats bobbing up and down in the harbour. 'We could use that,' she said, pointing at a rowing boat tied up near the end of the slipway.

'That one belongs to the rowing gig club.'

'So? They won't mind. We could have it back in the morning before they find out.'

'Tide'll be out by morning.'

Miranda considered for a moment, although she was way past the stage of considering anything and onto the stage where jumping off a cliff sounded rational. 'You're right; bugger the gig club, our need is greater than theirs.'

Jago climbed down the steps into the boat and held out his hand to her. Miranda looked down at the stone steps, slippery with weed. She stood on the top one and held out her hands. 'I feel like Louisa Musgrove. Whee!' She wobbled deliberately and made as if to leap into the boat.

'For God's sake, no. Be careful!'

'Only joking but I had you going, didn't I?'

His face, pale in the moonlight, stared up at her. 'Just get in the boat, wench.'

'How dare you call me a wench?'

'Because I'm his lordship. Now, come here.'

Taking Jago's outstretched hand, she let him help her down into the boat and sat on the thwart. Jago clambered back up to the quay, untied the boat and sat opposite her. He took the oars in both hands and pulled away from the harbour wall, grunting with effort.

Miranda giggled. 'Put your back into it, St Merryn.'

'How dare you speak to me like that? I'm the captain and I'm in charge.'

Miranda wagged her finger at him, insanely happy. 'I think not. You're incapaciiattated. I'm the one who's driving.'

The harbour wall glided by them and they were out in the bay, with the Mount ahead of them. 'I think you mean rowing,' said Jago.

'Driving, rowing. What–evahh,' said Miranda.

'If you're going to be criticise the skipper, you can take over.'

'I could do better.'

'OK then.' Jago let go of the oars and tried to stand up. The boat swayed precariously.

Miranda let out a squeal. 'Whoaa! Sit down, St Merryn.'

He plonked back down and she had to grab the sides for support.

He gathered the oars in his hands again. 'You know,' he said. 'If this was the Navy, I'd have you thrown on the brig for insubordination.'

The boat wobbled as Miranda gave him a cheeky salute. 'Do you know what Winston Churchill said about the Navy?'

'Funnily enough, no.'

'He said,' Miranda declared, 'that the Navy was "nothing but rum, sodomy and the lash".'

There was a pause. Miranda saw Jago's eyes sparkle wickedly. 'Well, we've had the rum, but if you fancy trying the other two, I'm willing to oblige.'

Oh er. Her skin burned like hot coals. Even in the half-light, even with the boat swaying and her swaying too, she recognised her trembly feeling as pure lust. Filthy thoughts rampaged through her mind, fantasies she'd never dare acknowledge and that, even through a groggy haze, both scared her and drove her wild.

'I think we should get a move on while the moon's out.'

Someone said the words and it must have been her because Jago said, 'Aye, Cap'n.' He then pulled on the oars and the boat bobbed forwards. Miranda gripped the thwarts as wavelets buffeted the boat. Lights from the quayside windows flickered on the water as the Mount grew closer. Miranda wrapped her arms around her trembling body as they reached the open sea and passed the halfway point between mainland and the harbour. She'd opened herself up to him in every way and yet it felt good. He'd made her cry and it had hurt and yet she felt as if part of a weight on her shoulders had been lifted. She hadn't realised that she'd been carrying a burden at all. Perhaps he was right; perhaps she should try to contact her mother again.

He stopped rowing and watched her. Did he know what she was thinking? Impossible but . . .

'What are you doing?' she asked.

His face broke into a grin. 'I feel a sea shanty coming on.' He opened his mouth wide and sang.

'Oh-hhh, there was a young lady of Kew who said as the curate withdrew, The Vicar is slicker and quicker and thicker and two inches longer than youuuu.'

Miranda clamped her hands over her ears.

Jago took a deep exaggerated breath then let rip. 'There was a young lady called Alice . . . '

'Nooooo!'

' . . . who used dynamite for a phallussss!'

'They'll hear you in Penzance!' Her stomach hurt. Tears of laughter rolled down her face.

'They found her – Arghhh!'

The boat hit a wave head on, Jago overbalanced and collapsed into the bottom of the boat on top of her. It swayed violently from side to side and Jago landed on her, taking her breath away.

'Shit. Have I hurt you?' he asked.

'Don't. . . know . . . yet. Ow.'

His face above her was horrified. 'God, I'm sorry. Call me a drunken tit.'

She opened her eyes and through her laughter, said, 'You're a drunken tit, my lord.'

He kneeled above her silhouetted against the moonlight, gazing down at her. 'Oh, there once was a girl called Miranda . . . ' he sang, out of tune, softly.

'And?'

'And nothing would rhyme with her ridiculous name.'

Her heart sank in disappointment. 'Oh.'

'And so there was only one thing to do.' His mouth came

down on hers, gentle, warm and smelling of Tinner's ale and bittersweet smoke. Miranda almost passed out, partly from the grog but also from shock and the sudden and wonderful realisation that that Jago was snogging her, deeply and tenderly. A real hero, she thought, would have tasted of minty fresh toothpaste but Jago was never going to live up to expectations and that drove her even wilder. He braced himself with two hands either side of her body. The wooden seat dug into her back painfully but she kissed him back. She explored his mouth with her tongue, seeking – who knew – just losing herself inside him.

When the kiss finally ended, she found herself inches from Jago's face. 'We're drunk,' she said, slowly.

He smiled. 'So?'

'Nothing. Nothing at all. Come here.' Did she really just say that? Was she really pulling his head back down to her and snogging his face off. Was he really joining in with just as much enthusiasm?

She shoved her hands up inside his T-shirt, desperate to touch him the way he had her in the armoury, only this time, without restraint. His skin was hot beneath her palms in contrast to the cold night air and she longed to press the whole length of her against his naked body. As she ranged her hands over the muscles of his back, his spine and shoulder blades, Jago explored her with his tongue. She gave a soft moan as he, Jago, trailed his tongue down her throat and her cleavage. The breeze left a trail of cool sensation where his tongue had been and her nipples stiffened.

She pushed her hands down the back of his jeans. For a

heartbeat, she thought he might protest and pull away but felt him arch against her.

He settled himself between her thighs, pressed himself against her and let out a groan. 'God, Miranda . . . '

Shouldn't we? Her words were carried away in a gust of wind or maybe she hadn't really said them at all, she was so lost in the feel and taste and smell of making love to the real Jago, not some fantasy figure. The real flesh and blood man, whose weight was pressing between her legs, whose fingers were popping the buttons of her dress and pushing aside the lace of her bra to suck her nipples, was a thousand times better than any figment of her imagination.

No matter how crazy, it seemed so exactly right that she was making out with Jago in a rowing boat in the middle of the ocean. It seemed right when he slid his hand under her dress and over her stomach. She shivered with pleasure as his fingers skated lower over her knickers and lingered at the nub of her as he kissed her.

His voice murmured in her ear, 'Yes?'

'Oh yes, yes, yes please.'

'Your wish is my command.'

Jago broke contact and the space between them was instantly cold. She gasped as spray flew from the waves and spattered her half-naked body. Jago loomed over her in the half-light, fumbling with the buttons of his jeans.

'Lie back, my lovely.'

She shuffled down into the bottom of the boat, not minding the puddle of seawater soaking through her thin dress. Her knees were bent and her thighs were open. She must look like a slut. She felt like one. She was as high as a kite and quivering with excitement. Jago tried to tug his jeans and boxers down his thighs, struggling and wincing as the boat wobbled alarmingly.

He cried out in exasperation. 'Give us a hand, will you?'

She laughed but reached up and yanked his jeans and boxers down. Her mouth gawped.

'I don't think there's time for any niceties,' he said.

'What about . . . you know?'

'In my wallet.' He tried to reach down to his ankles and the boat swayed dangerously.

'I'll get it,' she said, unable to bear the frustration and ready to burst. She sat up and groped in his jeans pocket for his wallet. Above her, Jago's cock jutted proudly like the prow of a ship and she laughed out loud.

'What's so funny?' he asked.

'Your . . . *thing* . . . it looks like a figurehead. A phallic figurehead.'

'Why, thank you on behalf of my "thing". Now would you please find the condoms before I explode?'

Dying with lust, she fumbled through the cards and notes for the condom. 'Sorry.' Her fingers slipped. The cards concertinaed into the bottom of the boat, landing in a pool of water.

'Sorry.'

'Forget it,' he said, briskly, and took the condom from her fingers and tore open the packet. How he rolled it on with the boat swaying, Miranda would never know. Or was that her swaying?

He smiled gently down at her. 'Miranda, my lovely, you need to take off your knickers.'

'Oh, yes. Of course.'

The boat bobbed as she shimmied out of her pants. Jago tugged the knickers over her feet and managed to get his knees between her legs as the boat bobbled alarmingly.

'Wind's getting up,' he said. 'Better be quick.'

He shuffled forwards and the boat lurched. He toppled into her, brushing against her thighs as he did so. 'Sorry. Bloody boat.'

Miranda felt his erection nudge her inner thighs. The wind howled and the boat lurched again. She felt her stomach turn over. Oh God, don't say she was going to be sick.

Jago's eyes were intent on her. 'Right. Ready to board, captain?'

The wind howled again. The boat rolled from side to side as a wave slammed into the bows.

'Shit!'

Water sloshed over the side. Miranda shrieked as a wave of cold water drenched them both. She shook her head to clear water from her face but another wave crashed over the boat, soaking them once again. Jago grabbed the sides of the boat as Miranda battled to sit up. A dark shape loomed ahead by the harbour wall, growing larger by the second. The moon came out from behind a cloud and a jagged mass appeared a few yards beyond the bows.

'Watch out! The rocks!'

'Bollocks!' Jago scrambled for the oars.

'Quick!'

He pulled hard on one oar, trying to steer them away from the rocks at the side of the harbour. Miranda paddled like crazy with her hands, heart thudding like mad. They were going to hit the rocks. 'Oh my God!'

She threw herself to the other end of the boat. Jago pulled on the oars but it was too late. The boat connected with the rocks with a sickening crash. Wood splinters flew into the air.

'Jump!' Jago grabbed her hand.

'No!'

He yanked her arm, hurting her and then she hit the water and went under into the cold blackness. The shock took her breath and froze her body. She gasped and burbled then bobbed up, gulping in air. She heard the boat cracking apart as it ground against the harbour wall. Frantically, she trod water and flailed her hands.

Jago bobbed up a few feet away. 'All right?' he spluttered.

She burbled in reply, her throat and eyes stinging from salt water, and struck out for the slipway. Her clothes weighed her down but suddenly her feet sank into the slimy weed on the bottom of the harbour. She floundered a few more yards to the slipway and hauled herself out of the sea, coughing and retching. She heard Jago behind her, splashing out of the water. The crushed and splintered boat began sinking rapidly.

Jago reached out a hand and pointed. 'Christ. Look at that.'

In the moonlight, she saw his wallet and one of her ballet pumps floating on the surface near the boat. She planted her hands on her knees and tugged in lungfuls of air like she wanted to suck up the night itself. Her dress was pasted to her thighs and she realised she had no knickers on. Shivering with cold and shock, she stood on the slipway and covered her face with her hands. What a disaster, what a bloody stupid, monumental disaster.

'Are you all right? Come here.' Jago touched her arm and tried to take her in his arms but she shoved him off her. 'No I'm not all right! We stole and wrecked a boat. We almost drowned! What are we going to do?'

He glanced at the boat. Full of water now, it hung grace-fully on the surface. 'Nothing for tonight.'

'But look at it!'

On cue, the boat disappeared beneath the surface of the harbour.

'I'll sort it out tomorrow. The most important thing is that you're safe but you need to get warm. Come on, let's get you back to your cottage.'

Miranda stared at him. Her lips were numb and she felt stone cold sober. She was also speechless with anger at her own stupidity. How could she have got so drunk that she'd been about to let Jago make love to her in a rowing boat in full view of the Mount? Lights twinkled now in some of the cottages.

'Oh God, people must have seen and heard us crash the boat.'

'Maybe, so let's get inside before they come out.'

Miranda stared at him in disbelief. 'Let *us* get inside? No way. I've made one huge mistake already tonight. I'm not going to make it worse.'

'But you're wet and cold. So am I.'

'Go and warm up in your castle then!'

She ran off, her bare feet slapping on the cobbles. She

realised that her bag was in the boat, along with her purse but, mercifully, not her keys. People rarely locked their doors on the Mount after hours, so she hadn't bothered taking them to the pub with her. She pushed open the door, closed and bolted it behind her. Water dripped off her dress and down her legs onto the tiles. She went upstairs to the bedroom and closed the curtain. She then went into the bathroom and stripped off her sopping dress and tossed it into the bath. She grabbed a bathrobe from the back of the door and wrapped it round her.

She found a towel and rubbed at her hair viciously as if she could rub away the fact that she'd opened up to Jago in so many ways. She caught sight of herself in the mirror and her pale, wet face stared back at her.

She went back into the bedroom, feeling slightly dizzy, and then heard voices outside the cottage. She dashed to the window and drew the curtain aside. Down on the harbour front there was no sign of Jago but two very large people were now walking along the quayside, one with a torch in her hand. It was Ronnie and Neem.

Miranda could hear their words clearly. Surely that meant they'd heard her and Jago?

'Shit.' Ronnie, swamped by Neem's T-shirt, flicked on her torch and shone it on the harbour. The beam swept over the surface of the water, just a few metres from where the boat had sunk. 'Can you see anything, Neem?'

Neem, wearing only his boxers, crouched down on the quayside like a huge Buddha. 'No.'

'There was definitely someone out here.'

Miranda drew back the curtain a little more. The moon

was fully out from behind the clouds, illuminating the whole harbour for a moment. Shivering, she tugged the robe tighter around her body.

Ronnie paced the quayside. 'I definitely heard voices.'

Neem touched her shoulder. 'Come back to bed, baby.'

Ronnie turned and kissed him. 'OK. But I'll have to report this as soon as the harbourmaster is up.'

Miranda closed her eyes in pure relief. I love you, Neem, she mouthed as he steered Ronnie back to her cottage. In the harbour, the waves rippled gently in the breeze but the water was black and there was no sign of the boat.

But in the morning, it would be exposed for everyone to see.

Chapter Fourteen

Miranda blinked against the light shining through her bedroom curtains. She felt as if Rage Against the Machine, the Fishermen's Choir and Ozzy Osbourne had all set up next to her head and were competing with each other.

She lifted her head from the pillow. She was wrong. They'd all set up inside her head. By the iPod station on her chest of drawers, it was just after 8 am. Her stomach turned over. Even if she'd stuck to mineral water all evening, she'd have felt nauseous this morning because, oh God, it was all coming back to her. She'd almost had sex with Jago in a rowing boat then they'd run aground in every possible way and everyone would know. They probably already did know.

She imagined Fred, the harbourmaster, tutting over the sunken boat in his harbour, possibly finding Jago's wallet and her purse in the bottom of it, or her shoes. She pictured

Fred, uttering a string of tabloid headlines about Youths and Vandals and Bringing Back National Service.

One phrase kept ringing round her head, even louder than the splintering crash as the boat had ground against the rocks. '*You need to take off your knickers, my lovely.*'

It was horrible. Excruciating. And all the more awful because she still felt turned on now. Every time her head throbbed, she heard him saying it. *Take them off, take them off. My lovely. Lovely Miranda.* She glanced at the clock again. It was only eight. Maybe Fred hadn't seen the boat yet; he wasn't due until half past eight. Maybe she still had time to at least rescue the evidence of her and Jago's personal belongings. She had to try.

She pulled on shorts, a sweatshirt and flip-flops and went down the stairs, ignoring her pounding head. If she could reach the wrecked boat and find anything incriminating, then she could deny all knowledge of the incident. As she walked to the door, there was a knock and a loud voice.

'Miranda!'

It was Ronnie. Oh God. Ronnie must have found the stuff or maybe she'd already deduced that Miranda and Jago had stolen the boat and was bringing the evidence back before the harbourmaster or one of the staff got to it. A wave of nausea washed over her.

'Are you OK, hun?' Ronnie spoke through the cottage door.

Miranda drew back the bolts and opened the door a crack.

Ronnie, her face scrubbed and crisply official in her uniform of black trousers, short-sleeved shirt and tie, loomed in the doorway 'Gonna let me in?'

Miranda opened the door, blinking as sunlight spilled in.

Ronnie put her hands on her hips. 'You look like shit.'

Her head throbbed sickeningly. 'I know I do.'

'Hangover?'

'Yes,' she whispered. *Get it over with. Get it over with. Just tell me you know . . .*

Ronnie grinned. 'I take it you haven't seen the harbour then?'

Miranda swallowed hard. 'What harbour?'

'You *are* hungover. The harbour – the one with the water and little boats in it. Except right now there's no water and one little boat that shouldn't be there.'

Miranda now knew how it felt to be in the dock at the Old Bailey. 'What about the harbour?' she asked weakly. With every word, she knew she could be digging a deeper hole. Ronnie was trained in interrogation techniques. Ronnie must be able to spot a guilty offender from ten feet. Ronnie must be able to smell her fear. Ronnie sniffed.

'What's up?' asked Miranda, panic rising.

'Hayfever season.'

Ronnie dug a tissue out of her pocket and wiped her nose. 'Anyway, you've clearly been comatose since you got home last night otherwise you'd have seen the mess in the harbour. Some total dork stole a rowing boat and ran aground on the rocks out there. Me and Neem thought we heard a noise last night and I phoned Fred this morning as soon as I saw the wreckage, but he'd already spotted it. It's dangerous, lying there in the entrance to the harbour.'

Miranda felt a glimmer of hope. Ronnie didn't know it

was her and Jago. Yet. 'Are you sure it was . . . um . . . left there last night?'

'Wasn't there yesterday evening so it must have been done last night. Total bloody wankers.' Ronnie stared at her hard. 'You don't know anything about it, do you?'

Miranda had to make a call. Fred might have found her purse and shoes since Ronnie had spoken to him but, on the other hand, they might have floated off. She decided to lie and face the consequences if they arose. 'Why would I know anything about it?'

'You must have got home not long after me and might have. I'm assuming you didn't go home with Theo because I've heard from Fred that the lifeboat was on a shout last night.'

So Theo had been risking his life while she and Jago had been playing at pirates. In fact they were lucky that the emergency services hadn't been called last night. Anyone spotting them capsizing from the shore would probably have dialled 999. 'No, I didn't go home with Theo,' she said.

'So you walked home? Mmm. You must have cut it fine. Hope you didn't get wet?'

'Ermm . . . a bit.'

Ronnie tutted. 'I knew you should have come with me and Neem. You know it's not worth wading over here. If anything had happened to you, I'd have blamed myself.'

'It's OK. I made it and I didn't want to cramp your style or play wallflower.'

'No.' Ronnie broke into a blissful smile. 'I can't tell you what an amazing night I had. As soon as we got through the door of the cottage – well, as soon as Neem had got through it, we couldn't wait to rip each other's clothes off. We were at it all night.'

Miranda clamped a hand over her mouth, feeling nauseous.

'Sorry, that's more than you need to know but I thought you might have heard something. Seems like you were dead to the world.'

Miranda managed a nod. All she could hope was that no one had found any evidence in the boat.

'Well, you look crap. I should go sick for a couple of hours. You'll scare the visitors in your state.' Ronnie checked her watch. 'I have to go. Get some coffee down you and I've got some Alka-Seltzer if you need it. Come and have a look at the boat if you can manage it before the harbourmaster shifts it. Bloody total twats to steal a boat and row off. Lucky they didn't drown'

'Very.'

'We've had to report the wreckage to the RNLI and the police, of course, but I bet they swam off. Fancy wasting people's time. I don't very often go all right wing but in their case, I agree with Fred. They should bring back the birch.'

Miranda coughed and grabbed the doorway for support.

'Miranda. You've gone green. Are you all right?'

Flapping a hand wildly, Miranda staggered through the kitchen for the downstairs loo.

She slammed the door. Above the sound of her retching, she heard Ronnie speaking on the radio. 'What? Who? You are joking? Well, that figures. I might have bloody well *known*.'

*

145

A few hours and several paracetamol later, Miranda dragged herself under the shower, got dressed and slunk out of the cottage. Fred, the harbourmaster, was busy supervising the removal of the boat from the harbour onto a trailer. Thankfully there was no sign of the emergency services. Miranda sneaked up the back path to the castle. Jago was the last person she wanted to see but she needed to find out what he knew about reaction to the wreck. She reached the castle terrace and guessed he must have seen her from the window because he waited at the door to the tower.

'Come up,' he said, unshaven and rough but still gorgeous. He shut the door of his study behind her. 'You look worse than I feel.'

'Thanks.'

'And before you say any more, you may as well know I've confessed.'

'Confessed? To wrecking the boat?

'No. To being Jack the Ripper. What else should I have confessed to?'

Miranda's head started to pulse again. 'Why have you told them? Ronnie said Fred didn't have any idea who'd stolen the boat. I was hoping we could keep it quiet.'

'No chance, I'm afraid. Fred asked me to go down to the harbour and said he was going to call the emergency services in case, and I quote, "the little bastards were washed up on some rocks somewhere". I had no choice but to say I'd borrowed the boat to get home, pissed as a newt, which was true, I suppose.'

'But what about our stuff?'

'I waited up last night until the tide turned and went down and picked up what I could at dawn. Everything's ruined, of course, but at least there's no evidence.'

He held up a plastic Mount St Merryn carrier bag. Water dripped from it onto the Chinese rug. Inside, Miranda saw her sodden purse, covered with mud, and both ballet pumps, now grey and sodden.

Miranda felt an unexpected rush of gratitude towards Jago. If he'd taken the blame for the previous night's debacle, he'd shot up in her estimation. 'Thanks for getting these,' she said, taking the bag. 'And you definitely didn't say I was with you?'

'No.'

'I really appreciate you taking the blame and –' she felt her heart rate quicken '– and for not mentioning the other thing.'

He looked annoyed and irritated. 'The other thing? I'm not sure I understand. Unless you mean us running aground in the boat.'

'I mean . . . you know, *the other thing* that happened.'

'Miranda, I really have no idea what you're talking about.'

Was he calling her bluff? Joking? Didn't look like it, he frowned as if he was annoyed with her. 'So you don't remember what happened . . . in the boat?' she asked, dying of embarrassment.

'I know that I'd had far too much to drink. We both had, although you were at least compos mentis. I remember the last pint of Tinner's and, possibly, the double whisky. I remember getting into the boat and hitting the rocks in the harbour.'

Miranda couldn't quite believe what she was hearing – or rather, wasn't hearing from him. 'Nothing else?'

'What else was there? Look, I was out of my skull. I haven't had a skinful like that for a long time and ... I may have accepted a slight stiffener while I went out for a smoke in the pub garden. Someone from the artist's loft offered me one of his roll-your-owns. Pretty lethal stuff.'

'You mean you were high?'

'Yes, Miranda. I probably was. You should try it some time.'

So he didn't remember snogging her? Pushing his hands up her dress? Trailing his tongue down her cleavage? Telling her she was beautiful? Asking her so tenderly to take her knickers off? Making her feel beautiful and wanted and so turned on she almost let him crash the boat just to feel him inside her.

She shuddered, on the verge of throwing up again, as Jago sat down behind his desk, picked up a piece of paper and started to read it. 'Is there anything else only I need to be at a meeting and I've got a head like a bag of shit.'

There came a point, thought Miranda, when you were so mad, so full of conflicting feelings of fury and crashing dis-appointment that your facial muscles just can't register how you feel. 'You know what, my lord?'

He lifted his handsome, hungover, arrogant face towards her. 'What?'

'This.'

She raised her middle finger, turned on her heel and slammed the door behind her.

*

Jago went to the window and watched her. Christ, she was livid with him. Her shoulders, as she stomped along his courtyard, were stiff with fury. Even her arse looked indignant. He would have laughed if he hadn't felt guilty enough to impale himself on the nearest pikestaff. He waited briefly for her to glance up at the window; when she didn't, he turned away with a sigh. It was for the best.

Back at the desk, he sat with his head in his hands, massaging his temples. Three of his mother's prescription co-codamol had failed to shift the monumental hangover or guilt at the previous evening's disastrous events. And the disaster had nothing to do with wrecking the boat and everything to do with almost wrecking Miranda's heart.

If they hadn't crashed, he was sure they'd have woken up in his bed – or hers – and, if he'd slept with her, it would have been ten times harder to sell the Mount and a hundred times harder to leave.

Chapter Fifteen

'Look at this? It's disgusting, the things people chuck into the sea.' Fred the harbourmaster held up a stick in front of Miranda's nose. A dripping piece of scarlet lace hung from its end, the label faded but clearly bearing the logo of La Senza. 'It's disgraceful to pollute the environment like this,' he grumbled.

'Dreadful,' Miranda agreed, having told so many fibs over the past few days that she didn't care any more. Two days after the wrecked boat had been towed back to the mainland on a trailer – at Jago's expense, Miranda presumed – the island was still abuzz with gossip. No one actually dared say anything to his lordship's face of course. On the surface, the island staff maintained a loyal silence, but, in private, there was talk of nothing else. And far from his name being mud, the fact he'd got pissed, nicked a boat and sunk it had only seemed to add to his rakish reputation.

She was about to change the subject before Fred got onto the subject of young people in hoodies when Jago passed the office.

'Wait! Lord St Merryn!' Catching sight of Jago passing the office, Fred waved the stick with its knicker flag in Jago's direction. The scarlet lace hung limply as Miranda's cheeks threatened to turn the same colour.

'Sir, look at what I found washed up on the slipway this morning.' He shook the pants under Jago's nose. 'It's disgusting, isn't it? Apart from the threat to marine life, what nice young girl wears drawers like those?'

Miranda stifled a gasp. She didn't wear drawers! Surely no one had worn drawers since 1950?

Jago tutted loudly. 'Not one I'd like to associate with, Fred, that's for sure. But I suppose we have to make allowances for the young. After all –' he lowered his voice '– we all make mistakes, don't we? High spirits and all that?'

What? So Jago *had* remembered trying to have sex with her and he'd recognised her knickers. Then why had he said he was too spaced out to remember?

A smile spread over Fred's craggy face and he winked. 'I see what you mean, my lord.'

'Boys will be boys, eh?' said Jago, patting Fred on the back.

'Yes, they will, sir. Indeed. Enjoyed a few high spirits myself in my younger days, I can tell you. Still do, when off duty, of course.'

She couldn't hold back. 'Gah!'

'Nasty cough, you have, Miranda. Can I offer you a Fisherman's Friend?'

Fred waggled his stick and the pants. Miranda caught sight of a figure approaching. 'It's Lady St Merryn. At least I *think* it is . . . ' She had to look twice because the woman walking towards them was wearing an orange and lime green kaftan. Lady St Merryn normally wore a knee-length skirt or a pair of slacks in a discreet taupe or navy. To see her in the flowing cotton garment with its tribal patterns was like spotting Margaret Thatcher in Vivienne Westwood.

Jago stared too. 'My God.'

Fred flipped the lid of a bin and dumped Miranda's knickers inside. 'We can't have your mother seeing those,' he said. 'Not at her stage of life.' Then he glanced up. 'Is that her ladyship? Bloody hell.'

Miranda thought that was rich, seeing Fred was five years younger and at least a century behind Lady St Merryn in his attitudes.

'I think we'd better head her off,' Jago said, looking genuinely shocked. 'Thank you for your vigilance, Fred, I know I can rely on you.'

As Jago strode off to the quayside, Miranda caught his arm 'Wait. I need to ask you something.'

'What?'

'You lied about not remembering what we . . . what we did . . . in the boat.'

'Almost did,' he corrected.

She panicked Lady St Merryn drew closer. 'All right, what we almost did. I don't have time to ask you why you thought lying was a good idea, but there's something else I have to talk to you about. Karen saw us leaving the pub together. If the story's out about you taking the boat, she must know we were both in it. Won't she have told people in the village?'

Jago stopped and shook his head. 'And your reputation will be in tatters? Theo won't want to have anything to do with one of the St Merryn men's fallen women?'

'Don't be any more of a bastard than I already think you are!' She'd raised her voice. She looked round her but no one had noticed. Lady St Merryn had stopped to talk to one of the maintenance team, giving her a precious few moments.

'Relax. You have no need to worry about Karen telling the world what a tart you are. I called her the morning after and asked her not to say you left with me.'

'You told her! Do you trust her?'

'With my life, but not my virtue.'

Miranda could barely believe it. 'You're surely not seeing Karen too'

Jago tutted. 'That's rather ageist, isn't it? Karen's a very attractive woman.'

'I didn't say anything about her being older.' But Miranda *was* thinking it. Karen must be twenty years older than Jago. 'And she's married, surely Ray will kill you if he finds out.' Karen's husband, Ray was a trawlerman, hard as nails and built like a tanker. Miranda couldn't believe what she was hearing.

Jago smiled. 'Don't worry, I'm not having an affair with Karen. I did, however, lose my cherry to her. It was on my seventeenth birthday and, don't worry, she was single at the time, but she's always had a soft spot for me. Karen is the soul of discretion; your secret is safe with her.'

Miranda was speechless at the thought that Karen,

however discreet, knew that she and Jago had stolen the boat. Karen must also think she and Jago were having an affair. Miranda hoped that he was right about her, otherwise the whole village would know, including Theo. And she *did* care what Theo thought. But, her conscience whispered, she *had* chosen to drop her knickers for Jago, she had wanted him to make love to her, even if she'd been drunk. She'd wanted him so much, she could feel the desire fizzing through her right now.

'Unbelievable,' she murmured, but she wasn't sure whether she meant Jago's behaviour or her own.

'Smile,' he said through gritted teeth. 'My mother's coming.'

He walked forwards to greet her, with Miranda close behind. As they closed the gap on Lady St Merryn, Miranda could see the outline of her slight figure through the filmy fabric of the kaftan. Lady St Merryn's hair, far from being restrained in a severe updo, was gathered back simply in a leather clip, like a silver-grey mane of a horse.

'Je-sus,' breathed Jago.

'I think she looks beautiful,' said Miranda, marvelling at the way Lady St Merryn sashayed along the quay, even with her stick.

'Mother?'

Lady St Merryn held up her hand to silence them. 'Not a word. In fact, I'll say it for you. I've gone off my rocker.' Her expression challenged them to deny it.

'Where did you get the kaftan?' asked Miranda.

'This old thing? It came out of the attic. It's an original Mary Quant from the King's Road – used to belong to an aunt of mine who handed it down to me. It probably smells a tad musty although I've had it airing for a couple of days.' She narrowed her eyes. 'Jago, you look like someone has slapped you in the face with a wet haddock.'

'I'm speechless, Mother.'

'Really? How refreshing. But no matter. As everyone is already talking about the St Merryns, I decided to come out and really give them something to talk about. You may as well know, Miranda, that I'm going to San Francisco at the end of the season and I thought I'd get into the spirit of things. When in Rome and all that.'

'Mother, I'm not sure that people are still wearing that kind of thing over there.'

'How do you know? Have you been there lately?'

'Not for a couple of years.'

'Then things might have changed. And besides, I don't give a fig if they're wearing suits of armour. I'm going to dress as I like.'

'But here? People will talk.'

Lady St Merryn looked at Jago as if she'd just caught him stealing from her purse. 'Talk? Talk about *me*? They're far too busy gossiping about you. Everyone within a thirty-mile radius knows about your unscheduled voyage. I hope you've settled up with the gig club.'

Miranda enjoyed seeing him squirm.

'Of course. I paid for the repairs to the boat and made a generous donation to the club.'

'You're damn lucky they haven't reported you to the police.'

'They obviously wanted the cash more than justice.'

Lady St Merryn sighed. 'And fortunately for you money can buy everything. And yet you think that by selling the Mount, you can rid yourself of your responsibilities and melt into the crowd. As long as you have money you have a burden. Running off won't help.'

Jago's expression darkened. 'I'm not "running off" as you put it, I'm making a business decision and, as you well know, money can't buy everything and I should know that better than anyone.'

'I ought to be getting back to the office,' said Miranda, horrified at being dragged into a family spat, even if she was partly involved in it.

'Yes, you do that. There's no point in you being embarrassed by Jago as well as the rest of the village.'

Miranda swallowed hard but Jago didn't even look at her. It was partly her fault that he and Lady St Merryn were arguing now.

'Yes, run along, Miranda,' he said nastily.

Miranda revised her opinion. The git deserved everything he got from his mother.

Lady St Merryn shook her head. 'What's happened to you? You know, sometimes I think I should stay here after all.'

His face fell as if he was genuinely worried then he set his jaw. 'Suit yourself, but I'm leaving.'

Miranda felt like a spectator. 'See you later,' she said quickly and escaped, full of relief and guilt.

Once she reached the office she risked a glance back. Lady St Merryn was being helped into a boat by the helmsman of the visitor ferry and Jago had vanished, either into the visitor areas or, more likely, up the back path to the castle.

If Lady St Merryn was having a midlife crisis, she was doing it in style. Her metamorphosis into Cher was a shock but it only signified that she had already left the Mount behind, psychologically at least. And Jago was clearly more determined than ever to sell.

A few days later, Ronnie staggered into Miranda's office, clutched the arm of the swivel chair and collapsed into it.

Miranda looked up. She'd been in the middle of typing up the Festival of Fools programme. 'What's the matter? Are you all right?'

'Not really. I've just seen her ladyship in a pair of jeans and a headband.'

'A headband!'

'Yup. One of those rainbow-striped, beaded ones like Native Americans wear. And the jeans were what my gran calls "bell bottoms". Reggie saw her. He said she looks like a white Bob Marley. He almost offered her a spliff. Not that I condone drugs, of course.'

Miranda knew for a fact that Reggie grew cannabis in a greenhouse behind his cottage, and that Ronnie regularly went round there to indulge, so ignored this.

'Fred says that Lady St Merryn told him she was going to San Francisco. What the hell does she want to go there for?' said Ronnie.

'Maybe for a holiday or to get some treatment for her arthritis?'

'I got the impression she was going away for good. I guess

that means we'll be left to Jago's tender mercies. The place will go to the dogs if it does but San Francisco sounds wonderful. I had some colleagues who went on an exchange trip to Californian penitentiaries. They were taken to Alcatraz on a day out.' Ronnie sighed longingly. 'Do they actually wear kaftans in San Fran any more?'

Miranda closed her Word document. 'I don't think Lady St Merryn cares.' But there was definitely something about reliving her lost youth in that kaftan. And the hair. Going back there must have something to do with the past. Even Jago had been surprised. 'Ronnie, did you want me for something because if not, hun, I have to try to finish putting the Festival programme together.'

'I saw that French bloke, Pierre, and his mate get off a boat again this morning. Do you know anything about it?'

Miranda felt goosebumps creep across her skin like little cat's feet. 'No ... I don't.' She felt a jag of unease and disappointment and then relief. Jago had invited Southcastle again and he hadn't involved her this time. That was a good thing, wasn't it?

'You see, I'm beginning to get a bit worried. What with Jago turning up out of the blue and Lady St Merryn off to spread peace and love and those two suits visiting the island ... you would tell me if there was anything I should know about, wouldn't you, hun?'

The phone rang. Miranda snatched it up hoping it would be an important call, preferably with a complicated issue to deal with at the very top of the castle. 'Can I help you?'

A few minutes later she put down the receiver. 'That was South West Television. I sent them a press release and they want to come to the Festival to do a piece for the regional news.'

Ronnie's eyes lit up. 'Excellent! Do you think they'll want an interview with me? Oh, I must go and phone Neem. He won't believe that we're going to be on telly!'

Chapter Sixteen

Since their meeting at the pub, Miranda had expected Theo to call, if only to discuss the possibility of the tug-of-war team coming to the Festival. Ronnie had been out with Neem but said that the whole team would have to make sure they had the date free before they could agree.

Of course, she'd also expected Theo to ask her out for a date but a week passed by and he hadn't called. She wondered if Theo had just been making polite conversation. Or maybe he really *did* think she was having a relationship with Jago and that's why he hadn't called. She didn't want him – or anyone in the village – to assume that because it just wasn't true. Oh what a tangled web, she thought. That was what happened when you got involved with Jago.

She was working in the office one afternoon when Theo's rich rolling burr came on the phone.

'Hi there,' he said.

Her pulse skittered. 'Hello.'

'Sorry I haven't called. It took me ages to get the lads to agree to be in the same place at the same time but they're all ready now; we'll definitely be at the Festival.'

Miranda, relieved at the normality of the conversation, started to gush. 'Oh, that's brilliant. I'm so thrilled. It will be fantastic.'

'Don't get too excited,' said Theo with a laugh. They discussed some ideas for bringing the inshore lifeboat, a display and a stall then Theo said, 'I hear Jago was up to his old tricks again after we met in the Pilchard.'

There was no use pretending she didn't know what Theo meant. Everyone in the village had heard. She laughed it off. 'I heard he got a bit pissed but I think he's squared it with the rowing club.'

'Yes, it's always easy to put things right when you've got the money,' said Theo. 'You can get away with pretty much anything and still come up smelling of roses. But I expect you've worked that out by now.'

Miranda squirmed with a mixture of discomfort at Theo's chippiness and at her own part in wrecking the boat. She listened for any hint of irony in Theo's voice or for clues that he'd guessed her part in it after all. Unlike Jago, she wasn't as confident in Karen's discretion and it was also possible that other people in the village or on the Mount had seen their drunken escapades.

She crossed her fingers, relieved Theo couldn't see her red

cheeks. 'Oh, I do my best to keep out of the family's private lives,' she said lightly.

'That's a very wise move. It's not really my business and I'm sure you're bright enough not to be taken in by Jago, but I thought I'd sound a warning note. The man's trouble and I wouldn't want you to get hurt.' He paused then added, 'And we must have that drink sometime. I'm going on a course at the Lifeboat College in Poole and then I've got a week's leave – I'm going to visit my sister in Scotland – but when I get home, we must get together. I'll call you as soon as I get back.'

Miranda made polite noises and put down the phone. Theo couldn't know what had happened, she was sure he would have dropped a hint if he had. He really disliked the St Merryns; she could understand it to a point. But Theo's animosity towards Jago seemed to go beyond general envy of the local landowner; in fact she had the distinct feeling that it was very very personal.

Over the next couple of weeks, Miranda hardly had a moment to spare as midsummer approached and the tourist season got into full swing. Lady St Merryn continued to float about the Mount in a succession of ever more vibrant hippy-inspired outfits, radiating her own regal brand of love and peace. Miranda might resent her for leaving, but she had to admit that it seemed the right decision for her lady-ship.

As for her son, Miranda knew it was impossible to avoid Jago; she saw him every day and, inevitably, they had to discuss a variety of issues relating to the finances and future events and plans for the Mount.

She hadn't seen Jumeau and Devlin again but that didn't mean they hadn't visited or that Jago hadn't been meeting them. In fact it was likely he had been to see them; he'd definitely been up to London twice and made no secret of it.

It hardly mattered. The sale was still going ahead and he'd assured her he would be announcing it to the staff as soon as the ink was dry on the contract. Miranda had thrown herself into her work, partly as a distraction and partly because she wanted to enjoy what could possibly be her last season at the Mount. Who knew what would happen to her role after the changeover? Even though she hated the idea of leaving, she couldn't get her head around working for Southcastle and had started looking at vacancies at other historic properties.

However, downloading the application form for a Scottish castle was as far as she'd got.

Work had enveloped everything else, which was inevitable at this time of year. Lunch breaks had almost evaporated and the chance to make small talk with the visitors had vanished. She still made her pilgrimage to see the last boat of the day off the island but, after they had left, there was still more paperwork to do in the evenings.

After working nine straight days without a break, she finally cracked. Having spent the morning dealing with an obese Manchester United fan who'd had been taken to the mainland with heat exhaustion, she retreated to her office with a thumping headache. She made the mistake of laying her head on the desk for a minute and the next thing she knew, someone shook her arm.

'Narrgh. Nooo . . . '

'Miranda?'

'Urghh.'

'Miranda!'

'Eh?' She blinked as a face came into focus. 'Is it morning? My alarm hasn't gone off.'

'It's half past three in the afternoon.' Jago's hand lay on her shoulder.

'Sorry. I didn't realise . . . '

He took his hand away and glared down at her. 'My mother says you've missed your last four days off and refused to take a break.'

'Have I? Oh God . . . well, we're too busy.' To her horror, Miranda felt moisture on her chin. Don't say she'd been drooling. She lifted her head and winced.

'What's the matter?'

'Bit of a headache. Do you mind getting me a glass of water, please? I've got some aspirin in my bag.'

She found the pills while he filled a glass from the staff kitchen. He came back and handed over the water and she took the pills and sipped.

He stood in front of her desk, with his arms folded. 'Better?'

'I will be in a few minutes.'

'Good. Then go home.'

'But there's tons of paperwork to do. There's a health and safety report to complete and I have to finish a proposal for a heritage grant by the end of tomorrow. Oh and the conservator needs to be briefed on the restoration of the tapestry in the library. Then there are the appraisals for the hourly paid staff and . . . '

He walked round to her and lifted her elbow. 'Go home, Miranda. Now.'

'But who will do all the work?'

'I will.'

She stared at him. 'You? You must be joking!'

'Thanks for the vote of confidence.' He pulled her to her feet.

'But you can't. You don't know how things work. No one does.'

'No one is indispensible, Miranda, even you. Now, I'll try my best and what I can't do, I'll ask for help from one of the staff.' He propelled her out of the door, still protesting.

'Hey, wait!'

Ignoring her, Jago marched her out of the office and onto the quayside.

'People are looking. I'll go quietly,' she said as Daisy stood, hands on hips, and an 'oh er, missus' expression on her round face.

He pushed open the front door of her cottage. 'In you go.'

'OK, OK. I don't need herding.'

But she had begun to rather enjoy it – until she remembered he would be in charge of her office.

'Sit,' he ordered as he led her into the sitting room. She was so surprised that she did just that. 'Now, I'll instruct the staff that you're not to be disturbed for the rest of today or tomorrow and if they see you in any of the office areas, I'll get them to report to me. Get some rest.'

*

165

Two days off to rest. Miranda faced it with a mix of pleasure, confusion and dismay. She had a ridiculously tingly feeling at Jago's concern. On the other hand, she dreaded what kind of chaos he might cause in the offices. The staff would be horrified, and Ronnie and Jago would be sure to get into a fight.

By late afternoon, she caved in and phoned one of her assistants to see how things were going.

'Hello.'

'Is that you, Miranda?'

Bugger. It was Jago. She hadn't expected him to actually answer the phone.

'Yes.'

'Go away.'

'But I only wanted to see how you're getting on. If you *needed* me.'

'No.'

The phone clicked off. Miranda flopped onto the sofa. Why was it so hard to do nothing? Even when you'd longed to do nothing? She was like one of those hamsters on a treadmill, still frantically running like the clappers even though her wheel had been taken away. She contemplated her mobile, fingers twitching. Perhaps she should text Ronnie and ask her how things were going. Her phone beeped and she jumped. The message was from Jago.

Don't even think about it.

Stay away from work, he'd said. She knew she should get off the island, Jago was right. The following morning, having pottered round the cottage and half-heartedly looked at in the application form for the Scottish castle and booked a massage at the health spa of a nearby hotel, she decided to catch some rays on the island's private beach. She made a sandwich for lunch, picked up a novel she'd been meaning to read and shut the door behind her.

She took a detour to the tiny beach via the offices and thought she could see Jago's head through the window. What on earth was going on in there? Should she just pop her head round the door and make sure all was well?

No. Jago would expect her not to trust him so it was probably better not to live up to his expectations. She set her eyes straight ahead and unlocked the gate to the private beach. Hidden from the main harbour by a narrow gated walkway through a rocky outcrop, it only had access from the staff route. The concrete walkway led to a small patch of sand and rocks, which was currently covered in shallow water.

She sat down on a rock by the water's edge, her toes dangling in the sea and the sun warming her cheeks. She could hear a faint buzz of voices on the nearby quayside, the chug of boats, the odd shout or shriek. But she was alone and enjoying a moment of peace.

So it was with a sigh that she heard the latch of the gate opening and heard someone else coming.

It was Jago.

'What are you doing here?' she asked, more brusquely than she'd meant.

He grinned. 'I own the place.'

'Oh yes. I meant . . .'

'Why am I bunking off?'

'Mmm.'

'I decided to give the staff a break from me.'

'Ah.'

He smiled ruefully and Miranda almost forgave him for denying they'd almost made love. He pushed his hair out of his eyes and frowned against the sun. She thought of the picture of the serious little boy with his fishing net.

'There's a photo of you in your mother's room that I think was taken down here.'

He frowned as if he didn't remember then nodded. 'Yes, I know.'

'How old were you?'

He shrugged. 'Six or seven. I'm not sure, but it was a very hot summer, I do remember that. I spent most of it down here on the quayside or beach, rock pooling.'

'With your father?'

He shook his head. 'God, no. He was far too busy running this place. We didn't have a property manager then.' He gave a wry smile. 'My mother came down here with me when she could spare the time, but I'm afraid to say that I also had a nanny until I went to prep school.'

Miranda tried not to laugh at the thought of a stern-faced nanny wiping the nose of a scrawny young Jago.

'I knew you'd find that amusing.'

'Not at all. I'm sure it's perfectly proper for the sons of the aristocracy,' she said with all the solemnity she could muster. 'What was her name? Binky? Tiggy?'

Jago treated her to a glare, which was strangely enjoyable. 'Insolent wench. I'm sure I needed watching. Her name was

Ursula, if you must know, but I'm afraid I called her Duckface behind her back. Don't ask. She kept an eye on me and sometimes my mother let me have a few friends over from the village. I don't think they were here with me that day. Maybe that's why I look so fed up.'

He looked sad then hopeful. Was he relieved that peace had broken out between them? She was surprised how happy that made her feel.

'What are you reading?' he asked, nodding at her book.

'An historical novel.'

'Of course. It's your day off. You know, I think my presence in that office is a mixed blessing. Ronnie keeps giving me death looks and the two women in the admin centre seem terrified of me. They're always making an excuse to go off together to the bathroom or to run errands. I feel as if I have the plague but there haven't been any major disasters yet so you can get on with your book. I'll go and make a nuisance of myself somewhere else.'

'No, don't do that!' He looked surprised and she shrugged. 'I mean don't rush off on my account. This is your beach.'

Her face grew warmer as his gaze slid over her from top to bottom. 'In that case, are you going to offer to share your lunch? I'm starving.'

She opened her sandwich box and held up a limp crust of bread. 'Ham or cheese?'

'What? No caviar or silver spoon? Never mind, either will do. I'm not fussy.' Miranda handed over the sandwich.

'Thanks. Shuffle up, then.' There wasn't really room but she shifted across the rocky surface towards a patch of barnacles. They ate in silence for a few minutes, Miranda keeping her eyes on the horizon. She could feel Jago next to her, his bare legs almost brushing hers. She knew the hair would tickle, she remembered that from the boat. Why had he pretended they hadn't almost made love? She swallowed her last piece of crust down furiously, wondering whether to confront him again now they weren't hungover and knackered.

'Can we have a grown-up conversation?' Jago asked.

She wriggled on the rock uncomfortably. Was he now opening the door for them to talk about what had really happened? 'Of course. What about?'

'The sale. Unless there's something else you think we should discuss.'

'No . . . should there be?'

'No reason that I can think of. We'll confine the discussion to business.'

'And leave pleasure out of it?'

'Perhaps that would be best.'

'I know we've talked about the sale before but please say you're not serious about it?' said Miranda.

'I am serious and I am going to sell.'

'But to *them*?'

'Who else but Southcastle? How many people are in the market for a white elephant like this? How many have the finance and the business acumen?'

'You could let a heritage charity manage it. I've thought about it. You don't have to sell; you could lease it to them instead. That way you could still live here in the castle apartments and at least oversee how the place is run.'

He smiled. 'As ever, a compromise from the sensible Miranda.'

'Don't patronise me, please. I deserve better than that.' And she hadn't always been sensible, she could have added, recalling their drunken night in the boat. Sometimes she could be completely crazy.

'Yes, you do. I'm sorry but I want a completely clean break with the place. Southcastle know what they're doing, and precisely because they're not emotionally attached to the Mount, they'll keep it going, make a profit and safeguard the future for everyone here.'

'Are you sure? Do you know how many of the staff will keep their jobs?'

'As many as possible, if Southcastle are as savvy as I think. I'll do my very best to make sure everyone's safe but, once I've sold, it's out of my hands.'

'Are you sure you just don't want the responsibility?' She knew instantly that she'd touched a nerve so raw that the sharp pain flickered across his eyes. 'I'm sorry. I probably shouldn't have said that.'

'No. You shouldn't.'

'I feel so passionate about this place that I don't want you making the wrong decision and regretting it. Oh, I know you won't believe me and you'll only think I'm thinking of myself – my job and the cottage. But it's not just me and it's not just the other people who work here. It's you. I could see you hated Southcastle and can't bear the thought of handing over the Mount to them.' She stopped.

He wasn't angry. His eyes were sad. 'Miranda, I know your motives are pure but I've thought about this for a long time. Longer than you know.' He reached out his hand, lightly resting it on her arm. Her skin tingled under the warmth of his touch. She wanted to kiss him again while she was sober and in her right mind and see if it felt as good as she remembered.

Instinctively, she leaned forwards a little and instantly he responded. His mouth closed on hers and she pushed her tongue eagerly inside. She felt every movement of his tongue in her mouth, his hands tangling in her hair, tasted the salt on his lips. She opened her eyes for a second to see him, filling up her vision, his own eyes closed. Then she shut them again, knowing this was real, not a fantasy or a drunken mistake. Only this moment mattered, not the past or the future. Nothing could take this away.

A seagull screamed overhead as Jago took her face in his hands and deepened his kiss. The gull cried again and, when she opened her eyes, Jago's were open too. He dropped his hands from her face. 'What's that?'

A scream seemed to tear the air, and it wasn't a gull. Shouts came from the harbour side beyond the gate. Miranda's heart plunged in disappointment that their kiss had been ended and also felt half relieved that it had stopped when it did. 'It's probably just teenagers messing about.'

'I don't think so.'

Wanting anything but for him to leave, Miranda knew he was right. 'I'll have to go and see what the matter is.'

Jago slid off the rock, splashing into the shallow rock pool. 'No. I'll go. You're supposed to be off duty.'

'I'm sure there's no need. It will be a fuss over nothing.'

The screams started again. Miranda scrambled to her feet as Jago climbed up onto the stone walkway that led to the gate. 'It's not nothing.'

He ran towards the gate, Miranda right behind, her sandwiches and book abandoned. As she followed him through the gate she saw the crowd clustered at the far end of the harbour. People stared down at the water, pointing, and one woman screamed over and over again.

Chapter Seventeen

'Braden! Someone please help my little boy!'

Jago started running and Miranda raced after him, tripping on the cobbles in her flip-flops. Her stomach turned over and over and her legs felt like they would give way at any moment. An empty pushchair stood on the quayside. Someone had fallen into the harbour. A child.

An elderly man started taking off his shoes but Jago laid a hand on his arm. 'Wait, sir. What happened?'

The man shook visibly. 'A little boy climbed out of his pushchair and must have fallen into the harbour.'

'How long ago?'

'A minute? I'm ... not ... not sure. I didn't see what happened.'

The mother grabbed Miranda's arm, squeezing it so hard, her nails almost pierced the skin. 'Do something, for God's sake!'

As Miranda comforted her, Jago peered into the water. 'How deep is it?'

'With the tide in like this, about five or six feet,' said Miranda.

'Anyone see him go under?' he demanded, pulling off his T-shirt.

The elderly man spoke. 'No. One moment he was in the pushchair, the next he'd gone.'

The mother let out a howl of pain and sank into the older man's arms. Jago kicked off his shoes and sat on the edge of harbour. There was a splash as he slipped off the wall.

'Anyone called an ambulance?' shouted Miranda, scanning the shocked faces around her.

A teenage boy handed her a phone. 'Not yet. It all happened so fast.'

Miranda snatched the phone from him. She had to stay calm but her fingers felt like sausages as she stabbed out 999. The controller answered straight away.

'Yes. An ambulance, please, at the Mount.' Her heart pounded harder as she gave the details to the emergency control. She couldn't believe she was saying the words. 'There's a child in the water. He's about two years old, I think. How long?' She tried to estimate the time that had elapsed from gearing the screams to now. 'A couple of minutes, I think . . . ' Yes, someone was trying to get him out. Yes, they were trained. No, there was no one else in danger. Yes, she'd stop anyone else from jumping in.

She gave back the phone to the boy and dropped to her knees, scanning the shifting surface to try to spot Jago. The water was murky but she could see his pale body, twisting beneath the surface, merging with weed and mud. He was searching right under the quayside where the pushchair stood empty. Surely the boy couldn't have drifted far? What if he was tangled in the weeds? What if he'd hit his head? What if he was already dead?

Jago popped out of the water, mouth open, gasping for breath. And he had something in his arms. 'Got him!'

The mother broke free of the elderly man and screamed.

'Come to the slipway!' Jago called to Miranda.

Jago towed the little boy towards the slippery stone ramp that led out of the water. Miranda raced to meet him as he waded out with the limp body in his arms. He seemed to stumble but then steadied himself and ran up the slipway. By now Reggie and Ronnie had arrived to help, ushering the gathering crowd back from the harbour wall.

'What's his name?' he shouted, running along the quayside. The mother dashed forwards, sobbing. 'Braden. Is he all right? He's not moving! Do something. Do something!' The mother let out a howl of anguish that brought bile to Miranda's throat, but she knew she mustn't throw up. It was her job to help, not fall to pieces. 'Please, someone help Braden's mum,' she ordered. 'Ronnie, we need some space here.'

The teenager stripped off his sweatshirt and spread it on the quayside.

Jago knelt down and carefully laid the child on the sweatshirt. The little boy's straw-coloured hair stuck to his face. His eyes were closed, his body still as if he were fast asleep. But he wasn't asleep, Miranda knew that. Not asleep.

'Miranda? You can do CPR, can't you?'

She heard Jago's voice and glanced at him, momentarily dumbfounded. It had been ages since her last first aid course and it had only gone through the basics, not a full-scale resuscitation. Even then, none of the staff had taken it seriously because none of them ever expected to use their so-called 'skills'. An instructor with halitosis had shown them what to do in a local community centre on the hottest day of the previous summer. The dummy had had a Hitler moustache drawn on it with biro and they'd all been too busy stifling sniggers to concentrate. She'd never thought that one day knowing what to do could mean the difference between a tiny life continuing – or ending here on the cobblestones.

Behind her, Braden's mother was sobbing and begging them to do something. She heard Ronnie trying to soothe the mother and tell her it would be OK. Miranda wished Ronnie wouldn't. It might not be OK, it probably wouldn't be. The cobbles were hard under her bare knees. She had to get a grip.

'What do I have to do?' she asked Jago.

'Kneel down here. Braden? Can you hear me?'

Gently, Jago inserted a finger inside the boy's mouth. 'There's something in here.' He scooped out a small piece of weed, a grotesque green strand and threw it on the cobbles. Then he listened at the boy's mouth. 'You need to help me. He'll have a better chance if we both do this,' he said softly.

'The ambulance . . . ' she whispered as the mother wailed above her.

'The tide's in and it'll be too late before help gets here. It's up to us.' Jago leaned in close to Braden's mouth. 'He's not breathing and his chest's not rising. I'll have to breathe for him while you do CPR. Do you know how?'

'Think I can remember.'

'Good.'

Jago tilted Braden's head back and lifted his tiny chin with two fingers. He closed his mouth around the boy's and gave two breaths into his tiny mouth. Miranda watched the bird-like chest. It was still as stone.

Jago blew into the mouth again but there was no response or movement, just gasps and sobbing from the crowd around him.

'You'll have to do chest compressions while I breathe for him. You know how?' He didn't wait for an answer. Miranda brought down the heel of her hand onto the Braden's chest. Her palm felt like a giant's. She would break him, surely? Her huge palm would crush the fragile ribcage? She pressed gently then brought her other hand on top. Just the way she'd been taught in the class. Back then she'd been shaking with laughter, and she was shaking now too, but with genuine terror and helplessness.

'Just one hand will do. He's only small ... that's right. You need to do fifteen compressions while I breathe for him. Ready? Now.'

Miranda tried to block out the mother's wails and just focus. This needed to be perfect. The rhythm of her compressions, the depth of them, had to be precise. She had to get this not just right, but absolutely *perfect*.

Sweat trickled down her back, just the way it had in the

stuffy first aid centre, except today it was fear not heat. Fear of failure. If she got this wrong. If she and Jago failed, the boy would die, his mother's life would be ruined. There'd be no future for him, any children or grandchildren, just a life wiped out.

'Wait.' Jago lifted his head and listened briefly for any sound of breath or movement of the toddler's chest. 'Carry on.'

Miranda's own heart tried to do the work of Braden and herself. It thumped away, and a pulse beat in her brain. Ohpleaseohpleaseohplease . . .

The little body twitched. Jago lifted his head. The boy coughed and spluttered. Miranda let out a cry. 'He breathed!'

The mother broke free from Ronnie's arms. 'Braden? Can you hear me?'

Jago turned him onto his side as he coughed. 'Good. Good boy. That's it.'

The mother collapsed on her knees. 'Is he alive?'

'Wait,' said Miranda. 'Hold on.'

Jago held the boy's head as he coughed again and vomited seawater onto the cobbles.

'He'll be all right, though. He's OK!' The mother stared at Miranda, begging her to give the right answer.

'He needs to get to a hospital fast. He needs proper medical attention,' said Jago.

'But he's breathing!'

Miranda glanced at Jago. The little boy had been unconscious for over two minutes. Even she remembered that from the first aid course. There could be all kinds of complications. Brain damage. Secondary drowning. Hypo-thermia.

'We need to keep him warm,' said Jago. 'And get him into the medical room.'

Ronnie brought a blanket. Braden started to sob with shock. Miranda didn't blame him, falling into the harbour and waking up to two strangers doing horrible things to him. He couldn't be kept down on the cobbles any more and let out a howl: 'Mummy.'

That was good, that had to be a good sign, thought Miranda.

Jago picked him up, from the quayside.

'Mummmmmyyyy!'

Jago grimaced. 'You'd better take him,' he said, handing him to the mother. 'What's your name?'

'Louise,' said Ronnie as Braden's mum hugged him and cried even louder than her son.

'Any ETA on the ambulance?' asked Miranda.

'Twenty minutes,' said Ronnie. 'But the lifeboat's on its way.'

'Good. Let's get him into the medical room.'

As Miranda led Louise and Braden to the medical room, she was amazed to see so many people with their phones and cameras out, filming. Bloody hell ...

'Show's over, folks. The little boy will be fine now,' said Ronnie, with a laser glare. She turned to the elderly man. 'Thanks for your help, sir. Can we treat you and your wife to tea?'

Jago was by Louise's side keeping a close eye on Braden who shrank against his mother, clearly disgusted with Jago. Miranda noticed Jago limping and the trail of blood spots on the cobbles where he'd walked. Inside the medical room, he gave Louise a blanket and, as she wrapped Braden up, he spoke quietly to Miranda. 'We need to keep an eye on him and the ambulance needs to get here as soon as it can. There could be a risk of secondary drowning.'

'I hope not. The RNLI are bringing the paramedics over. They'd have called an air ambulance but there's no place for it to land with the tide in.'

'This damned place,' said Jago then shut his mouth.

'The mother . . .' she said.

Braden's mum, Louise, hugged her little boy as if she would never ever let him go. Miranda was still shaking. There would have to be an inquiry as to how he'd ended up in the harbour. There'd be an incident report to complete; the police might have to be involved. Filling in forms seemed ridiculous after a little boy had almost lost his life but there was no getting away from it.

Right now, she was too concerned about the little boy to care. As Louise soothed her son, Miranda turned her attention to Jago. He sat on a plastic chair in a corner, grimacing at his foot. Blood streaked the tiles and led out of the door. 'What happened?' she asked

'I don't know. Suppose I must have stepped on an old can or some glass on the bottom of the harbour. I didn't notice with all the adrenaline pumping.'

Miranda pulled a green first aid box from a shelf and opened the lid. 'Here press this to it.' She handed him an absorbent dressing.

'I'm fine.'

'You're making a mess on the tiles.'

'True.' He ripped open the pack and pressed the dressing to the wound.

Miranda let him be and went back to Louise and Braden. 'How are you both doing?'

Squirming against his mother, Braden sucked his thumb and glared at Miranda. Miranda didn't blame him.

Louise held out her hand. 'I just can't stop shaking.'

'No wonder. Do you want a glass of water?'

'Got any vodka? I don't mean that. Yes, I do but – I need bloody something. Braden could have ... Oh Christ, I don't know how to thank you both.'

'Really. You don't have to.'

'But he could have ...' Her words tailed off. She obviously didn't want to frighten her son any more than he already had been. 'You must think I'm a terrible mother, letting him fall in but I swear I only took my eyes off him for a second to answer my phone. I thought he was strapped in. Maybe I'd forgotten or he must have undone the straps. He's like that; I never know what he'll do next. But this ...'

Miranda smiled. 'It's an adventure he'll never forget or perhaps it's better if he does. I'll get you a drink.' She filled a glass from the tap and handed it to Louise, who drank it with her free hand while keeping the other tightly around Braden.

Jago watched carefully as Louise gulped down the water and handed the glass back to Miranda. Her hands were still trembling as she turned to Jago. 'What you did – jumping in and saving him – was amazing, thank you.'

Miranda saw him visibly shrink into the corner.

'No need,' he muttered.

'Have you hurt yourself?'

'Just a graze. It's nothing.'

Ronnie popped her head round the door of the medical room. 'The lifeboat's here with the paramedics.'

In seconds, the small room was filled with people in green and orange overalls, all calmly and swiftly going about their work. Quietly, Miranda and Jago gave the details of how long Braden had been in the water as the paramedics took Louise and her son outside. One of the female medical team stayed behind and pointed to Jago's foot. 'That looks nasty. Want us to take a look at it?'

'No.'

'You can come with us to A&E if you like.'

'I said no.'

The medic shrugged, justifiably annoyed at his rudeness. 'Suit yourself but by the amount of blood, it needs stitches.'

'Take care of Braden and his mother. I need the bathroom.' He hopped into the bathroom at the side of the medical room and locked the door.

'I'll try to get him to go to hospital,' said Miranda, following the paramedic outside.

She shrugged. 'Good luck to you. I was only trying to help.'

Outside, the inshore lifeboat waited alongside the harbour wall. Theo was at the helm, and two of his colleagues helped the medics into the boat. Braden's eyes widened in excitement at the sight of the bright orange RIB. He looked remarkably well considering his unscheduled exploration of the harbour. Miranda cringed to think of the crap that was down there; her own brief experience of it had been horrible enough. He pointed to it. 'Boat!'

For the first time, his mother smiled.

Theo took Braden from her arms. 'Let's have you, young lad.'

'Thanks for getting here so quickly,' said Miranda as he handed the boy to the crew and the medics climbed aboard.

'Where's Jago got to?' he asked.

'I don't know.'

There was no time for any more talk. Theo jumped aboard and piloted the boat out of the harbour, while the visitors took pictures on their phones, chattering excitedly. To them it was just another episode of *Seaside Rescue* with another happy ending. Miranda felt like she'd been put through an old-fashioned mangle and wrung out. Braden could have died; he was almost dead when he was pulled from the sea.

She watched the boat power back to the mainland where the blue lights of an ambulance flashed. She saw the crew carry Braden into the ambulance and heard the sirens start up. It pulled away and people began to disperse from around the harbour, the drama over for the day. All she could do now was clear up the mess and hope Braden stayed as well as he'd seemed. She went back into the medical room, stepping over the streaks of blood and water on the tiles.

'You can come out now. They've all gone.'

The bathroom door opened and Jago limped out, the blood-soaked dressing stuck to his foot with sticky tape. He grimaced. 'I can't stand a fuss.'

'I know, but you are bleeding everywhere and making work for the cleaning staff. Can I at least take a look at your foot?'

He hesitated.

She patted the exam couch. 'Come on, get up here, Long John Silver. You can trust me. I'm a trained first aider.'

With a sigh, he hopped over to the couch and let her help him onto it. Carefully, Miranda peeled away the dressing and forced herself to look at the jagged wound. She bit her lip. The paramedic was right. 'You definitely need a couple of stitches.'

Jago pulled a face, and then nodded. Miranda replaced the dressing with a fresh one, fumbling with the adhesive tape as she tried to attach it to his skin. 'Sorry, my hands are shaking.'

'Mine too.' He held out a hand. It was rock steady.

She pressed down the tape on the blade on his foot, feeling the veins and bone under her fingertips. 'You've done that before, haven't you?'

'Cut my foot on a can or saved someone's life?'

She glanced up. 'You know exactly what I mean.'

'I've never saved anyone before. Not when they'd stopped breathing. When I worked in Australia, we pulled out a lot of people, but mostly ones who were very much alive. The rescues you see on TV are the happy endings. CPR doesn't always work, you know. In fact, it usually doesn't work at the stage Braden was at.'

'But you got lucky today.'

Jago reached out and touched her arm and all the invisible downy hairs rose. Her lips tingled at the memory of their kiss. '*We* got lucky. Braden's alive because of you too.'

Her face warmed up. She stepped back from the exam couch. 'I'll come with you to the hospital.'

He gave a sigh. 'Christ, what a pain in the arse.'

'We could see if we can find out how Braden is.'

'OK, it's a deal.'

Chapter Eighteen

'I fucking hate these places.'

Jago rested a hand on the door of the Land Rover and grimaced at the hospital buildings. His tan had visibly paled and perspiration beaded his forehead. He looked like he'd rather chop his own foot off than be here. Miranda wasn't surprised, the cut probably hurt him a lot more than he'd admit and all his bravado after the rescue had most likely disappeared as the shock set in. She'd had to take a motorboat off the island to the harbour. Her handling skills were rusty but she'd managed to get it safely tied up at the mainland quay. One of the estate vehicles had been parked on the quayside and she'd used that to drive the dozen or so miles to the county hospital.

She left him by the car as she collected a ticket from the machine. She'd had to trawl around the parking area three times before she'd found a space and it was still going to be a long walk – or hop – in Jago's case to the Accident & Emergency department.

'You know, it would have been easier if you'd gone with the paramedics,' she said.

'I could have driven myself.'

'You can't even bear the weight on your foot.'

He responded by attempting to hop from the car park to the entrance of the hospital. After toppling into a flower display funded by the Hospital League of Friends, he finally accepted her arm. Once inside the doors, seeing Miranda grunting under his weight, a nurse hurried forwards, her face full of concern.

'What's happened here?'

'I hurt my foot,' said Jago.

'How did you manage to do that?'

'Paddling,' said Miranda, trying to hold him upright. 'At St Merryn's Mount.'

The nurse looked surprised. 'That's two of you then. We've had a little boy brought in from there not long ago.'

'Really?' said Miranda.

'Yes, he fell into the harbour there. Luckily, someone pulled him out and he's OK. Didn't you hear about it, if you were there?' She frowned and beckoned to a porter. 'But I shouldn't be talking about it, as you're not relatives.'

The nurse smiled as a porter arrived with a wheelchair. Jago's face fell. 'I don't need that.'

'I think you do. Your friend looks done in. You must be heavy.'

'He is,' said Miranda,

'I can walk,' said Jago.

Miranda let go of his arm. 'He can't.'

Jago swayed and the nurse and porter grabbed him just in time, easing him down into the wheelchair. Miranda looked down at his sulky face, trying not to laugh. He reminded her very much of his photo, all he needed was the fishing net.

'Don't worry, I'll take care of him,' said the nurse cheerfully. 'Do you want to hold his hand while we stitch him up or wait here?'

'She can wait here,' he growled.

The nurse raised her eyebrows. 'My, we are a grumpy pants today, aren't we? I should get a cup of tea, love. I'll bring your friend back when I've finished with him.'

Jago put out his tongue but was wheeled away.

Miranda sat in the waiting room. She bought a cup of tea from the machine but couldn't drink it. She tried to leaf through an old copy of *Country Life* but found the mating habits of the woodcock were no distraction from the events of the afternoon. The accident, the rescue, the kiss that was cut short.

That kiss. The rescue. She'd had enough adrenaline to power a relay team, no wonder she felt like a wet dishcloth. Jago seemed to be ages and she was just thinking of putting another car park ticket on the Land Rover when he hobbled out of the treatment room, with the aid of a pair of crutches.

His foot was expertly dressed and bandaged and the nurse followed him out. 'Be careful the next time you go rock pooling, young man.'

'Yeah. Sure.'

'Thank you,' said Miranda.

'Almost a pleasure,' said the nurse. 'If you think it's getting infected, see your GP or, failing that, come back here.'

'I don't have a GP,' said Jago, after she'd left. Miranda realised why immediately. He wasn't planning on staying so why should he register with a practice?

He tried to put his weight on the injured foot and grimaced.

She watched him. 'Does it still hurt?'

'My foot's fine. It's my arse that's sore. That sadist of a nurse gave me a tetanus jab and shot me full of antibiotics. Just couldn't wait to get my daks down I guess.'

She laughed.

'It's not that funny.'

'I know. But you're a big boy now. You can take it.'

A half-smile spread over his lips then he returned to grumpy mode. 'I can't stand the smell of this place any more. Let's see if we can find out how Braden is then get out of here.'

They made their way from the minor injuries unit to the far end of the emergency unit. It had grown much busier since they'd arrived, with several rows of people in shorts and flip-flops all waiting glumly to be attended to. Kids dashed about, throwing Lego bricks at each other while fractious toddlers clambered over the seats.

She nudged Jago's arm. 'There's Braden over by the nurses' station.'

Braden wriggled on a trolley while his mum tried to stop him from climbing over the side. 'I want to go home. Home!' he wailed.

'Soon, love. But we have to stay for a bit longer so we can make sure you're OK after you tumbled into the sea.'

'I want to go home!'

A young doctor with a pink stethoscope round her neck tried to soothe him but Braden opened his mouth and wailed. 'Homeeeeeeee!'

Miranda shook her head in disbelief. 'Looks like he'll be OK.'

'Hopefully. No wonder he came round. He's got an amazing pair of lungs.'

Braden launched into full tantrum mode, screwing up his face and banging the sides of the trolley with his chubby little fists. The porter winced and started to wheel the trolley towards Jago and Miranda.

'Oh, shit. Quick. I don't want them to see us.' Jago hobbled off as fast as he could towards the doors. He shuffled right past Louise but every eye in the waiting room was now on Braden, yelling at the top of his not-so-tiny voice.

Outside, Miranda couldn't wipe the grin off her face, she was so relieved that Braden was fine and amused by the sight of Jago hopping along at an insane pace. He hopped towards the Land Rover like a man spotting an oasis in the desert, but suddenly overbalanced without warning. Miranda caught him, his weight almost taking her with him. She gasped out loud. 'Hey!'

His unexpected grip was tight around her arm. In an instant, he released her and regained his balance with the aid of the car bonnet. 'I'm sorry. I've hurt you,' he said.

'No. I'm fine. It's you I'm worried about.' She laughed. 'Long John Silver.'

'Pieces of eight!' he squawked pathetically.

She laughed and opened the door for him. 'That was the parrot.'

'Bloody nuisance, these things,' he said waving the crutches. 'But at least Louise didn't see us, thank God. I don't want any more fuss.'

'I'm well aware of that but you do realise this story might get into the papers? I might have to answer some questions from the press about it and they'll want to know who the rescuer was.'

'I'll sack you if you tell them.'

'Thanks.'

'I don't really mean I'll sack you but ... Oh, can't you just tell them to piss off?'

'Great idea. I can see it now. "So, Miranda, does Lord St Merryn have any comment for South West Television on the incident in which he saved a toddler from drowning?" "Oh yes, he says you can all just piss off." Southcastle Estates would love to hear you saying that. In that case, maybe I definitely should quote you.' Jago rolled his eyes in despair. 'I suppose I could say the identity of the victims is confidential and we can't comment. That might fend them off?' He brightened. 'But you know, there were plenty of people with phones taking pictures. It might even get onto YouTube.'

'Jesus, I hope not!'

She decided he'd had enough torture for one day. 'You'll just have to keep your fingers crossed. Come on, Long John, let's get you back to the ship.'

He shook his head. 'Not yet.'

'No?'

'You know that thing we did before Braden fell into the sea?'

He meant the kiss. Her lips tingled at the memory. 'So you remember this time?'

'Yes. I do. I shouldn't have done it. Not earlier and not in the boat.'

She felt angry, even though he'd finally acknowledged what went on between them. 'Like you said we were pissed,' she said, the hurt making her sarcastic.

'Not that pissed. In my case, not very pissed at all.'

She wanted to scream. 'Then why deny it? Why?'

'Because I'm a bastard and because I was afraid of what might happen if we'd carried on, but that stops now. It's time I faced up to my responsibilities, as you keep telling me.' He touched her arm gently. 'But please, not here at the hospital and not at the Mount. Let's drive. I need some fresh air.'

Chapter Nineteen

Miranda pulled into a cliff edge space above the Towans, the great sand dunes that backed St Ives Bay. Puffs of dust from the dry gravel rose under her sandals as she slid down from the driver's seat. It was late in the afternoon; most people were hauling their tired bodies off the beach, wetsuits turned down to their waists, carrying boards. A few people sat outside at the Surfer's Café, basking in the late rays after a day riding the waves. After opening the door, she handed Jago his crutches from the back of the car. He took them and then stopped.

'What's the matter?'

'I need a minute.'

Shading her eyes, she followed his gaze out over the Atlantic, dark blue and seemingly boundless. To the west, the bay swept in a vast curve along the coast towards the headland. Towering white clouds raced across the sky and the air was clear and fresh and pure. She had the feeling that she would never want to move forwards or back but stay here, frozen in one moment where the past and future didn't matter and yet she felt her skin prickle with dread.

'I'd forgotten ...' His voice was barely audible above wind and sea and crying gulls.

She knew exactly what he meant, and felt exactly what he felt. Just for a few seconds. 'How beautiful this place is?'

'Yes.'

She walked beside him as he hopped down the path, ignoring the pitying and amused glances of surfers passing by. 'How long has it been since you were up here?' she asked.

'Years. You?'

'Months. I think that November was the last time. I came up here with the manager of Trevarra House on our way back from a tourism seminar in St Ives.'

There was a shriek as a bunch of young surfers ran past, high on adrenaline and endorphins. A fleeting smile crossed Jago's face as if he was remembering how they felt. 'How often do you even get off the island?' he asked.

'Whenever I can spare to the time. I walk to the village shops and the Pilchard, of course.' She waited for a reaction but got none. 'I get my hair cut, then there are historical conferences, visits to other properties ... and Ronnie and I go into Penzance to the cinema and the bars with a few mates as often as we can.'

She had the distinct impression he was merely making small talk, before delivering some unwelcome news. '*How's the family? Lovely weather and, by the way, you've just lost your job and your house has burned down.'*

She almost smiled. 'Jago. This isn't about me. You said you wanted to explain why you're so desperate to get rid of the Mount. Is it because of something that happened at university or while your father was alive? Is that why you went to Australia, to get away from something awful that happened here?'

Jago's stomach tightened. He fought to wipe out a vision of Rhianna, a dried-up husk just like the driftwood littering the beach. Then he compared her with Miranda, with her glowing cheeks, sunlight reflecting in her eyes, hair shining in the sun. The contrast with his last memory of Rhianna was still painful. He ought to be over her death but coming home to the Mount again had made him realise he might never move on, not in the way he'd once planned. Or, his heart whispered, that he *could* move on but that the risk of getting hurt again was more than he could face.

He spotted a bench and stopped. 'I don't think I'm going to make it down to the beach.'

'Do you want to sit here?'

'Yes.'

He sat down before he fell down. He felt so tired, suddenly. Maybe it was the rescue, or the hospital or hopping about like a bloody penguin or maybe it was the nights at the Mount. They'd all been long and many of them sleepless, as he'd turned his decision to sell over and over in his mind and, lately, he'd added a new dilemma: his growing feelings for Miranda. They were undeniable now and they weren't part of his plan at all. If they had only been physical, he might have coped. Looking back, he thought the first spark had started almost when he'd first laid eyes on her, feisty, scared and beautiful, in the armoury. He should never have messed around with her feelings, coming on to her and then behaving like a shit, playing up to the image of the lord of the bloody manor.

He'd got his comeuppance though, got his own heart singed a little.

A lot, actually.

Shit.

In the days since they'd almost made love in the rowing boat, he'd tried to keep away from her, but their kiss on the quayside today and the business with Braden had brought them frighteningly closer. They'd shared an empathy that had made him contemplate the unthinkable: staying at the Mount and making a home there.

A home with *her* in it.

He'd glimpsed a future where he would, after all, be a father to his children, perhaps a little boy like Braden, who he would love and care for. They would poke around in rock pools together and eat too many ice creams. Then the sight of the hospital, the nurses and doctors, the sights and smells of sickness and futility had uncovered raw, jagged memories he didn't want to face.

He laid his crutches on the ground as Miranda perched on the far end of the bench. 'Good idea,' he said. 'Keep away from me.'

'What do you mean?'

She seemed nervous of even getting close to him. She had good reason. 'Your first instincts about me in the armoury were right. I'm a dangerous bastard.' He shoved his hands through his hair. 'Christ, I sound defensive. I don't mean to. Coming back here has done that to me and I don't want this . . . what's happened already to go any further. I want to tell you the truth about me now, not at the end.'

'The end?'

'Yes, the end. After we've kissed, made love, after I've held you and said stuff I shouldn't when we're in bed and made you think there's hope and that we're all going to live happily ever after at the Mount.'

She gasped. 'Now wait a minute, Jago. I never said wanted any of that. I've never even given you a hint of it. How can you assume . . .'

'I know you want me to stay.'

'Yes, to run the Mount! But one kiss and an almost-shag doesn't mean I want to play happy families with you and be Queen of the Castle!'

Was she playing devil's advocate? Telling him she didn't want to get involved with him? She was right to be furious at his assumptions but he was right to have them. She wanted him, he knew that from the way she'd pressed herself against him when they'd kissed. He knew from the way she'd closed her eyes and invited him deeper inside her. She'd trailed her fingers over his back, exploring, almost begging him to pull her against him, wanting *more* from him.

'Well, you knew I was an arrogant bastard. Maybe I'm

assuming too much but you can't deny that if we let things go any further things would get bloody difficult. You don't know what I'm capable of – or rather what I'm *not* capable of and I don't want to let things get that far and then you wake up one morning to find I've turned into Mr Hyde. Waiting until the end of the story would be a huge cop out and you deserve better than that.'

She folded her arms. 'Oh really? So, are you going to keep me in agony any longer before you tell me your Big Secret?'

'No, I'm not going to make you wait any longer,' he said, so calmly, he surprised himself. 'Cutting a long story short, my wife died.'

It was so unexpected that Miranda physically flinched and gasped out loud. She stared at him.

'It's OK. I mean, it's not OK, obviously, because it ripped me apart but it's been ... was a while ago. I ought to be able to say it now without making people want to get the hell away from me.' He felt as if he was floating, as if another man was speaking now. Maybe it was the shots the nurse had given him, or maybe he was simply distancing himself from the story: telling her about another man or else he would pass out with the grief and pain of it. 'I'll say it again. My wife died. Rhianna died. And, please, don't say you're sorry.'

He thought he'd cut off any response but she tried anyway. 'I will say it because I feel it. I *am* sorry. How could I not be? But I don't understand ... please, forgive me but what has that got to do with you not wanting to come back home?'

'Because I was supposed to come back with her, with Rhianna, with our family.' He smiled because she was kind and beautiful and thought she would change his mind by talking. 'You see, once upon a time, I couldn't wait to get back to the Mount but it's a long story and you'll walk away when you hear it.'

Chapter Twenty

Was that what Jago hoped for? That she would just get up and leave him? Leaving him now was the last thing she intended. If a tidal wave had rolled in from the ocean, she'd have stayed with Jago on that bench.

'I'm not going anywhere, so you'd better get on with it,' she said lightly, as unease crawled up her spine like some hideous insect.

He shook his head. 'Miss Whiplash, eh? I should have known you'd show your true colours.'

'Jago . . . don't try and joke and get away from this now. Tell me.'

He took a deep breath. 'It started when my father died just after I'd finished my A levels. I came home from boarding school and helped my mother manage the Mount as best as I could. I'm sorry to say this but, with my father gone, I suddenly saw the place in a new light. It was like a burden had been lifted from us both. This will probably sound hard but Dad had been a total shit, frankly – to me and to her.'

'Did he . . . ?' she couldn't say the word.

'Abuse me? No. He beat me a few times until I got bigger than him, but largely he just ignored 'me. I was away at school most of the time but my mother bore the full brunt of him. He didn't lay a hand on her, as far as I know, or I would have killed him myself, but he had his own way of torturing her. He had a string of other women and he didn't care that she knew about them. I heard him once, the bastard, taunting her with a new woman he'd met in London, telling my mother she was old and past it and that he could get a divorce any time he wanted.' He clenched his fist.

Miranda wanted to comfort him but didn't dare. 'I'm so sorry. I had no idea.'

'No one really does though the older staff have an inkling. But what really went on behind closed doors is private. That's how we deal with things, the St Merryns. You see I am my father's son in that way.' He laughed bitterly.

'So you wanted to stay at the Mount when you got back from university?'

'Yes but Mother was having none of it. Back then she was still fit and more than able to run the place without my help. She told me to go off and "see the world". She obviously thought it would be a good idea if I sowed my wild oats for a while and then came back in a few years' time. I was only twenty-one so it was a good plan in theory but I think she fully expected me to return and take up the reins.'

'And did you? Sow your wild oats, I mean?'

'I suppose so. I bummed round the world for a while,

doing the usual. Grape picking, bar work, surfing, having a lot of filthy sex.' His gaze slid to her, perhaps hoping he'd shocked her and she'd have to glance away.

Heat flooded through her up to her cheeks but her reply was cool. 'Go on.'

'I enjoyed it, I'll admit. No one knew who I was and, frankly, no one gave a toss anyway. Who gives a shit that you're an earl when you're riding a half pipe in Oahu?'

'How did you end up in Oz?'

'I hooked up with a couple of guys and we ended up in Bells Beach where I worked as an instructor for a couple of years.' He swallowed and stared at the breakers thundering up the sands. 'I always intended to go back to the Mount sooner or later, I just stayed a little longer than I'd expected.'

'Is that where you met Rhianna?'

He nodded. 'She was a physio, someone recommended her to me when I damaged a disc in my back. I visited her and, well, it's hard not to fall for a girl when you're laid face down at her mercy with your pants off.' And that, Miranda knew, was code for Jago having fallen crazily in love with Rhianna. 'Six months later we got married.'

Only six months? He really was crazy about her, then. 'Did she know who you were?'

'I told her after she'd accepted me, but she didn't give a toss, in the way of most Aussies. She only cared that I was a half-decent surfer and that ... well, we were loved up, I suppose.'

He supposed? Miranda could see how much Jago cared for Rhianna. The love and pain were etched onto his features.

'We'd been married a couple of months when there was an accident.' He paused briefly. 'We were in the water when she wiped out and hit her head on a reef. I managed to pull her out and the lifeguards brought her round but when we got her to hospital, we found out she was paralysed from the neck down.'

'Oh my God.'

'Shit happens as they say. But until then I'd thought it happened to other people. Not to me or Rhianna. She was young and fit. I thought we were both invincible.'

Miranda longed to comfort him, to hold him but he was not the kind of man you hugged or comforted and she didn't know if she was the kind of woman who could hug or comfort anyone. She floundered, confronted by conflicting feelings. Sympathy for him, and yet a horrible sense of dread at what it all meant for her. 'I'm so sorry. It must have been terrible for both of you,' she said, lamely.

'I kept on believing she'd get better and walk again and I kept on telling Rhianna that too. I spent a fortune trying to find some cure for her and, when that failed, I fitted out a house and I nursed her.'

A laughing group of girls carrying boards trotted past them down to the surf.

'So you bring me here to tell me this? To a surfing beach?'

'I know it seems crazy but I'm like a burned child drawn to the fire. You have to understand that I don't mind being reminded of Rhianna or of what happened. It focuses my mind.'

Her body tensed, suspecting his focus was not a good

thing. His hand was next to hers on the bench. She wanted to close her hand over it and comfort him but she didn't dare. 'Can I ask how she died?'

'Not soon enough, unfortunately and I'm sorry if that makes me sound like a heartless bastard. She was young and fit, and all she had to look forward to was a lifetime hooked up to a machine, pumped full of drugs, with me wiping her backside. She asked me to stop lying to her that she would get better, and I shouted at her. I couldn't face what she'd accepted; that she *wanted* to die.'

He wasn't being heartless, in fact Miranda thought the opposite, as he ploughed on bitterly, as if unable to stop himself, or else afraid that if he did he would clam up entirely.

'Rhianna lived for the waves and the outdoors. She was an athlete and she couldn't face life as the person – the physical husk – that she'd become. The doctors hoped she'd come to terms with her condition in time but, after eighteen months in that bed, she begged me to finish her off.'

Miranda held her breath as his voice quietened. 'Every day she asked me to get her some pills or put a pillow over her face, but I couldn't do it. I *wouldn't* do it. Maybe I hadn't grown up enough to do that. Maybe I didn't . . .'

She knew he was going to say 'love her enough'. She bit back tears as he turned to face her. 'Could you have done it?'

He wanted Miranda to absolve him, like a young boy asking for approval. Had he done the right thing? It was gut-wrenchingly painful and impossible to answer. Not when she'd asked herself that often enough recently. She'd been so sure, for so long, that abandoning her mother was the right thing but, lately, she'd questioned herself.

'I don't know what I'd have done but I'm gutted that she suffered and that you still hurt so much now.'

He removed his hand as if she'd hurt him. 'Me? I didn't give a toss about me! Rhianna hurt, more than any human being should ever hurt. I was just there, watching, waiting, useless.'

'Not useless. What happened . . . at the end?'

'A miracle happened. She caught got pneumonia and she went quickly. Even the doctors were surprised how fast she went downhill, once she knew she had an infection. It was as if she'd grabbed on to the chance to go with every ounce of strength she had left.'

Miranda could hardly bear to look at his face. 'How long ago did it all happen?'

'Since she died? Two years. Three months.'

'And how many weeks?' she asked softly, hoping he wouldn't be able to tell her. If he'd forgotten that kind of detail, then maybe there was hope.

'Two years, three months and six days.'

'You must love her very much.'

His silence answered her question. No 'loved'. No denial. No 'I *did*'. Jago was still in love with his dead wife, grieving for the family he couldn't have. There was no argument with his reasons for selling and leaving; she had to accept it. She could almost hear the bell tolling, the bell that some said they could hear from beneath the waves off the coast, booming out from the seabed for the lost souls of sailors.

'We wanted kids, you know . . . Lots of them. After we'd surfed some more and travelled some more, we were going to have some children and then I was going to come back here to the Mount and we were all going to live happily ever after. I told her all about it and she said she'd come with me.'

'And now you hate the place?'

'Not hate but I can't live there now. I need to be anywhere but there.' He glanced behind him, miles away to where the Mount stood on the other coast, out of sight but still huge, solid and eternal. 'Does that make any kind of sense?'

Sense? For him, not for her, but what *could* she say? He'd dragged these painful memories from some raw place inside him and it must be hurting him. It definitely hurt her to hear them, because she empathised with his pain and because of their finality. She managed another question in reply. 'What will you do after the sale?'

'I'll make sure my mother is secure for the rest of her life, of course. I'll set up a charity trust fund with the proceeds and with the rest I'll buy a boat and just see where it takes me.'

'For how long? You can't do that forever.'

'That's just the point, I don't know where I'll go, or for how long. There will be no plans or responsibilities and that suits me for now.' He hesitated then said: 'I should be over it now, over her, shouldn't I?'

'Since when did "should" make any difference to the way we feel? There's no time limit on grief,' said Miranda. Or guilt, either, she could have added but was too kind to. In truth, that was Jago's biggest demon, she thought. His guilt at being helpless at the end of Rhianna's life. Or perhaps his guilt at feeling ready to move on – with another woman, with her?

But saying any of those things felt so wrong, it was almost laughable. The only thing she could do, she did instinctively: reached out and touched his arm in empathy and reassurance. Possibly a big mistake on her part for his skin was warm under her fingertips, the muscle in his forearm solid and she wanted him more than she ever had. He stopped seeing refuge in the surf and turned to her, his expression gentle but reining back a dam of emotion. His hand reached for hers and held it lightly as if he was sending a signal: I care about you but not too much, not enough to stay. 'You and me. It has to end because it can't go anywhere. I'll only hurt you. You do understand?'

Her heart felt as if it had stopped. The wind slapped at her body. She wanted to kiss him again and feel that warm mouth on hers. 'You can't hurt me.'

'Don't deny you have feelings for me. I do – I care about you.'

It cost her everything but she wouldn't give into him. 'As you said yourself, sod me. It's the Mount I care about. The people. I don't matter.'

He stared at her and shook his head. 'You are impossible, Miranda.'

'Not impossible. Just honest and realistic, as you've been with me.'

He took his crutches and struggled to his feet. 'You don't have to lie.'

'I won't lie. There's no point. I don't like what you're

doing and I happen to think it's the wrong decision but I'll respect it. For the sake of your mother and the staff, I'll try to make the process as smooth as possible, but if I can, I'll still try to fight it.'

'Suit yourself, but you're wasting your time. Try if you like, fight me if you want, but in the end, you'll lose.'

Chapter Twenty-One

She'd lied about not caring, of course, because she felt so hurt and devastated. He cared for her? What? Like a puppy or a faithful retainer? A lapdog? She was way, way too proud to settle for that. But pride would only carry her so far. It kept her going as she drove him home and back along the causeway to the castle. She offered to help him back up to the castle but, as she'd expected, and hoped, he refused.

Over the next few days, there was no point trying to keep out of his way; they had to work together every day and, since he'd found her asleep in the office, he'd taken it upon himself to spend more time 'helping' out, hobbling around the office and literally getting under everyone's feet. Miranda longed for a wand to magic Jago out of the office. After their conversation at the beach, she'd rather have worked round the clock on her own than in such close proximity to him.

He kept things strictly professional, of course, and, she had to admit, the extra help had given both her and her staff a little more time to devote to the Festival and she could hardly kick him out.

Late one afternoon, Miranda sat enjoying a rare moment of relative peace while Jago worked in his study when Ronnie popped her head round the office door.

'Someone to see you, Miranda.'

'Who is it?'

Ronnie tapped her nose. 'Surprise.'

'I don't like surprises.'

'You'll love this one.'

For a heart-stopping moment, Miranda imagined that somehow her mother was standing outside on the quay. Yet that was impossible because her mother probably had no idea what she was doing, let alone any desire to see her again. And Ronnie wouldn't have been grinning like a Cheshire cat if that had been the case, or teased her about who was waiting. She followed Ronnie out onto the quayside.

An empty pushchair stood outside the office door. Louise Dixon was crouched down by an old anchor with her son tightly held between her legs. He reached up his hand and touched the anchor, his mouth opened in an 'o'. Miranda's stomach did a little flip. He was a chubby little boy but tiny all the same next to the huge iron anchor. She walked forwards, smiling. 'Hello, again, Braden.'

Louise stood up, clutching Braden's hand tightly. She seemed embarrassed. 'Hello. Bet you hoped you wouldn't see us again but I – that is me and Braden – wanted to say thank you for saving him. Didn't we, Braden?'

Braden didn't look grateful. He grasped his mum's hand and slunk behind her legs, peeping warily out at Miranda as if she was the Green Goblin.

'You didn't have to thank us that but it is lovely to see you, and nice to see Braden looking so ...well. How's he doing?'

Braden thrust a chubby finger up his nostril.

'Don't do that, Braden! I've told you your head will cave in if you dig out all the bogeys.' Louise scooped him up and swung him towards Miranda. 'He's right as rain now. Kiss the nice lady who saved you from the water.'

He shook his head so hard Miranda thought it might fall off and then buried his face in his mum's neck.

'He's shy.'

'It's fine and I don't blame him. We're the funny people who did all that weird stuff to him.'

'You saved his life,' said Louise. 'You and the dark-haired guy. Jacob or Jamie something, is it? Sorry, I can't remember. I heard some of the lifeboat people saying he lived on the island but, to be honest, I was so worried about Braden, I didn't take anything in. Does he work here? I'd like to say thanks to him. He's a real hero.'

Miranda cringed inwardly. Jago would hate a fuss but she could hardly refuse to let Louise see him. Besides, she thought wickedly, he oughtn't to get out of this one. 'He won't think he's a hero but you can have a word with him if you like. He's called Jago.'

Louise's face lit up. 'Shall we go and see the nice man who dived into the sea to get you out?' Braden pushed his face into his mum's shoulder. 'I'd like to meet him again, even if Braden doesn't. One day he'll be grateful,' she said.

'I hope not. It's maybe just as well he won't remember. Come on, then, I'll see if we can find him.'

Jago's foot was healing well. In fact, he'd abandoned the crutches the day after he'd got back from the hospital. She'd seen him from a distance only that morning, crossing the courtyard, limping slightly. In fact, Miranda thought he was fit enough to be called to the quayside to spare Louise and Braden the steep walk to the top of the Mount, but she suspected he'd never come down if he heard who was here to see him. She also knew he was preparing for his meeting with Southcastle. Her distraction wasn't entirely a charitable act but she didn't care.

''kin hell. Oh, sorry.' Louise stopped to lean against a wall, depositing Braden on the steps but still keeping a tight hold of his hand. 'How do you do this every day?'

Miranda wondered if she should radio Jago after all. 'It is very steep. I'd carry him for you if you like but I don't think he'll come to me?'

'Will you let the lady take you, Braden?' He hid behind his mum and she let out a big sigh.

'I wish there was an easier way up here but it's not too far now. Let me carry your bag, at least.'

By the time they got to the castle, Louise's face was almost crimson. Miranda had tried to keep chatting to her to pass the time. There didn't seem to be any mention of Braden's dad and Miranda wondered if she had to cope with her little boy on her own. Must be tough. Apart from a fascination with picking his nose, he was a gorgeous little boy, all big blue eyes and curls as pale as moonlight. The picture of innocence. She smiled to herself, imagining that was how Jago had looked once, when he was a toddler. Maybe he'd picked his nose too. Lady St Merryn would have rapped his knuckles for that.

She bit her lip so she didn't laugh out loud. They'd reached the castle door.

'What does he do, here, this Jago?' asked Louise as Miranda hesitated in the archway to the courtyard.

Should she warn Louise who Jago was? Trouble was there didn't seem an easy way of saying it.

'Is he a workman? He didn't sound local but then, I had other things on my mind. He might have been Matthew McConaughey crossed with Brad Pitt for all I cared. Or is he one of the gardeners? I love gardens but I've got a flat . . . Oh look, Braden! There's that man who pulled you out of the water.'

Jago trotted down the steps from the castle to the courtyard just as Miranda, accompanied by Louise and Braden, puffed up the flagstones and under the archway. Fleetingly, and Miranda guessed only she'd noticed, a look of dismay crossed his face, but he managed a smile and walked briskly across the courtyard towards them.

'Hello there, Braden,' he said. 'And Louise, isn't it?'

'Louise Dixon,' said Miranda as Braden took his finger out of his nose and stared at Jago. 'Louise, this is Jago St Merryn, the owner of the Mount.'

Miranda had seen plenty of jaws drop at the sight of the Mount but rarely had she seen one plunge quite so dramatically as Louise's.

214

'Shit. I mean, shit, your lordship.'

Jago laughed out loud. 'Oh God, please call me Jago or I'll have to have you clapped in irons. I hate all that formal stuff.'

'Right.' Louise's eyes were out on stalks at Jago's dishevelled appearance. He'd obviously been doing a spot of decorating, judging by the paint-spattered overalls. I am a lost cause, thought Miranda, wondering if he'd got anything on underneath.

But Louise recovered faster than she had. 'Ermm . . . I've brought you something. It seems really daft now, considering who you are, but I thought you worked here you see and . . . anyway, it was all I could think of.'

She pulled out a plastic carrier from her baby bag and handed it to Jago. Miranda smiled. It was from the Mount's gift shop.

Jago opened it and pulled out a print. It was a Victorian scene, dramatic and detailed. It showed a sailing ship tossing in a stormy sea beyond the Mount, a rowing boat by its side, local fishermen trying to rescue the stricken sailors.

His face lit up with pleasure and Miranda could see he was deeply touched. She thought she might cry as Jago turned the print round so that Braden could see it. She wondered if Jago was thinking what might have been if Rhianna had lived and they'd had children.

'Thank you,' he said. Braden opened his rosebud mouth and reached out a hand to touch the picture. 'And thank you, Braden.'

'Boat! Boat!'

Louise set Braden down on the cobbles and Jago

crouched down so he could show the little boy the picture. 'Yes. It's a big boat from a long time ago and here's the castle. Look.'

Braden toddled forwards. 'Cattle,' he said. Jago laughed. 'Yes, it's the castle. Here's the tower.'

Braden's face creased. 'Trowur. Cattle.' Then he chuckled so hard that they all burst out laughing too. 'Boat. Man.'

Unexpectedly, Braden placed his small, sticky hand in Jago's large one. Jago glanced at him and Miranda saw him struggling to hold back his emotions. Miranda's own throat tightened and her eyes prickled. Don't say she was going to blub? Not here in front of Louise who seemed oblivious to the effect Braden was having on her and Jago.

'Is it all right if we have a look round the courtyard?' Jago asked Louise.

'Yeah, sure. Braden, you can have a walk with Jago, if you like. I'll be here watching, so it's all right.'

They walked off towards the corner of the courtyard where Jago bent down to show him a gargoyle spitting water into a trough. Both boys, big and small, splashed their hands in the stream of water. Louise chatted away to Miranda but she had trouble concentrating, unable to banish the feeling that she was on the brink of tears.

She'd missed so much in her relationship with her own mother. Could she have made more of an effort to understand her mum when she was a teenager? Many times since then, she'd wondered if she'd done the right thing by leaving in such a brutal, final way but perhaps she could forgive herself for that. She'd been young, hurt and angry, and her mother's final betrayal had been the straw that had broken her.

But staying away for twelve years had killed any relationship she might have had with her mother stone dead. Long ago, she'd decided there was no point in trying to contact her mum. It was too late for them now, just as it was for Jago and Rhianna.

She chatted to Louise for a little while about the island until Jago carried Braden back towards them in his arms. The little boy looked sleepy, rubbing his eyes with his fists and then wiping his nose on Jago's overalls.

'Sorry,' said Louise, looking embarrassed.

He grinned. 'No problem. I think the walk up here has whacked him out.'

'It's done me in but you're really lucky to live here,' said Louise. 'You too, Miranda.'

Miranda's throat was still scratchy with emotion but she made a joke. 'Keeps me fit, that's for sure.'

Louise lowered her voice. 'Heating bills must be shit, though?'

Jago was momentarily taken aback then a grin spread across his face. 'Bloody shocking, if you must know.'

Braden's head was lolling.

'He's tired out. I'd better get him home.'

'I'll help you down to the quay,' Jago offered.

The journey down was ten times easier. Miranda followed Jago down the steps, carrying Louise's bag, pointing out a few things as they went. Jago carried Braden to the door of the visitor centre where his pushchair was stored and one of the staff appeared.

'Lady St Merryn just phoned the office. There's an important call for you, Lord St Merryn.'

'Can't it wait?'

'Her ladyship says not. She told them you'd call back immediately. Do you want to phone from the office?'

Jago frowned and hesitated. 'No. I'll go back up to the castle. Thanks.' He ruffled Braden's hair as Louise took him and strapped the sleepy boy into his pushchair.

'I'm afraid we have to go to catch the boat, it's the last one of the day,' said Miranda, wondering if the call was from Southcastle.

Jago smiled. 'Goodbye then, Braden and Louise. Come back and visit any time you like.'

'We'd love to. I know Braden would.' Louse looked so delighted that Miranda felt almost guilty. It was their harbour that Braden had fallen into. When Jago had gone, Miranda escorted Louise and Braden to the boat, helping Louise to lift the pushchair over the cobbles, so as not to disturb her son. His long lashes brushed his chubby cheeks as he slept in his chair.

'How d'you keep your hands off him?' asked Louise as Miranda helped her lower the pushchair onto the gangway.

'Who?'

'Oh come on, you must fancy the pants off him?'

Miranda gave in pretending she didn't know what Louise meant. 'He's my boss.'

Louise straightened up. 'Not gay, is he?'

'Oh God, no!'

Louise raised her eyebrows. 'Got some posh totty lined up to marry?'

'I ... um ... don't know much about his private life.'

''Scuse me but that's crap. You live here, don't you? I bet

you know everything that goes on and you've gone bright red. Well, I don't blame you. I'd shag him. He is totally hot.'

Braden yawned and opened his eyes. 'Poo, Mummy . . . I want a poo.'

Louise groaned. 'I'm trying to potty train him. Oh God, not here. Not now. Go to sleep. I'll take you when we get off the boat. Goodbye, Miranda, and thanks again.'

'A pleasure. Come to the Festival of Fools. Ask for me when you get here and I'll make sure you have a good time.'

Chapter Twenty-Two

The season was in full swing. Even with Jago lending a hand when he could, even with him actually becoming useful, Miranda's free time was almost non-existent. Lady St Merryn had taken more and more of a back seat, leaving the running to Jago and Miranda, while she made more trips off the island to London and to visit friends.

The Mount was now open even longer to take advantage of the school holidays. By the time the last visitor had been persuaded and cajoled to leave, it was usually well after six, then there was clearing up, locking up and a final security sweep to organise. The rhythm of the days was exhausting but Miranda had convinced herself that was a good thing.

Not such a good thing was Jago's frequent presence in her office.

One morning, his one-fingered typing, which consisted

of squinting at the screen, punctuated by periodic bashing of the keypad and swearing under his breath, had been driving her slowly mad. She was also trying to dispel a series of alarming and very un-PC *Secretary*-type fantasies. The phone rang and Jago glanced up, a frown on his face because his concentration had been broken.

Miranda snatched up the handset. 'Hi, it's Theo. How's it going?'

She glanced at Jago. He was doing his screen staring thing. 'Fine, thanks,' she said, trying to sound neutral yet friendly, unwilling to alert Jago to her caller's identity.

'I was calling to discuss a few more details about the tug of war. The guys are looking forward to it, especially Neem. The bloke will do anything to have an excuse to spend time with Ronnie,' said Theo.

'Yes, it all seems to be going very well,' Miranda agreed breezily.

'We also need to arrange a precise time and a space for the tug of war. We'll need a flat surface and a fair bit of room for the guys and the spectators.'

'I'd already thought of holding it in the lower courtyard in between the visitor centre and the café. There's plenty of room for everyone there.'

Jago jabbed his keyboard again, concentration creasing a deep line between his eyebrows.

At the other end of the line, Theo went on, oblivious. 'OK. What time do you want us? Afternoon is best as the guys have training in the morning.'

'What about mid-afternoon when everything's in full swing? Say three o'clock?'

'Sounds like a plan. Have you got a team from the Mount sorted yet?'

Miranda twirled the telephone cord in her fingers. 'It's in hand. Reggie's going to be team captain but he's still recruiting and training people at the moment. How many did you say we need?'

'Officially we need eight people per team, and the weights have to be roughly even, but that might be difficult for you, considering the size of our lads. One of us will drop out on the day, if things look totally unfair to your lot.'

'We can hold our own!' Miranda exclaimed. Big mistake. Jago glanced up at her, If he'd been a Jack Russell, his ears would definitely have pricked up.

'Don't worry. It's only a bit of fun,' said Theo, chuckling softly. 'We won't take it too seriously if you don't.'

Unlike Reggie, thought Miranda. He'd already been drilling his team of gardeners and handymen like the hard-nosed sergeant from *An Officer and a Gentleman*. Miranda had seen them jogging up and down the castle steps, and performing press-ups in the courtyard. She fully expected them to have buzz cuts and a platoon chant by the day of the Festival.

'Is Jago in the team?' asked Theo.

Miranda glanced at Jago, now engrossed in a report from English Heritage. 'Not as far as I know,' said Miranda.

'Can't stand the heat, eh?'

'I don't think he's been asked.'

Jago *must* know she was talking about him. She sounded guilty as sin but, still, he didn't look up at her.

'OK, thank you for calling,' she said, eager to end the

call. She could phone Theo back when she was on her own.

'Miranda, wait.'

She squirmed. 'Yes?'

'I've put this off for far too long. Would you like to come out for a drink with me sometime? Not the Pilchard, somewhere away from the Mount and the village so we can talk properly.' Miranda glimpsed Jago, eyes still riveted on the report as Theo went on. 'What about Wednesday? That would be best for me as I'm definitely not on call and we won't be interrupted.'

'Wednesday?' She scrabbled through her mental diary. 'Well, I was hoping to go to the see the Fishermen's Choir that night. They're appearing at the Festival and I wanted to meet them in person and thank them for donating their fee to the Lifeboats.'

'Where are they doing the gig?'

'Porth Ivo.'

'That's not far. Why don't I sail you there, weather permitting? One of the lifeboat crew has a cousin who sings with them.'

'But do you really want to see them? Won't it be a busman's holiday?'

Theo laughed. 'You know I love sailing and I can put up with a few sea shanties for one night. I'll pick you up by boat or in the car, depending on the tides and weather. I'll phone you again when I know which.'

'Wednesday. Of course,' she repeated.

'Miranda, are you all right?'

'I'm fine. See you then.'

Gently, she replaced the receiver. Surely, Jago must have realised she was setting up a date by now but he still appeared to be absorbed in his work. *Too* absorbed, in Miranda's opinion. Had he guessed that it had been Theo on the phone? Of course, it didn't matter if he had. It was none of his business and of no relevance whatsoever to his life or Miranda's. And there was no earthly reason for her to refuse Theo's invitation. Jago had made it brutally clear he wasn't interested in taking their relationship further and she wanted to prove to herself that could move on from her crush on Jago.

Ten minutes later, after she'd stared at her own screen without taking in a single word, she heard Jago snap shut a box file and replace it in the cupboard.

She treated him to a beaming smile that was as much guilt as relief. 'Taking a break?' she asked.

'I need to go up to the castle. I've got a video conference with my legal team about the Southcastle contract.'

'Oh.'

He came over to the desk and glanced down at her. 'Have a lovely evening, Miranda. You know, Theo is right; you really should get away from this place.

The tides and weather being fair, Theo arrived on schedule at the Mount, allowing plenty of time to sail to the busy harbour at Porth Ivo. Ronnie and Neem waved them off from the quayside. Ronnie almost danced with glee because she'd finally 'got Theo and Miranda together' as she put it. At least, two people were happy; not all love affairs were doomed, thought Miranda at the unlikely sight of Neem giving Ronnie a piggyback to her cottage. Tonight, she hoped that getting to know Theo better, away from work and the Mount, might mark a new start for her.

Miranda wasn't a great sailor but she knew the ropes well enough to help Theo crew his small yacht safely in to the mousehole-sized harbour at Porth Ivo. After tying up, they joined the crowds heading to one of the harbourside inns where the choir had set up ready to sing.

It was a repertoire Miranda had heard before yet still loved; Cornish standards like 'Trelawny', sea shanties, folk songs and the odd modern track, given an unusual twist. The choir had rich, evocative voices that told of people lost at sea and the pride of local fishing communities; Miranda could almost feel the sea spray whipping her face as they sang. It should have been cheesy, but it wasn't, not sung here by people who really did live, work and die by the sea.

'I have to go and thank them,' she said as the applause died down after their first half set and everyone dived for the bar.

'Sure. Let's say hello.' Theo slipped his arm around her back, his hand firmly on her waist. Miranda asked herself how that felt. Sexy? She wasn't sure. Comforting? Not really. Proprietorial? Where had that word come from? She tried to relax as they wandered among the audience in the interval. She was sure his grip tightened when they stopped to chat to his friends and realised that Theo obviously wanted people to know she was with him. She was with him, for that evening anyway, and it was flattering, but she didn't feel ready to be labelled as his girlfriend.

She managed to fight her way through the crowds to the singers, enjoying pints of cider and Doom Bar ale. After thanking them for their generosity and saying how much she enjoyed the gig, Theo bought some of the singers a pint and Miranda slipped away to the loo. On the way back, she bumped into Karen from the Pilchard.

'Hello there!'

'Oh hello, Karen.'

Karen smiled. 'What's up? You look like you've seen a ghost. Or is it a guilty conscience?'

Miranda laughed. 'No . . . um . . . I'm just surprised you got a night off from the pub. You're always so busy.'

'That's the pot calling the kettle black. I got Ray to hold the fort while he's not at sea. I wanted to see this gig. One of my regulars is in the choir.'

'Oh.' Miranda moved out of the narrow corridor that led to the toilets in the pub. Karen followed. Theo saw her and waved.

'I didn't know you were with Theo,' said Karen. 'I saw him with his arm round you earlier.'

'Well, I'm not actually *with* him.'

'You could have fooled me. You two seemed glued together.'

Miranda managed a laugh, but she knew that it wasn't only her who had noticed Theo's casual ownership of her. 'Theo wanted to come and meet the choir before they sing at the Festival and he offered to sail me here.'

Karen held up her hands. 'It's OK, you don't have to explain. It's really none of my business.'

Miranda thought she *did* have to explain, having been seen with Jago one week and Theo the next. Apparently dating two men hardly made her the village bike but the bad

226

blood that existed between Jago and Theo somehow made the situation seem worse. She hadn't forgotten that Karen knew most of Jago's intimate secrets, either.

She lowered her voice and plunged in. 'Karen, what happened that night with the rowing boat and Jago. It was a one-off. I was three sheets to the wind.'

Karen winked. 'It's OK. My lips are sealed. To be honest with you, a one-off sounds about right where Jago's concerned. I heard about his wife's accident, you know. My second cousin runs a bar in Bells Beach near where they were living. It was a terrible business and it sounds like it's messed Jago up for good. He's always been a complicated boy, shall we say, and now he's pure trouble.' She smiled. 'He's completely gorgeous trouble, of course but you're better off with Theo.'

'And Theo isn't trouble?'

Karen laughed. 'Aren't all men? Yes, Theo's a handful, but he's very loyal. When he takes a liking to someone, he sticks by them – and the reverse is true too. Cross him and you've made an enemy for good.'

Miranda thought about asking Karen if she knew why Theo disliked Jago so much. After all, she was involved with Jago when both he and Theo were lads and still living in the village. Perhaps the rivalry had started then? But Miranda couldn't think of any way of asking that didn't sound incredibly intrusive and showing such an interest in Jago's past really would ring Karen's alarm bells.

'Theo seems like a nice guy. He does a lot for the community,' said Miranda, hoping Karen would take the bait.

'And he's sex on legs, honey, unless it had escaped your

notice. He's a man who knows what he wants and gets it. Catch of the year is Theo and you hooked him.'

Miranda wasn't quite sure she liked this analogy. It sounded like she'd cast her net, hauled Theo in and had him floundering at her feet, gasping for air. 'Maybe,' she said, going for enigmatic and failing. 'I'll see you soon,' she said, and walked back to Theo.

'Miranda. You look cold. I'll warm you up.' Theo handed her a pint of cider and Miranda tried to relax and enjoy nestling in the arm of the unofficial hottest guy in Cornwall. A quick scan of the women in the audience showed more than one pair of envious eyes turned in her direction.

Unexpectedly, the cider and the rousing second half of the gig helped her unwind and she was laughing all the way home as Theo sailed back to the Mount. It was dark when they tied up in the harbour, with a few lights shining in the cottages and castle, revealing who was still awake. There was a glow from the bedroom of Ronnie's place, Lady St Merryn's bedroom window was dark but Jago's lamp was on. He must be in his study working late.

Theo followed Miranda up the ladder from the boat and onto the quayside. They stood in the night air, both a little breathless and unsure what to say.

'I had a nice time tonight,' she said eventually.

'Me too.' Theo reached out, pulled her gently to him and kissed her. It was a long, slow, wet kiss. A kiss that might possibly have been enjoyable were it not for the fact that when she opened her eyes Jago was watching from barely ten feet away.

She dropped her hands from Theo's back and pulled away.

'What's up?' Theo's eyes were puzzled then he turned. 'Oh, I see. His lordship.'

Jago's face was half in shadow. 'Hello. Had a good evening?' he asked.

'A fantastic evening, thanks. Didn't we, Miranda?'

Her heart sank. 'It was lovely. The Fishermen's Choir did a brilliant gig.'

'And Theo sailed you home?'

'No, we walked. What do you think?' said Theo not bothering to hide his sarcasm.

'How lovely. Miranda loves boats, don't you?' There was no mistaking the dangerous edge to Jago's voice.

'I've had a nice time,' said Miranda firmly.

Theo took her hand in his. 'Good. I aim to please. Now, I'm sorry I can't come in for coffee but I've got an early start. Work has to come before pleasure for some of us.'

Someone turned a light on in the harbourmaster's cottage and Jago's face was illuminated. There was a momentary flash of fury on his face then it settled into blankness. Miranda stopped herself from pointing out she hadn't asked Theo back to her cottage. That would have delighted Jago and she wasn't in the mood to give either one of them an inch.

'Now, I hate to leave but I must get home before the tide turns.'

'Yes, we wouldn't want you to get stuck here for the night, would we?' said Jago.

Miranda felt like a bone being fought over by two Jack Russells. She freed her hand from Theo's and threw him a brief smile, ignoring Jago. Theo brushed her lips with his and said, 'I'll call you.'

Miranda longed for a bucket of cold water to chuck over them. 'Yes, you do that,' she said sweetly.

'I can see I'm intruding. I'll see you tomorrow, Miranda,' Jago muttered.

Theo threw him a triumphant glare. 'Goodnight, your lordship.'

Miranda half held her breath, sure that Jago would shout or swear or show some reaction but instead he gave the slightest inclination of his head, almost as if he was admitting defeat to Theo. Then he turned his back and stalked off towards the path to the castle.

As Theo sailed off to the mainland, Miranda watched him, first from the quay and then from her cottage window, all the way back to the harbour. She flopped down on her bed, trying to make sense of the evening and the encounter between Jago and Theo. Theo had clearly wanted everyone to know she was 'his' at the gig; in fact, she had the distinct impression she was his trophy – his war trophy. But, she reminded herself as she shivered in the draught from the open window, how could there be a war if one party wasn't interested in fighting for her?

Chapter Twenty-Three

The following morning, Miranda hovered in front of Jago's desk, having been summoned to his study by a message on her radio. When she'd arrived, he'd peered at her through a pair of wire-rimmed glasses as if he'd forgotten he'd asked her to see him. Then he took them off and lifted his thick, dark hair back from his temples, revealing threads of grey. The gesture and the glasses made him seemed more real and vulnerable and sexy than he ever had before. She felt her resolve to ignore him collapsing like a sandcastle swamped by a wave.

'You're wearing glasses.'

He frowned. 'Yes. Did you expect me to have superhuman powers or something like X-Men?'

She laughed at him. ''Course not, but I haven't seen them before.'

'I wear contacts normally but my eyes are sore. All that

typing, I guess.' As he pushed the glasses aside, he brushed a pile of papers and a heavy object rolled from under them. Jago scrabbled to catch it but it fell off the desk and landed on the floorboards with a crash. Both he and Miranda dashed to pick the object up, ending up on the floorboards at the same time. Miranda saw it was a telescope and closed her hand around it. Crouched on the floor, inches from him, his eyes, amber-flecked brown without his contacts, held hers.

His breath feathered her face. She ached for him to lean forwards and kiss her and make love to her on the boards. Instead, she pushed herself to her feet, still keeping hold of the telescope. He straightened up too and she held out the scope, now warm from her hand.

'Thanks.'

He deposited it in his wire in-tray as if he kept one there every day, but Miranda couldn't take her eyes off it. She recognised it now. It was an antique brass piece from the nautical room and it had no place in Jago's study. The cogs in her mind whirred.

'Jago. Were you watching us last night?'

'What do you mean?'

'You know exactly what I mean. Your study light was on when we sailed into the harbour so what were you doing down on the quayside when we tied up?'

'Firstly, I came out for some of fresh air and, secondly, I do own the place, so I have a right to be down there.'

'So you weren't spying on me?'

A smile spread over his face. 'With my little telescope? Ah, Miranda, you have a wild imagination. No, I wasn't spying on you. I was working late and I had a headache, so I went for a walk. It is pure coincidence that I caught you and Theo snogging on the quayside.'

'Snogging? We weren't snogging. And as for catching us? We're not naughty schoolkids!'

He shrugged. 'Snogging, kissing, have it your way, I don't care. Or rather I do care as long as it – he – makes you happy.'

Miranda simmered with a mix of anger and, she had to admit, of hope. Jago *was* jealous.

'Now can we actually discuss the reason I asked you up here? Southcastle are coming over.'

Her stomach turned over. The last thing she needed was another visit from Southcastle Estates. 'What for?' It was a dangerous question and the moment it was out she fully expected him to say he was signing the contract. She felt sick.

'It's a final visit to tie up any loose ends before I go to London to sign the deal in front of the lawyers and money men.'

That answer brought no relief. 'When?'

'Tomorrow. You won't be required but I thought it only fair to warn you.'

The next morning, Miranda was in the castle courtyard checking there was space for the fire-eaters and jesters to perform. Pierre Jumeau came across her as she blew an imaginary flame at an imaginary audience. 'Whooshhhh!'

'Miranda. *Bonjour.*' She cringed as he strode up, obviously amused. 'Sound effects, non? Very good.'

Goosebumps popped up on her arms. 'We have fire-eaters at the Festival. I was just checking out the space. Um ... I didn't know you'd arrived. I thought you'd be here a bit later than this.'

'I decided to catch an earlier train and walk over the causeway.'

'Oh. Is Andrew not with you?'

'No. He's tied up in London and sends his apologies.'

'Has Jago seen you yet?'

'No. I was on my way into the castle now.' He smiled. 'I have paid my entry fee.'

'Paid? I must reimburse you.' She shoved her hand in her pocket for some cash but Jumeau laughed.

'Don't think of it. I wanted to arrive as a normal visitor and just wander about.'

Shit, thought Miranda. She was torn between a hope that Fred had been rude to him or that he'd been impressed. She was past the stage of trying to put him off buying the Mount. Once was enough as a joke, now she had no choice but to try to make the best of a bad job. 'So, how was your visitor experience so far?' she asked, fighting to sound neutral.

'Quirky ... very British, polite, amusing.'

'Oh.'

He patted her arm, making her goosebumps almost explode. He really made her skin crawl. 'And exactly as I'd have expected and hoped. We don't want to change the character of the place, Miranda. I feel passionate about this property too. It has the potential to be the biggest asset we own. We may take a slightly different approach in the short term but I'm sure you will appreciate what we are trying to do.'

Asset? Different approach? The hairs rose on her scalp now too. Jumeau had the same effect on her as some suave but creepy character from a vintage *film noir*. 'I . . .'

'I empathise with your loyalty and your passion, believe me, but you can see that Lord St Merryn does not want to take on the responsibility of this place. It is a huge enterprise, one that has become far bigger than one family should have to cope with – one man, in fact, now her ladyship is so frail and planning to leave. I think you know Lord St Merryn –' he smiled '– or should I say, you know Jago very well indeed. For everyone's sake, and his, you must realise this is the right decision.'

Jumeau glanced behind him. Miranda saw Jago standing by the wall on the other side of the terrace, staring out to sea. He looked tired, bowed down, almost broken. She felt like her own heart, her spirit even, might shatter at any moment. Then she saw Jumeau's smug half-smile. Bugger that. She'd still fight, for the staff if not for herself.

'What about the staff?' she demanded, finally giving up on the niceties.

'Hmm. Now, if I promised that no one would lose their jobs and that things would stay exactly the same as they are now, would you believe me?'

'No.'

'I thought you'd say that. Well, my dear Miranda, that is why I have no intention of lying to you. Of course, things will change when we take over management of the Mount but we'll have you to guide and advise us. I'd like to offer you a bigger role, not just here at the Mount but within our organisation. There would, of course, be a serious salary to go with it.'

She held her clipboard tighter as her skin grew icier. What was happening here? Was he trying to get rid of her so she wouldn't cause trouble? Or was it a genuine opportunity? 'Not at the Mount?' she asked.

Jumeau was as close as he could get without actually touching her. 'Do you not want to broaden your horizons as Jago does?'

Jago turned to look at her, an agonised expression on his face. She had the distinct impression he was caught between the devil and the deep blue sea. He didn't want to broaden his horizons, he wanted to escape but she wasn't telling Jumeau that.

Jumeau took a step back. 'It's a big decision and you need time to think about it. I'll leave my card in your office; it has my private number on it. Now, I must speak to Lord St Merryn about signing the contract.' He smiled. 'I think it is more than time we had this deal wrapped up.'

Jago watched Miranda scuttling down the steps from the terrace, pain stamped all over her lovely face. He saw Jumeau smiling after her then turn towards him. What had he said to her? What had the bastard done to her? Then he laughed at himself. It was ridiculous to be jealous of Miranda and Jumeau. His feelings of jealousy towards Theo, he could understand, if not handle, but Miranda wouldn't be interested in Jumeau, not in that way.

But what the hell *had* the slimeball been saying to her?

236

He strode forwards to meet the man, hand outstretched. 'Good morning, Pierre.'

'*Bonjour*, Jago. What a beautiful day, *non*?'

'Very. Shall we go up to my study for coffee?'

Face thine enemies, he reminded himself, like generations of St Merryns before him, except he wasn't repelling Southcastle, he'd invited them in with open arms. He was being overdramatic and, worse, letting his emotions rule his decisions. The irony darted through him. Wasn't selling the Mount the ultimate in emotional decisions on his part? Immediately, he shut out that paradox; it was too complex and painful to deal with.

An excruciating hour later, Pierre occupied the Chesterfield sofa in his study. The Frenchman closed his laptop with a sigh that could have been satisfaction or relief, but drove Jago irrationally crazy. 'So we have the contract ready, all the details of the transfer are in place,' he said.

Jago replaced his coffee cup in his saucer and, with infinite care, placed it on the mantelpiece. 'I still need my own legal team to go through it a final time.'

'Of course, and I will have copies sent to all our people, but that is a formality. We agree on the deal and that is what matters.'

Jago's gaze drifted to the window. He heard children playing on the terrace. 'Yes, of course.'

Silence hung in the air as Jago listened to the laughter in the courtyard, wondering when he'd hear it again, knowing he never would, not in this time, or place, not here in his home.

'You know you don't have to worry about her?'

Jago turned sharply to find Jumeau watching him, hawk-like, as composed and calm as he was in turmoil. 'What?'

'Miss Marshall. I have a role for her.'

Inside, his stomach plunged like an out-of-control elevator, but he managed to feign a casual shrug. 'Jumeau. You're paying umpteen million for the place. It's your concern what you do. I can't worry about individual members of staff.'

There was a smile on Jumeau's lips, a smile that was knowing and amused. 'Come now. That's not quite true, is it? You are a realist and appreciate we will have to make changes. There will be casualties but we'll do our best to soften any blows.'

'Casualties?' Jago's fingers tightened.

'I can see that Miranda is . . . special to you. We are men of the world, Lord St Merryn, and I can assure you she will be taken care of.'

Men of the world? Whose warped, archaic world would that be? Jago crossed to the window, gripped the stone ledge and closed his eyes. He didn't care what Jumeau thought, he just wanted to punch the bastard's urbane face in. 'I'm not sure what you're implying,' he said to the open window as he struggled to control his fury.

He turned to find Jumeau with concern on his face. 'I implied nothing beyond we will behave with the utmost professionalism.'

'I'm glad to hear it.' He almost spat out the words.

Jumeau got to his feet. 'Then we understand each other. We will be back in a few weeks' time with a date to sign the contracts. It is our main priority now and we will set a date to meet in London. Jago, you have no doubts about this?'

Doubts? He had so many doubts about every decision he'd made over the past few years that he could barely contemplate them. The biggest was that Jumeau had said that Miranda would be taken care of. In what way? Financially? Sexually? He shouldn't care about what happened to her but he did. He cared so much it was influencing the biggest decision of his life. One he had been set on, since his mother had called him back. He did not want to be lord of the island, he didn't want the responsibility, the burden of a place and its people, their hopes, fears and livelihoods He didn't want to commit his life and his heart, everything, to one woman ever again. It had ripped out his heart to lose Rhianna and yet here he was again, thinking of giving everything he had to the Mount and its people – and more importantly to one of them. To Miranda.

It was impossible. He couldn't afford to care and, more to the point, he didn't have that kind of commitment left in him. Grief had utterly destroyed it.

He took a breath. 'No. No doubts.'

The bell of the chapel clock tolled. *Traitor. Coward.* Each chime seemed to mock him for his weakness but he shut out everything and walked Jumeau down the steps and onto the boat. To his horror, and before he'd realised what was happening, Jumeau leaned forwards in the French way and kissed him on both cheeks and Jago felt like Judas.

Sod work. Miranda escaped to her cottage after her meeting with Jumeau, locked her door and told the office she wasn't to be disturbed. She simply couldn't stay at the Mount, not with Southcastle in charge. Jumeau had as good as said he wanted to remove her from the position by making her an offer she couldn't refuse. Well, she would tell him to shove it up his smooth arse and she would get another job, no matter how long it took. She'd clean toilets again and work in the ticket office if she had to, and live on baked beans like when she'd left home. She snatched the application form for the Scottish castle from under the pile of magazines on the coffee table, grabbed a pen and tried to fill it in.

Her hands shook too much.

An hour and an obscenely large whisky later, she'd managed to fill in most of the form. She went to the window of her bedroom and looked out. Jago was on the quayside, showing Jumeau onto a boat. As the Frenchman stepped onto the gangway, a seagull swooped low over his head and spattered him with muck. Miranda heard his angry shout from her room.

'*Merde!*'

She remembered Braden shouting 'Poo, Mummy! Poo!' She saw Jumeau wiping at his suit and Jago's astonished face and she started laughing. She laughed until her stomach ached, her sides hurt and the tears poured down her cheeks and turned to long, racking sobs.

Chapter Twenty-Four

No one was more surprised than Miranda when Jago knocked on the door of the cottage a few days later. She'd been having a proper day off, again, even in the midst of all the Festival preparations because Jago had finally admitted he wasn't the ideal assistant and hired in part-time help.

He followed her into the sitting room and asked, 'How do you feel about getting out of here?'

The answer that should have been 'No, thanks I've booked an appointment with a gay man in town who's going to give me an aromatherapy massage' turned into: 'Where?'

It wasn't the most gracious of answers but, in fairness, her brain did seem to have been taken over by another woman – a reckless one who wanted to spend time with him despite all her better judgement. The last time she would spend with him, alone.

Jago didn't seem to notice, or else was used to her brusqueness by now. 'I'd like to have a day out at the seaside. Call it going back to the egg or the last meal of a condemned man.'

'On this occasion, you have the power of reprieve,' she said softly.

'Nice try and I take your point but this isn't the same situation as Rhianna.'

'I didn't mean that!'

He gave a sigh. 'I know. Now, please, humour me and come out.'

'Just let me make a phone call and I'll meet you at the staff car park.'

Her hands trembled slightly as she dialled the beauty therapy centre to reschedule the massage. She had the feeling that everything was slipping away from her, the rope sliding out of her hands as she prepared to let go and just fall.

So why not enjoy one last hurrah? The prospect of spending time with Jago, one last time, just as friends, even though they were enemies, was impossible to resist.

She wasn't the least bit surprised when, an hour later, Jago guided the Land Rover through the narrow dune-banked lane into the car park at Godrevy and slotted into a spot overlooking the beach. It was not the best of days; the sky was swathed in clouds of grey, white and steel, with the odd patch of blue struggling in vain for attention. The wind blew fiercely, buffeting the car from time to time.

She struggled to push the door open. 'Not ideal for the beach,' she called.

'It looks perfect to me!' he shouted back and she realised

why when she saw the white surf rolling onto the shore below them. Oh bloody hell, was that really what he had in mind?

Jago had no choice but to hire the wetsuits and boards from the Surfer's Café. He wasn't entirely happy with the board, the café staff who doubled as instructors had done their best to find him the best of their hire kit but it bore no comparison to the custom-made board he'd owned in Australia.

He could picture it now, in its bag inside the garage at the house he'd once shared with Rhianna. He hadn't used the board or lived in the house since her funeral. He'd moved out straightaway, gone travelling and then returned briefly to Bells and rented an apartment in the middle of a town. 'Don't you want a view of the ocean, mate?' the rental agent had asked, clearly guessing that Jago could afford a prime location. But Jago hadn't wanted a view of the ocean. It reminded him of Rhianna too much.

So why was here now, with Miranda?

Simple lust was one reason, although he'd be lying if he said he'd brought her here simply to watch her wriggling her body into a wetsuit. That had been hugely enjoyable, of course, as had finding that she owned a startlingly small bikini. He even took some pleasure in seeing in her face now, in her body language: apprehension, excitement, a little fear as they walked towards the water. The way she glanced at him as they walked towards the shore, carrying the boards, felt like a demon was scouring his heart. She relied on him; trusted him.

If only she knew that her natural fear and anxiety about this new and possibly dangerous experience were nothing to his. His heart pounded as hard as the surf. It had been three years since he'd been on a board, since Rhianna's accident, and they'd been the longest and darkest years of his life. He stopped on the hard wave-rippled sand, his heart thudding. He wasn't sure he could overcome either fear but he had to try.

'Here?' she asked.

She looked at him. She trusted him and he wanted to tell her she shouldn't, not in the water and certainly not out of it. He steeled himself. He shut out the roaring clamour of guilt and fear that told him to turn away from the ocean and from her. He closed his ears and heart to the conviction that he was playing with Miranda's life and heart to assuage his own grief and he smiled.

She needed reassurance. 'Yes. Here will do and don't look so scared. The lesson starts before we go into the water.'

'I'm not certain I can do this. Remind me again why I'm here?'

Jago had asked himself the same question. Was he using Miranda to exorcise his demons? A twisted logic told him that if he could overcome his fear of taking her surfing, in this symbolic way, maybe he could overcome his fear of commitment and stay at the Mount.

He tucked the board under his arm and grabbed her hand. 'Let's just suck it and see.'

Suck it and see, thought Miranda as she battled through the surf to the beach for the final time. She'd certainly sucked enough of the Atlantic into her in the past hour, or was it two? She'd lost all sense of time. All she knew was that an invisible sea creature had silently sucked the bones from her body and replaced them with mush. She didn't know who or how but it had. She lay flat on the board, staring up at the sky. All the dark clouds had flown away while they'd been in the water and been replaced with bright sunlight. She closed her eyes against the rays then opened them to see Jago silhouetted against the light.

'Time to go. We'll be late getting the boards back to the Surfer's Café,' he said.

'I don't think I can get up.'

'Good. That's how it should feel.'

'Really?'

'Yes.' He shifted his body and she blinked as the sunlight dazzled again. Every muscle in her body had given up the ghost. She didn't ache; she was simply drained of every ounce of energy. Before she'd even got into the water, her thighs and arms had ached from practising paddling and jumping up to crouch on the board.

Once in the surf, she'd felt as if she was fighting a battle; struggling with the waves; wading out, paddling through the breakers, trying to crouch, falling off, getting wiped out, being hauled out of a giant washing machine of swirling surf by Jago. She'd wanted to just give up, ten, twenty, countless times by the end. Just once, when she thought she couldn't take another minute of pounding, she'd managed to get to her feet and ride a wave. Just for a few seconds, awkwardly but gloriously, before she'd wiped out in spectacular fashion.

'You did well,' he said, as she grinned like an idiot at the memory. 'For a virgin.'

'Thanks!'

He thrust out a hand and she reached for it. As he hauled her up, she swayed and then steadied. 'My God. I'll never walk again.'

'You will.' He picked up her board and his, tucked them under each arm, 'Eventually.'

They handed back the kit just in time and, after a quick shower, Jago waited for her, his hair damp and tousled, a couple of days worth of stubble shading his jaw. He looked so sexy that Miranda wanted to leap on him. Somehow, she would have found the energy. She quickened her step then half stumbled as she got nearer. Shit, her legs wouldn't bloody work. Most of her joints appeared to have rusted.

'Sore?' There was amusement in Jago's eyes.

'What do you think? Oh,' she groaned as she tried to straighten up and her back protested. Briefly she thought she knew how Lady St Merryn felt.

'You know, back in Oz, we'd have got a body massage after a session like that.' He flipped his thumb in the direction of the rolling dunes behind the car park. 'We could do that now, unless you have any objections.'

She could think of at least ten reasons not to accept such an offer, but the chance to lengthen this glorious fantasy day was impossible to ignore. The thought of Jago's warm hands massaging her tired muscles, of him touching her made her want to explode with lust.

'OK.'

His mouth opened in surprise.

'Don't look so shocked. As a matter of fact, I had a massage booked for this afternoon. Ronnie gave me a gift voucher for the Kynance Hotel Spa and I'd booked an aromatherapy session with their therapist. He's called Dave,' she said, enjoying his expression.

'Dave? I wouldn't have thought they allowed male masseurs to handle female clients at the Kynance. They're far too strait-laced.'

'Of course they do. There's absolutely nothing sexual about a massage. It's purely therapeutic as you said yourself, and besides,' she had to admit, 'Dave is very gay.'

Jago gave a sigh. 'Then I shall try very hard to replicate the experience though I can't promise pink towels and pan pipes. Let's find somewhere more private.'

They headed into the sandy *towans*, the rolling heathland that stretched out on the cliffs above the beach. A few hardy walkers were heading towards them after hiking through the dunes.

'Afternoon, mate,' called a man taking a chubby Labrador for a walk. 'Nice day for it, eh?'

Jago nodded. 'It is.'

The hiker winked and Miranda's cheeks grew hot. The walkers probably guessed what she and Jago intended and had taken it one step further. She shivered with anticipation as they reached a hollow in the dunes, surrounded on all sides by blades of rippling marram grass. It smelled divine.

'You know these dunes are one of the last places to see the great crested sand lizard?' she said. 'I read it in the nature magazine at the hospital and . . .'

'Really? That's interesting,' Jago said brusquely. 'Take off your shorts and T-shirt.'

'Take them off? You didn't say anything about that.'

He tutted loudly. 'How the hell do you expect me to give you a massage through your clothes? I'm sure you wouldn't have objected if Dave had asked you.'

'I don't know, but you're not Dave and I really don't think this is such a good idea after all.'

'As you pointed out, there is absolutely nothing sexual about massage, if that's what you're worried about.'

'I'm not that immature.'

'Then take off your top and lie down. I'll go away for a few minutes while you undress.'

When he'd gone, Miranda couldn't hear another human sound, just the hum of insects, the whisper of the breeze in the grass and the seagulls crying far overhead. Glancing around, she unzipped her shorts and let them slip down to her ankles. She stepped out of them and her flip-flops. Surely, at any moment, someone would come along and see her? Or worse, Jago would come back and find her half undressed. She wanted him to touch her so much. So much, she thought, for vowing to keep Jago at arm's length. She was burning for him to touch her, even it was meant to be 'therapeutic'.

She pulled her T-shirt over her head, unhooked the back of her bra and shrugged it off. Quickly, she lay face down, her breasts sinking into powdery sand.

She heard him coming back a few minutes later and closed her eyes, trying not to feel awkward about being topless.

'Now, try to relax and just think of me as Dave,' he said. 'Only bigger and hairier.'

Miranda giggled.

'That's good,' he said, kneeling beside her. 'This might be a bit sore to start with but that's a good thing. It's a shame I have no oil with me but I didn't come prepared for this.'

Miranda ignored his remark and tried not to tense her bottom or press her hips into the sand. He'd said the massage might be painful and that hadn't helped her relax. Then it began. His hands were smooth, not calloused like in her fantasy. They were also warm and swept over her shoulders and spine, lightly and rhythmically. The pressure was gentle and didn't hurt at all. She began to relax.

'Ow!' She let out a cry as his fingertips probed the flesh between her shoulders.

'Sorry. But this is the best way, believe me.'

So the first few strokes had just been a warm-up. Or exploratory. She tried not to tense as he started the massage proper and now knew why he'd warned her. His strong fingers sought out every knot of fatigue and tension, kneading until she could hardly bear it. She bit her lip, determined not to make any sound, but every so often she twitched in discomfort.

'Try to relax,' he said softly.

Relax? She would have laughed if she hadn't been too busy wincing. 'Ouch!'

She heard the laugh in his voice. 'You needed this, Miranda. You're as stiff as a board.'

He was merciless in seeking out the stiff flesh and muscles and kneading it away. When she didn't think she could stand any more, suddenly, he changed rhythm and pressure. His hands swept down the length of her back, either side of her spine. She felt her flesh relaxing, the tension ebbing slowly but surely away. She sighed softly as he pressed the skin around the small of her back, his fingers probing just above the waistband of her knickers. Now, *that* was much nicer.

'Better?'

'Mmm.'

'Good.'

She closed her eyes. He definitely wasn't Dave. And she definitely *mustn't* want him to go lower or turn her over and touch her breasts or hold her to him and kiss her. Or make love to her. Both hands swept firmly down the backs of her thighs. She felt deliciously relaxed and soothed.

His voice reached her from far away. 'That's good.'

His hands swept from her shoulders, along her back, over her bottom and down her thighs and calves. She waited for the next sweep along her skin, for the next touch but there was only the cool breeze whispering over her skin.

'OK, that should do it,' he said.

She stifled a protest. No, she wasn't ready for this to be over yet. She wanted more, of his fingers moulding her flesh, touching her everywhere, exploring.

'I'll leave while you get dressed.'

He was going away. She pushed herself up until she was kneeling. 'Jago. Wait.'

He was squatting beside her a few feet away, about to stand up, but, as she called his name, he froze. She glanced down at her breasts, sprinkled with bone-white sand, her nipples dark and stiff. Jago stared at her, his lips parted, his breathing louder. Miranda felt powerful and she wanted him so much, she ached. She was ready to make love with him without worrying about the past or the future.

She just wanted the moment. He met her gaze with eyes that seemed full of pain, not the pleasure at seeing her body that she'd expected. She reached out a hand to touch his arm but he sprang to his feet, her fingertips brushing the hairs on his arm.

His voice grated like waves dragging over shingle. 'You'd better get dressed. Let's go and get something to eat.'

Chapter Twenty-Five

At the café, Miranda bagged a table on the terrace over-looking the coast while Jago ordered. He came out carrying a tray laden with mugs of steaming hot chocolate topped with whipped cream and a plate piled with slabs of fruit loaf, flapjacks, brownies and lemon drizzle cake. Miranda thought it hardly made up for being left cold in the dunes, but it was a start.

'Is someone joining us?' she asked, as he unloaded the plates onto the table.

'Not as far as I know. I wasn't sure what you liked best but I knew you'd be hungry. And I don't think Dave would have done this for you.'

She laughed. 'Thanks but I can't eat two great slices of cake,' she said, but proceeded to do exactly that. She was just dotting up the last few crumbs with her fingertip when

Jago asked, 'Miranda, what exactly happened with your parents?'

No preamble. No request to ask a personal question. Jago just dived straight in. 'Was the surfing and cake to soften me up?'

He shook his head. 'Not at all. Now simply seemed the right time. I want to try to understand why the Mount means so much to you.'

'It's too late for that. It won't make any difference to your plans.'

'No.'

Miranda pushed her plate away and fiddled with her paper napkin.

'You don't have to tell me,' he said. 'Only if you want to.'

She wasn't sure she wanted to talk about something so personal but perhaps she needed to. More than anything, she didn't want their day to end and if this was the price to pay so she could stay here with him, she'd do it. 'My dad might be dead for all I know. I never knew him. I told you he left us before I was born.'

'I'm sorry.'

'Mum brought me up,' she said, 'Although "bringing up" is being generous. She made sure I didn't starve, or at least made sure there were either baked beans in the cupboard or a pound to buy some with . . . ' Her voice tailed off. But as actual bringing up, as in emotional support, guidance, love? Her gran had done that, for a time at least.

'And?' he asked, probing again.

'My gran helped in the early days, until I was about ten or so, but then she died.' She felt a corkscrew of pain in her guts even now at the loss. She'd adored her gran and had often stayed over at her Victorian terrace with its tacked-on bathroom and narrow stairs. 'I loved her and I would have lived there permanently if I could.' Sudden insight hit her. No wonder her mother had felt sidelined, guessing her own daughter preferred her grandmother. It wasn't Miranda's fault; at ten she'd loved Gran with all her heart without thinking who it might hurt, but her mother must have felt pushed out.

'I wanted to stay with Gran but Mum wouldn't let me. I suppose she wanted me in her own way – then my gran died.'

'That must have been tough.'

She screwed the serviette into a ball in her hand, crushing it. 'Yes. I loved her.'

'I'm sorry you didn't have a relationship with your mother. I know what it's like when parents turn out to be a disappointment.' Jago gave a rueful smile. 'And children even more so.'

Miranda guessed he was referring to him leaving his mother to run the Mount alone and not going back as expected. Yet Lady St Merryn *did* love her son; she was prepared to give up her own life and dreams to look after his future. At least, she had been, until recently.

'I'm not complaining. Mum wasn't cruel to me and, if she was, maybe she never meant to be. As you say, I just wasn't what she expected, I think. Maybe she'd been hoping for a friend or a younger sister because she was only seventeen when she had me. But I didn't like boys and make-up and all that stuff. I preferred books and reading. I liked hiding away in my bedroom instead of hanging round the shops and going to discos and Mum found that hard to understand. She blamed Gran for encouraging the books too.'

'So what made you leave home?'

'Gran left me some money when she died. She always told me about it and she said it was "for my education". I wasn't sure what that meant, at ten. I thought it was for school but as I got older I realised she'd meant it to help me through university.'

Miranda was plunged back to those days again, when she'd hidden under the duvet, battling the dragons. They were roaring fire and St George was raising his sword arm and, funnily enough, he looked a lot like Jago now, in her memory, but back then he hadn't looked like anyone, just some unspecified knight in shining armour.

She had to smile at herself. Jago was so far from a knight in shining armour, it was laughable, but she went on. 'One day, when I was in the sixth form, there'd been a meeting at school about funding for university. Some of the parents had come along, in fact, most had come, but not Mum. I was used to that and I'd worked out what I needed to do for myself. And I knew I had Gran's money to help me out. It wasn't that much, but enough to ease my path a little bit so I wouldn't have to ask Mum for handouts that I knew she couldn't afford and wouldn't give me. When I got home from school, I asked Mum where the money was and how I could get access to it. But she just told me it had gone.'

She was back in the lounge of the caravan now, hearing

her conversation with her mother, feeling the crushing sense of loss again when her mother had turned to her and shrugged. She'd shrugged away all Miranda's hopes and any faith in her mother.

'*Gone? What do you mean? What have you spent it on?*'

'*Stuff.*'

'*When?*'

'*Over the years. We needed it, Miranda. Money doesn't grow on sodding trees.*'

'*But Gran said there was over ten thousand pounds. It was in the building society. It would have added up.*'

'*Well, it hasn't so tough shit.*'

She'd exploded, screaming at the top of her voice, losing control and hating herself for showing how much she cared.

'*I bet you drank it, you bitch! I bet you spent it on the fucking tossers you call your boyfriends. I hate you. I hate you!*'

'I went berserk, called her all the names under the sun, cruel names, but I thought they were true. Still do. Then she slapped my face,' she told Jago. Her fingers rested on her cheek briefly, remembering the shock and the sting. 'I expect I deserved it.'

'No, never!'

Miranda shook her head. 'Yes, I did. We both deserved what we got, her and me.'

'And then you ran away?'

'Not immediately. I ran to my room and slammed the door and didn't come out. Mum must have thought I'd got over it and that's what I wanted her to think. Over the next few weeks I kept on going to school, finished my A levels and scraped together a bit of cash from a Saturday job in the tea room in the town museum.' She shook her head. 'You see, I've always had a soft spot for dusty old relics.'

Jago didn't smile back so she went on. 'At the end of term, Mum thought I'd gone to the sixth-form leavers' afternoon but I took the chance to run away and I never went back.'

'You don't mean you let her think you were dead?'

'For a while, yes.'

'Christ.'

'I was terrified of her or the social coming after me and terrified of what I was going to do or where I was going to go. I was shit scared of what I'd done. It was a cruel thing to do. A weird thing to do. Maybe I wasn't normal and Mum was right.'

'Where did you go?'

'I ended up at the housing office in Winchester.'

'Why?'

'I liked the cathedral and Jane Austen had died there. In Winchester, I mean, not the housing office. You see I told you I was weird.'

He touched her arm, still not smiling, even though she'd managed to make a joke.

'No. You were angry and upset,' he said.

'Yes. Maybe a lot more even than I'd realised.' She remembered the feeling of bubbling bitter anger inside her, boiling away like a kettle but never running dry. 'For all Mum and her latest bloke knew, I was dead. But I cracked first. I phoned after a couple of days but only in case she called the police. Not for her sake, I remember. I just didn't want them wasting their time and most of all I didn't want them looking for me. But I wanted her to suffer. That makes me evil, doesn't it?'

'Of course not.'

'I think it does. After seeing what Louise went through when Braden fell in the harbour, thinking he was dead, I hated myself more than I've ever done. It was a wicked thing to do, to make her suffer like that. You didn't want Rhianna to suffer, did you? You would have helped her to die if you could?'

He hesitated before replying. 'This is different, Miranda. Very different.'

Was it? Miranda wondered what Jago really thought of her, if he was just being kind.

'What happened when you called home?' he asked.

'She shouted and told me to get my arse back home, but I was too hurt to do that. I kept expecting to be less hurt as the days went by but I didn't. I felt just as angry and still didn't want to go back and that's how it started. I stayed away forever.'

Jago gave a sigh. 'What amazes me is how you ended up at Mount. How did you manage with university – you obviously got your degree?'

'I got the university to defer my place; they understood in a way Mum wouldn't. I got a job in my gap year – three jobs, actually. I worked in the café at a National Trust place, in a pub kitchen and in a vinegar factory for a few months packing bottles.' She laughed. 'I went home every night stinking like a chip shop, with people avoiding me on the bus, but I learned to manage. I worked in the vacations in the university bar, the college gave me hardship grants and I ate beans on toast.'

'And you've had no contact with your mother at all?'

She shook her head and sat on her hands. 'I've never spoken to her, not from the day I phoned to say I was alive and was never coming home. I haven't seen her since. I'm not sure I'd even recognise her now and I've no idea what she's doing.'

'She might recognise you.'

Miranda shrugged. 'I doubt it. I shouldn't think she ever thinks about me.'

'I think you're wrong but I won't argue.' Jago fiddled with a fork as if he wasn't sure he should be probing. Miranda's heart felt almost overfull with the relief of telling someone what had happened to her, what she'd done. 'So the Mount is an escape from the real world? That's why you love it so much.' He gave an ironic smile as he added, 'For the stability?'

He didn't need to add that he was snatching that stability away and Miranda was too tired to fight any more. It was too late.

'You were right, Jago. Growing up as a little girl, it was my dream to go to university and then run somewhere like this. Gran supported and encouraged me. The money would have helped, it would have made things so much less difficult and hard, but that wasn't all. When I knew the money was gone and no one was going to lend a hand, I was on my own. I managed to get my dream anyhow; it was just a lot harder.'

She touched his arm. 'You were right about me playing safe in staying here for so long, but I'm only trying to protect myself and what I've fought for. Once I got it, I was never going to let anyone take it away from me again. Even if you don't want it as a part of your future, I wasn't prepared to listen or think about what you needed. That was wrong. I can't make you do what I want and I'm going to stop trying. You've won.'

Chapter Twenty-Six

On the morning of the Festival, Miranda pulled aside the curtain and peered out onto the harbour. Well, thank goodness something had finally gone right, or was in the process of going right. The sun shone, still pink, from a sky streaked by a few early morning clouds. A gentle breeze wafted her cheek through the open casement. Even though it was barely 7 am, she knew the crowds would flock to the event.

Today, at least, she could forget that the place was being sold and that its residents and staff's lives would soon change forever. None of the thousands of visitors who were even now packing picnics, loading up the car, calming excited children or cajoling cynical teenagers, knew that the course of history was actually being changed when the St Merryns sold it.

Most of today's visitors wouldn't give a toss about the sale;

perhaps a few of the older ones, the history buffs, the local MPs and old-fashioned sticklers for tradition would really mind and might complain. In the end, the Mount was someone else's problem and who would shed a tear over the angst of its overprivileged owners and their hangers-on? Not Louise and Braden Dixon, that's for sure, they had far too much to worry about surviving each day.

Theo might even be pleased. He'd phoned her to confirm the final arrangements for the tug of war and asked her to go for a drink after the Festival was over. She'd agreed, deciding to give him another chance – and give herself another chance to like him. Soon the news would be out about the sale and whether she was staying, or more likely, leaving, it was time to get on with life. She hoped that by thinking the words often enough, they might one day come true.

Miranda shook her head. What had she said about forgetting about the sale today?

After bolting down a piece of toast and a cup of coffee, she headed straight to the office, rubbing still-gritty eyes and sucking in lungfuls of seaweed-scented air as she strode over the cobbled harbour side from the cottage. She hadn't slept much. Her mind had waltzed its way through the night, whirling with a list of undone jobs to do before the festival opened and a maelstrom of thoughts that had nothing do with the event at all. Yet as she passed the staff and entertainers, she held her head high, determined to make this last event her best. For it would be her last. Even if she didn't leave, she wasn't sure if Southcastle would keep up the tradition, unless it made money for their organisation.

Or maybe they *would* keep it up, she second-guessed.

They'd probably keep on doing it for the PR value and wasn't that why the Mount did it too? As a gesture to the community? No one kidded themselves that the place was run entirely for the benefit of the local people. And yet somehow it felt that way and she really believed that it mattered to the local people, beyond the tourist pounds it brought in.

The Festival, like the Mount and its people, was a living thing.

By half past ten, the early birds were already making their way over the causeway. Costumed staff swarmed about, helping the entertainers set up and the charities lay out their stalls and the smell of toffee apples competed with hog roast and candy floss. Miranda threaded her way through the growing crowds and up to the storeroom in the castle tower where the Mount kept a collection of costumes for interpretation days, school visits and special events. She'd much rather have stayed in her shorts and polo shirt but she had to enter into the spirit of things.

Bugger. The costume rail was almost empty. But that was her own fault – she should have got here sooner. Hanging from the rail was a jester's outfit, complete with three-cornered hat with bells on it and curly-toed slippers. No way was she wearing that. She'd probably trip over the slippers and jingle wherever she went.

The other choices weren't good, either. A bear suit – in this heat? A peasant's sack and what appeared to be a tavern slut's outfit.

Miranda went into the washroom, slipped out of her uniform and held up the costume. Maybe it would fit if she breathed in hard but it looked as if it had been made for a very underfed wench indeed. The skirt had a stretchy waist and Velcro so that was OK but the blouse was a nightmare. She worried about ripping it as she pulled it over her head. It had a lace-up bodice that, drawn as tight as possible, just about covered her bra and almost covered her modesty. When she got down to the quayside, she would absolutely have to fetch a tank top from her cottage to wear underneath.

'Miranda!' Lady St Merryn's voice boomed through the door. 'Is that you in there?'

Stuffing her clothes in a carrier bag, Miranda opened the door of the cubicle. 'I'm here. Wow. You look ...'

'Fulsome?' offered Lady St Merryn.

'Regal,' said Miranda, taking in her boss's emerald velvet dress, blonde wig and wimple.

'Do you know who I am?'

'Um ... The Lady of Shalott?'

'Guinevere, actually, but you were close enough. As long as you didn't say Rapunzel, I'm happy.'

Miranda let out a sigh of relief and felt the laces on her bodice creak.

'The walking stick somewhat ruins the illusion but they say that King Arthur came from Cornwall so I feel it's appropriate on this occasion. I was damned if I was going to dress up as some fusty old matriarch. For a day, I can pretend I'm the woman whom Sir Lancelot risked life and honour for.' She paused. 'Forgive me asking, Miranda, but can you actually breathe in that frock?'

'Not really but it was this or a bear suit.'

'Hmm.' Lady St Merryn raised an eyebrow, as if the bear should have won. 'Have you seen Jago?'

'Not yet.' Miranda had been too busy to think about him for the past two hours. She was too busy now. Her radio crackled. 'Yes? OK. We'll be right down. The mayor's arrived to open the fair,' she told Lady St Merryn.

Her employer adjusted her wimple and sighed. 'Shall we go and meet her?'

Down on the quayside, after the formalities with the mayor were over, Miranda ran straight into Jago. She didn't know whose eyes popped out further – hers or his.

'Bloody hell! Where the hell did you get that outfit?' he asked.

Miranda's heart sank and her cheeks heated up. 'It was either this, a bear or a jester so please don't make any comments.'

He held up his hands but he couldn't wipe the smile off his face. 'I wouldn't dream of it.'

'I see you got to the dressing-up box first.'

Jago glanced down at his own outfit. 'I thought you'd find it appropriate in the circumstances.'

He was dressed as a pirate in a billowing white shirt, leather waistcoat, dark fitted breeches and black leather boots. On his head he wore a tricorne hat topped with a feather and, over one eye, a black patch. The other eye seemed to have a touch of guyliner but she resisted the urge to ask him where he'd got it from. 'You need a parrot,' she said briskly, hoping he wouldn't notice the pink in her cheeks.

'It must have flown away.' He lifted up the eye patch and blinked. 'Do you think I look wicked enough to rape and pillage the local populace? Not that I know what pillaging is.'

'It means looting and plundering. Taking what you shouldn't have.'

'Or selling it? Let's not start the day like this.'

The laces on her bodice creaked again. She still hadn't had time to get a tank top to wear underneath so that would be the very next task on her list. 'I have a feeling it's going to be a long one,' said Miranda. 'And I'll see you in the stocks.'

A few hours later, the quay swarmed with visitors. The great weather, the attractions and the publicity had all combined to lure a record number of people to the Festival. The Fishermen's Choir had been a huge hit with the older visitors and a hat had been passed around which had raised even more money for the lifeboats. Theo and some of the crew had even joined in with the rousing finale of 'Trelawny', a Cornish anthem guaranteed to stir the blood.

Amid the non-stop mayhem, Miranda's still-untamed bodice was the least of her worries as she dashed about, fielding radio calls, looking after the entertainers and dealing with a stream of minor problems that always happened at such events. She'd just finished judging a children's pirate fancy dress contest when she spotted Louise Dixon on the fringes of the crowd. It was almost time for the tug of war but Miranda decided to take the time to say hello.

'Hello again!'

Braden sat in his pushchair with his mouth ringed with

chocolate ice cream. He poked a finger into a tub, inspected his sticky finger then shoved it in his mouth, sucking off the cream.

Louise grimaced. 'The lady in the kiosk gave him a free tub but I was worried he'd try to swallow the little wooden spoon. Thanks for the free Festival ticket. He's having a great time. We both are, and Braden's just been in the lifeboat.' She hesitated. 'Um ... that guy who pilots it seems nice. The captain, or whatever he's called. Theo, isn't it?'

Miranda hid a smile. So Louise fancied Theo. 'Yes. Theo's the coxswain of the boat. He's organised a tug-of-war today. It starts soon. Are you going to watch?'

'Do you think I'd miss all those blokes getting hot and sweaty. Are you mad?'

Braden let out a chuckle.

'I guess that's a "yes" to staying.'

A large crowd had gathered on the quayside, ready to watch the highlight of the day. A tug of war between a combined rugby/lifeboat team and the staff from the Mount. Miranda didn't fancy her side's chances. The gardeners, boatmen and maintenance men who made up the team were fit and captained by Reggie, but the rugby team had Neem. Miranda glanced at her staff and decided it was like putting Alan Carr in a cage fight with Vinnie Jones.

She heard Ronnie's voice at her ear. 'Don't look so worried. Reggie's been training our team using his SAS techniques.'

'That should be good if they need to live on bugs and kill a man with a rolled-up newspaper,' said Miranda. 'But I don't think it will be much of an advantage against Neem.'

'Neem's promised me he'll try not to hurt anyone too badly.'

'That's good of him.'

'Miranda!'

Reggie jogged over, sweating buckets before battle had even commenced. 'There's a problem.'

'What problem?'

'One of the gardeners has put his shoulder out and had to go to hospital.'

Miranda winced. 'Is he OK?'

'Yes, but we're one short for the team.'

'Can't one of Theo's team drop out?'

Reggie looked at her as if she'd suggested he assassinate the Queen. 'Drop out? I'm not letting his lot know we're one man down! You never show weakness to the enemy. We need someone else. Someone fit and strong and preferably very large.'

His eyes rested on Ronnie who returned his questioning look with a glare that could have turned a whole tug-of-war team to stone. 'Say a word and you die, Reggie.'

'Wouldn't dream of it. But who can we ask? I've already roped in every fit member of staff who's not on medication.'

Ronnie pointed at Jago, doing a stint in the ice-cream kiosk next to very flushed Daisy. 'What about his lordship?'

Reggie seemed doubtful. 'D'you think he would?'

'If someone asked him very nicely, he might. After all, it is his island.'

If there was an emphasis on Ronnie's last phrase, Miranda couldn't have sworn to it but she was swiftly despatched to drag Jago out of the kiosk and persuade him to take his part on the rope. She was convinced he'd refuse, having already agreed to be in the stocks later.

Leading him behind the kiosk, she began her pitch. 'I know you won't want to do this and it's so not your thing and we're completely desperate or I wouldn't have asked you and in the circumstances you might not want to get involved in any more of the activities today but ... would you mind being in the Mount's tug-of-war team? One of the gardeners is injured and you are our last resort.'

Jago took off his tricorne and gave a little bow. 'Gosh, Miranda, that's such a flattering offer. How could I resist?'

Chapter Twenty-Seven

To Miranda's complete astonishment, the staff team, with Jago at the front, won the first of the three tug-of-war sessions. Sweat poured off torsos onto the sawdust-covered cobbled court and the grunting rivalled a ladies' tennis match. Miranda spotted Lady St Merryn, pigtails flying, screaming at the Mount team like a spectator at an all-in wrestling match. Any moment now, Miranda expected her ladyship to jump into the fray and batter one of Theo's team with her stick.

As for Miranda, she now knew the meaning of being between a rock and a hard place. Naturally she wanted to the staff to win, but she didn't want to cheer too loudly in case Theo thought she was shouting for Jago. On the other hand, it would be disloyal not to egg on the staff. On the other hand – bugger, that was three hands – she ought to support Theo and his lifeboat and rugby friends as they were the main reason for the event.

After an epic second tug, a great roar went up and Theo raised his arms in the air. 'Yessss!'

His team cheered as the Mount team collapsed on the cobbles, gasping. Jago, sitting on his backside, put his head in his hands.

'Oh, knickers!' cried Miranda. Then, 'Well done!'

Ronnie nudged her. 'Hard, isn't it, knowing who to support? I want our lot to win but I want Neem to win too. Life's just so complicated sometimes.'

'Tell me about it,' replied Miranda

The teams gulped down bottles of water before taking up their positions again. Jago faced Theo and Miranda could feel the tension emanating from the edge of the crowd as they squared up. Both men glared at each other but Miranda guessed she was the only person watching who knew the animosity was real, not put on for effect. Her skin pricked. She had a horrible feeling something was going to give today.

'Ready!' Fred the harbourmaster, acting as adjudicator, raised his hand as the crowd simmered.

'This is it then,' Jago shouted across the line.

'May the best man win,' called Theo.

'Shouldn't that be best men?'

'You know what I mean, mate.'

Miranda closed her eyes briefly. *Oh, bloody hell.*

'Testosterone is a mixed blessing,' murmured Ronnie. 'I think I might have to practise some restraining techniques after this.'

'Pull!'

At Fred's cry, the teams took up the strain. Their faces grew scarlet, veins stood out on their arms and their grunts became almost bestial. It might be only a game but the sixteen men at either end of that rope were treating it like all-out war. The lifeboat crew's supporters yelled at the tops of their voices, the staff's families bellowed even louder. First, Jago's team, then Theo's, inched close to the line. Reggie's eyes bulged alarmingly and one of the rugby team had turned puce. Miranda wondered if the new defibrillator in the medical room was working. Just in case.

Theo edged closer to the line, heels digging into the ground, as the Mount team had the upper hand. The Mount team were going to win! She held her breath and her hands flew to her mouth. Another few feet and Jago's team would have dragged Theo over. Suddenly, Neem let out a great roar and, in seconds, Theo had shot backwards. Jago staggered forwards, stumbling over the line and falling flat on his face in a cloud of sawdust. Theo's team had won and the air was filled with cheering and whistling and clapping.

Neem grinned, looking as cool as if he'd been for a walk in the park, until Ronnie hurtled into him and almost strangled him with her hug. Miranda had the distinct impression that Neem had been toying with them; he was barely out of breath. As Jago lay sprawled on the cobbles, she ran forwards to help him but Theo got there first.

He held out his hand to Jago. 'Sorry, mate, but the best men won.'

Ignoring him, Jago pushed himself to his feet. Sweat poured off his forehead and he was red-faced with effort, anger and humiliation.

'Are you OK? Both of you?' asked Miranda.

'Fine. Well done to your team,' Jago squeezed out, finally extending a hand to Theo.

Ignoring it, Theo put his arm around Miranda's shoulders and Jago's expression turned stormy.

'We thought it would make better entertainment for the crowds if we let you win the first round,' said Theo.

In despair at both of them, she freed herself from Theo's arm and stood apart.

Jago tried to smile but only managed to snarl, 'Excuse me, I need a shower. Miranda's promised to lock me in the stocks later.'

Theo's response was a snort. 'Really? Well, maybe that's just what you need, a nice long sit-down, mate. See you later.'

Miranda almost gasped. They were pathetic, both of them.

'Right. The tug-of-war is over,' she said. 'And if you two *gentlemen* don't mind, I've got things to do.'

An hour later, the crowds showed no sign of thinning. Some of the densest were over by the coconut shy where Lady St Merryn twirled her plaits like Rapunzel meets Ride of the Valkyries. 'Roll up, roll up!' Miranda heard her shout, then smiled and felt a pang of regret. She squashed it down, determined to enjoy every last moment, even though the day was racing faster than the tide.

Ronnie found her hiding behind a shed at the back of the offices, drinking a bottle of water and bolting down a rather squishy Mars bar.

'How's it going?'

Miranda swallowed her mouthful of chocolate. 'It's crazy, but look at all the people. It's going to be a record year. How are you doing? Any incidents I should know about?'

'One heated argument over at the coconut shy; one attempt to dive off the terrace Acapulco style.'

Miranda groaned. 'You are joking!'

'No. Couple of kids from the village thought they'd move on from tomb stoning, but they've been shown the error of their ways. Look, I'm sorry to disturb your break but we need someone to supervise the stocks and take the money for half an hour. Do you have time to do it?'

Miranda threw the last part of her Mars bar into a rubbish bin. 'Not really but I will. Who's in there?'

'One of the lifeboatmen but it's Jago's turn soon. Have you seen him?'

'No. I'll try and track him down.'

Maybe he'd backed out, thought Miranda, as she fought her way through the crowds to the stocks, licking chocolate off her fingers on the way. But she was wrong – Jago was already waiting.

'Bet you thought I'd bottled it?'

'Of course not,' she lied, hoping he wouldn't mention Theo.

'When you didn't come, I thought you might be otherwise engaged by now.' Jago left her in no doubt of whom he was referring to.

Miranda bit her lip and pointed to the stocks. 'Get yourself in there, villain.'

'Whatever you say, Miss Whiplash.' After he'd positioned himself on the wooden block, worn shiny by hundreds of unfortunate bottoms, Miranda slotted the wood on top of his ankles and locked it, pocketing the key. Already a new crowd had gathered, all eager to have a turn at soaking and taunting someone fresh. The fact that the someone was the owner of the castle had not escaped a few of the visitors.

'I can see I'm going to be popular,' said Jago as Miranda filled a bucket with water to soak the sponges.

'One thing you can rely on is that a thirst for public humiliation never goes out of fashion.' She held up a dripping sponge and shouted to the eager-eyed crowd, 'Ladies and gentlemen, boys and girls, I'm here to tell you that this pathetic-looking miscreant has been sentenced to half an hour in the stocks.'

Jago's jaw dropped. 'Half an hour? I thought you said ten minutes!'

'Oh, you've been far too wicked for that, you dirty, wicked, horrible pirate scum.'

'That's going too far,' he growled.

'Be thankful it's only wet sponges, not rotten fruit and veg.'

'What's a miscreant?' asked a small boy.

Miranda wrung out a sponge. 'It's a very naughty person. So, who will help this terrible pirate get what he deserves?'

A chorus of 'me's' filled the air and a dozen arms shot up

in unison. Miranda handed the bucket to a teenage girl in exchange for a pound coin.

'Do ye worst, varlet,' Jago snarled. 'I'm Cap'n Jago and I . . . bloody he—'

His words were cut off as a wet sponge hit him smack on the nose. Miranda clamped a hand over his mouth. 'Sorry for Pirate Jago's language, ladies and gentlemen, but I did warn you he was *very* wicked.'

Umpteen sponges later, Jago's hair was plastered to his head. He licked water from around his lips and snarled, 'I'll have you keelhauled, boy!'

The little boy shrieked in delight, wound up his arm and launched his final sponge. It flew through the air and knocked off Jago's eye patch as the crowd cheered.

'Yay! I got him again! Mum, can I have another go?'

Jago shook his head like a dog, sending droplets of water spraying into the air.

'Mum, can I smack him again?' The boy hopped up and down like Tigger.

'Not now, Jake. I want to go round the craft stalls.'

'But, Mum!'

Taking his hand, his mother dragged him away from the bucket. Jago sighed in relief.

A man rolled his sleeves up and grinned. 'It's my turn, now. I think Pirate Jago needs a good going over. I used to bowl for my school, you know.'

Shit. Miranda was getting worried. She'd wanted Jago to suffer but he'd taken over twenty minutes of punishment from children, teenagers, grannies, mums and dads. Three times she'd had to ask some of the fathers in football shirts to show a little restraint but Jago had ruined any of her efforts by growling pirate oaths and insulting their chosen teams. One man, with a huge belly and barbed wire for hair, had spent six pounds on sponges and would have carried on if Miranda hadn't put a limit on the number of goes.

'Do you have a death wish or something?' she hissed as she switched on the tap and thrust the hose in the bucket to fill it. Her ballet shoes and clothes were soaked, but she was more worried about Jago.

'I just want to make as much money for Theo's good cause as possible.'

She shook her head. 'The tug-of-war is over, you know. This isn't a battle.'

'I've no idea what you're talking about, wench.'

Miranda turned off the tap and stood up. Six rounds of sponges later and there was still a queue lining up. Jago shook away water droplets from his hair and growled menacingly. He reached his arms into the air, laced his fingers together and stretched. The sodden shirt clung to his chest and stomach. His breeches were soaking. He must be freezing because his nipples were showing through the white cotton. Jago caught her staring at him and she rolled her eyes and mouthed 'You're crazy.'

A teenage girl jingled coins. 'Me next!'

Miranda shook her head. 'I'm sorry but think Pirate Jago has taken enough punishment for now.'

The crowd groaned in disappointment.

A little girl said plaintively. 'I want to throw a sponge at the pirate, Mummy!'

Miranda smiled. 'We'll put someone else in the stocks later. There are lots of other attractions and they're all in a good cause for the lifeboats.'

A large woman huffed. 'I've been waiting for twenty minutes to do him.'

'I am sorry, madam, but he's had enough for now. Please, come back later. I'll allow three more turns but for under threes only.'

The teenagers thumped off in disgust but the little girl hopped up and down so Miranda took the money from the girl's father.

'I make children walk the plank!' Jago bellowed.

Not ten, but at least a dozen turns later, Jago finally gave in and allowed Miranda to unlock the wooden plank that held him in the stocks.

'Are you OK?' she asked as the crowd dispersed, muttering.

He straightened up, wincing. 'Yes, but I'm not sure I have a coccyx any more. Jesus. Some of those kids could be in the England first XI.'

'It was the fathers I worried about. Why on earth did you have to taunt them?'

Jago put his hands on his hips and circled his pelvis. Miranda knew he was only stretching his back but she wished he wouldn't. 'It got more money for Theo's boat fund didn't it?'

'You're acting like a spoiled boy,' said Miranda.

He grabbed her arm. 'Am I?'

The silence hung between them for a moment. 'Jago, what happens between me and Theo is none of your business.'

'No. Of course not. I just don't want you to get hurt.'

'Isn't it a bit late for that?' She could have bitten out her tongue.

'What the hell has he done to you?'

So, Jago thought *Theo* had hurt her. 'He hasn't done anything to me.'

'Then what did you mean, that it's a bit late?'

'Nothing. I meant nothing. No, no, I do mean something,' she said, exasperated beyond the limit. 'I hate it when you two act like dogs scrapping over an old bone!'

Jago's startled expression was quickly replaced with a bitter smile. 'An old bone? That's brilliant, Miranda. Now I know what you've always reminded me of.'

'It's not funny! You and Theo are like stroppy teenagers when I'm around. It's as if you've never grown up past fifteen. It's ridiculous.'

The smile disappeared from his face as quickly as it had appeared. 'You're absolutely right. I am behaving like a teenager but I promise to stop from now on. I can't answer for Theo; you'll have to ask him why he seems to hate the sight of me though I can hazard a guess. I expect he thinks I've come home to claim my *droit de seigneur* over you.'

This was so close to Miranda's one-time fantasy that she felt her face grow red. 'I can't stand here arguing. I've got enough to do.' She picked up the bucket and shoved it at him. She saw Ronnie in the distance, pushing her way through the crowds, waving frantically at her. She didn't want to get caught arguing with Jago. 'Please, leave me alone and find something useful to do.'

Jago, with a face like thunder, ignored the bucket and stalked off towards the castle path.

'Security coming through, folks. Thank you very much!' Visitors parted like the Red Sea as Ronnie shouldered her way through. Red-faced and panting, she reached Miranda. 'Bloody hell, where have you been? We've been looking everywhere for you. You don't have your radio.'

Miranda patted her skirt pocket, still reeling from her confrontation with Jago. 'Haven't I? I must have left it in the office. What's up?'

'South West TV want an interview with his lordship, or failing that, they said someone in charge will do. Have you seen him?'

'Um. Not since we finished the stocks. He should be back soon.' Or maybe not if he found out the TV wanted an interview with him, she guessed.

'Tough. We can't wait for him. The telly people are getting pissed off and I think they'll leave if someone doesn't speak to them soon. Can you do it?'

She glanced down at her damp clothes. 'Looking like this?'

'I expect the ratings will go through the roof. And our visitor numbers. Shit, that's them, coming over now.'

The cameraman, a sound recordist and a presenter, who Miranda recognised from the evening news programme, headed straight for them.

'Oh no.'

'Smile,' hissed Ronnie.

The reporter thrust a microphone in Miranda's face and beamed. 'Well, you look as if you've been enjoying yourself!

Miranda Marshall is the property manager of St Merryn's Mount, where the annual Festival of Fools is in full swing. Miranda, we're live on South West Television's afternoon bulletin. How's the day gone so far?'

Live? Oh no! Miranda didn't have time to think. 'Um. Fantastic. We've got even more visitors than we'd expected and everyone seems to be having a great time.'

Ronnie hovered by, almost bursting with glee, as Miranda did her duty. She'd given interviews and presentations before, but never wearing a wet wench's outfit. She felt her hair tickling her face and her neck where it had long ago escaped its ponytail.

But the way she looked was the least of her worries. Her blood went cold as a sudden dread struck her. What if any rumours about the sale had reached the press? She didn't see how they could have done, as none of the staff knew, but it was always possible. That would be an absolute disaster.

The presenter beamed in her face. 'I hear Lord St Merryn was in the stocks. Was that a highlight of the day?'

'It certainly raised a lot of money for our nominated charity, the local lifeboat station . . .'

She hesitated. Jago had materialised again and was standing behind the reporter, grinning fit to burst. Ronnie's mouth opened in an 'o' of surprise and she pointed at her chest, then at Miranda's. She felt the laces loosening over her bosom and almost fainted. Oh no, not now.

'And what do you think about the future for heritage attractions like the M–'

The reporter might as well have asked her if fairies

existed because Miranda could no longer concentrate. She glanced down at her bust for a split second then heard a creak and a ping. The camera wobbled. Ronnie's hand flew to her mouth. Jago's grin melted away and reporter's eyes nearly popped out. The laces had snapped and her cleavage was on view to half a million viewers of South West Television.

Chapter Twenty-Eight

'OK then, I think that's all we have time for. Thank you for joining us, Miranda. Now it's back to the studio from St Merryn's Mount. We'll have an extended report on the festivities here on the evening edition of *South West Tonight*.'

'That's it,' said the reporter as Miranda tried to tug her bodice together.

She groaned. 'What a disaster.'

The reporter was beaming. 'Oh, don't worry. That's one for the blooper reel. You'll probably end up on out-take shows for years to come. Sorry to spring on you like that, but we've got to rush back to base.'

Miranda wasn't the least bit comforted and, ignoring Ronnie, she dashed off towards her cottage past grinning visitors. Jago ran after her and grabbed her arm.

'Get off me!'

'Calm down. Come here.' He led her behind the visitor centre.

'I just showed my rack to half the population of the South West!' Miranda wailed.

'Not *half* the population. I'm sure the station only has a few thousand watching at this time of day. Maybe only a couple of blokes in the pub and a little old lady in Penzance at a guess.'

'It's not funny. Look.'

He let out a sigh of admiration. 'Believe me, I did and I am.'

'I hate you sometimes.'

'I'm well aware of that. Here.' He took off his waistcoat and slipped it over her shoulders. 'That should cover your modesty until you get to the cottage.'

Under the relative safety of the waistcoat, she made it to the cottage and unlocked the door. 'I need to get a new top.'

Jago followed her into the sitting room. 'I'll wait here.'

She turned. 'Please, there's no need. I'll get changed and see you later.'

For a moment, she wasn't sure he would leave. He seemed about to say something and she half held her breath but then he said: 'OK, I'll see myself out.'

Upstairs, she found a faded peasant-style blouse at the bottom of her drawer. After she'd changed, she brushed her hair and secured it back in its ponytail. She stood in front of the mirror and took a few deep breaths. With Jago and Theo following her around like warring brigands, she ought to feel like Cornwall's luckiest woman but it wasn't a happy experience. She hoped that the rest of the day could go without incident but that hope was crushed when she finally emerged from the cottage to find Theo hovering in the doorway.

'Ah. Now I see. I've been wasting my time, haven't I?' he said as she ushered him out and relocked the door.

'What?'

'I saw Jago come out of the cottage earlier. I saw you with him in the stocks and I saw him put his arm around you. Most of all, I saw your face. You're in love with him.'

She opened her mouth to deny it then realised it was hopeless. 'Theo, I like you but . . . '

'As a friend?' His lip curled sarcastically.

'Yes. As a friend. I know that makes me the only woman for miles around who likes you only as a friend but . . . ' She smiled to try to defuse his hurt.

'Slept with you, has he?'

'Now wait a minute!'

'He'll finish you, you know.'

She was getting angry now. 'I don't know what you mean.'

'Yes, you do, Miranda. You've got it bad for Jago, haven't you? I'm worried about you because he'll only let you down. He'll fuck you up and then he'll be on to some other woman, just like his father. And you'll be here in five years' time, still cleaning his toilets while he marries some rich horsey type.'

Miranda wanted to tell him how wrong he was in every possible way. About her staying and about Jago loving and leaving her but she couldn't tell Theo that. She couldn't tell him because she'd made a promise to Jago, a vow that, she knew now, she could no longer keep. The day was drawing to a close and the time had come when he had to let everyone know his plans.

So, she shook her head and ran a finger over his shoulder. 'Theo, has anyone ever told you to brush that chip off your shoulder?'

Theo's mouth twitched in anger. 'As a matter of fact, they have. But before you accuse me of being jealous of Jago, you should ask my mother if you want to know what the St Merryns really are. Ask her what happened when Lord Patrick sowed his wild oats. He'd only just got married to Lady St Merryn when he came sniffing round my mother. She had a nervous breakdown after he'd finished breaking her heart and then my dad left us.'

'That doesn't mean . . .' Miranda shut her mouth firmly, almost having been drawn into a trap. The revelation answered some of the reasons why Theo seemed to hate Jago. But the sins of the fathers weren't always visited on their sons, she thought, or the sins of mothers on their daughters. This was a path she wasn't prepared to go down with Theo, or Jago, or anyone. 'Theo, not that it's any of your business but I haven't been having an affair with Jago and I'm never going to and, on that, you can trust me. And we can't be together either.'

'Why not?'

'Because . . .' *Because I'm leaving, I'm running away again. I've had enough of this place and things can never ever be the same.*

'We just can't. Believe me.'

'No. He grabbed her arm.

'You're hurting me.'

There was desperation in his eyes and anger, resentment burning like a fire. 'Now that bastard's come back, he thinks he can take and own anything he wants to, you included.'

'Me? I'm not some kind of trophy, Theo, and I'm never going to be Jago's and I can't be yours either.'

'My trophy? You? I think you're living in fantasy land.' He laughed in derision. She took an involuntary step backwards and saw the dismay in his face. 'Shit, Miranda, I didn't mean to say that.'

'Yes, you did. You've always meant it. You wanted me to make Jago jealous. To spite him.'

'It's true. I did want to make him suffer and I do like you, Miranda, I really like you but ... I just hate this fucking family even more.' Even though she'd suspected Theo had been using her, Miranda was still hurt and angry to hear him admit it. Her ego was bruised but his nastiness cut deeper than that. It was calculating and it diminished him. He was a smaller man than she'd thought, no matter what his reasons.

'You hate the St Merryns because Jago's father had an affair with your mother?'

'Because the St Merryns almost ruined my family. My dad left my mum after she had the affair and she had to bring us up on her own. That bastard, Lord Patrick, just cut her out of his life when he'd finished with her. When she tried to confront him and go to his wife, he threatened to turn us out of the cottage where we lived. My mum was a tenant and desperate to stay living in her own home so she decided she had no choice but to keep her mouth shut. Now, as soon as Jago comes back here, he thinks he can just have anyone too.'

'Including me?'

'Yes. Including you. I want that tosser to learn he can't just take what he wants and then chuck it away when he's bored, leaving a trail of bloody destruction.'

How did he know Jago would get bored? She couldn't say that to Theo, she couldn't say it to herself because what he had predicted had already come true. Jago had already hurt her, but not in the way Theo thought. 'I'm really sorry about your mother and I know Lord Patrick was a bastard, but have you thought how Lady St Merryn felt about her husband's affairs? Or how Jago felt? You really don't know about him. What he's been through.'

'You mean his wife dying. Yeah, I heard about that from Karen. Tough shit.'

'You don't mean that. This isn't you, Theo.'

'Maybe I don't mean it and maybe I do.'

There was no helping him in this mood. The bitterness and resentment was gnawing away at him until there wasn't much of the real Theo left. 'Theo, I can't carry on seeing you, but you can be sure of one thing – I never have and I never will have an affair with a St Merryn.' She dug her nails in her hand.

'Miranda, I'm sorry . . .' he began, as the true realisation of everything he'd revealed started to dawn on him.

'Not now. You've got visitors.' She turned and waved as Louise Dixon wheeled Braden towards them. The little boy bounced in his reins as he recognised Theo. Miranda watched as Theo's expression changed. She realised how much it had cost him to show his true feelings and how deep his hatred of Jago ran. In his job, he must be used to

288

hiding his emotions and pretending everything would be all right when it often wouldn't.

Theo headed for Braden. Louise freed him from his pushchair and Theo swung him into his arms and Miranda heard him say, 'How are you, sunshine? No swimming today I hope?'

She rubbed her hand across her eyes as visitors swarmed past, one or two glancing at her in puzzlement. The day was by no means finished, and she had to go back and join in with it, just as Theo had done. He'd stripped off every veneer to tell her how he really felt and the saddest thing was she'd hadn't much liked what was underneath. Some other woman would get to the heart of Theo again one day and hopefully, probably, find a different man, but it wouldn't be her.

Chapter Twenty-Nine

Miranda crawled up the steps to the castle keep. The sun had sunk now below the horizon, the last of its light staining the sky crimson and pink and the castle rooms seemed eerily silent after a day of unrelenting mayhem.

Her arms were tired, not least because she was carrying a Tudor helmet that had been on display in the visitor centre. Miranda had offered to put it back in its place in the armoury, but the truth was that she'd wanted to escape to the top of the castle and think. Surrounded by clear air and sea and silence, she hoped to make some space and sense of a day that had started with so much sun and hope and ended, for her, in a damp fog of despondency.

The exhausted staff had headed home to the mainland or to their cottages, leaving the remainder of the clear-up until morning. Lady St Merryn had been driven off to Penzance for dinner with a friend from her bridge club. Ronnie had the night off and had gone to Neem's studio. As for Jago, Miranda hadn't seen him since he'd walked out of the cottage and Theo had kept out of her way for the rest of the afternoon.

She hesitated at the entrance to the armoury, the heavy oak door seeming like the entrance to a dungeon. Even though it had been the best Festival ever, she had never felt more desolate.

Did Jago know the real reason why Theo hated him so much? Miranda didn't know whether it would help Jago to understand or if telling him would simply be chucking petrol onto a bonfire. As for revealing that Theo had used her as a pawn to make him jealous, that would be lethal for both of them. She'd decided to say nothing, in the hope that the both men would leave her alone from now on. She certainly wouldn't see Theo again, and Jago would probably be leaving within a couple of months – if Miranda didn't quit first.

With a sigh, she crossed the flagstones and placed the helmet on its stand, repositioning it until it was exactly right.

'Hello.'

Her heart did a huge flip as she turned to see Jago silhouetted under the stone archway. He'd changed out of pirate mode and into a loose shirt and black jeans. His hair was damp and slicked back, as if he'd recently come out of the shower.

'Shouldn't you be putting your feet up by now?' he asked.

'Believe me I will be, but I wanted to put this helmet back first.'

'That could have waited.'

'I couldn't leave it lying around in the visitor centre.' She glanced at him. He was fresh and seemed composed. In contrast, her own skin was gritty and hot and she felt strangely vulnerable.

'Are you going out?' she asked, returning her gaze to the helmet, repositioning it. She could see her face in it, distorted and shiny.

'No. Why?'

'You've got changed. I thought . . .'

'Miranda. I think you should know that Theo spoke to me earlier.'

'Really?'

'Yes. He warned me off you.'

Miranda turned and laughed as her heart pitter-pattered. Her hope of avoiding confrontation ebbed away.

'Why is that, do you think?' He crossed the flagstones towards her.

'I have no idea, your lordship.'

'Then I'll enlighten you, shall I? Theo thinks I'm going to turn into my father and defile you and break your heart, but we both know that's not possible, don't we?'

Miranda swallowed down a lump in her throat, wanting to laugh his comments away but finding it impossible. 'I don't know.'

Jago stopped a few feet from her. 'I think you know that I'm not going to break your heart because neither of us will let the other within a hundred miles and rightly so. As for defiling you, I believe I'm too late. I believe there was an archaeology student on a dig who beat me to it?'

Her pulse raced. 'How do you know that?'

'At the Pilchard the evening we took our boat trip. You were very chatty.'

'Oh, shit.'

'There was an incident with a vet too and his Labrador, I understand.'

She smiled but ran her hands through her hair. Her scalp tingled, along with every other part of her. 'What did you say to Theo?' she asked quietly.

'I told him he was living in fantasy land and that he has nothing to fear from me.'

'Did he believe you?'

'I don't care.'

'And did you mean what you said to him?' Her heart thumped now, her mouth dry. How did she dare speak like this? So recklessly? She felt as if the barriers between her and Jago were crumbling away.

'Unfortunately, for both of us, I didn't mean any of it. Because he does have something to fear from me. I want to take you to bed, and I know that's what you want too and I can think of a dozen reasons why we shouldn't, and I'm going to ignore every single one of them.'

'You know we can't,' she said but knew she was just going through the motions.

'We can, we're just too scared to, but I can't take this dancing around each other any more and I don't want to. I told Theo to mind his own business, by the way.'

A thought struck her, a horrible thought she didn't want to be true. 'Are you playing with me too, Jago, to get at Theo?'

He gasped. 'Playing with you? You think the way I feel is playing . . . Jesus.'

'I don't know how you feel. You keep changing your mind; I don't know what to think. This could all just be some kind of game!'

His eyes were angry but then he let go of her arm and stepped away. 'OK. If you think it's a game, let's make it one. A make-believe game where we forget about tomorrow and just pretend. You like doing that, don't you? That's what you were doing up here, and what you often do. I've seen you, daydreaming up here, imagining.' He touched her arm and the skin prickled with delicious sensation.

'This is the real world and there will be a tomorrow,' she said, knowing already that she didn't care about anything beyond this moment, or outside of this room. She'd already crossed the threshold.

'Tomorrow?' He laughed gently. 'I think I know that there's no use worrying about tomorrow. Screw tomorrow.'

'But there will be consequences. If we do this.'

'There may be, will be, but are you that afraid of them? How do you know what they will be?'

She knew. She knew what would happen if she let Jago in so deeply, so intimately, but the balance between caution and temptation had shifted. It was too late, she'd tipped over the edge.

'Let's have one night before it's too late.' He was inches away and gently ran a finger down her cheek. 'One night, one night of fantasy. Do you dare?'

She picked up the signal, a tremor in his voice that made

her want to abandon sense and caution and let recklessness take over. She lifted her chin upwards and looked at him defiantly, already caught up in a game that was dangerous for both of them. 'What if I refuse?'

'Then it will be the worse for you, wench.'

'And nothing will change afterwards? Tomorrow will be business as usual?'

'Business as usual. Nothing will change.'

'Then I've made my mind up. I want this.'

She closed her eyes, anticipating his lips on hers and his fingers tangling in her hair and his tongue flicking inside her mouth. Instead she heard his footsteps ring out on the stone flags and opened her eyes to find he'd crossed to the other side of the armoury.

'This? What exactly do you think "this" is going to be, Miranda? Have you any idea?' He reached behind him and picked up the cutlass.

Miranda laughed.

'You find this funny?'

'Yes. Captain Jack Sparrow wielding his sword. Is it meant to be some kind of metaphor?'

Jago glanced down at the blade glinting in the light. 'It looks like a lethal weapon to me. And I don't think you're taking this seriously.'

He stepped forwards, holding the cutlass by his side. A million nerves zinged her from head to toe as he stopped, barely two feet away from her, and raised the sword to chest height, the lethal tip pointing right at her breasts.

'This must be breaking every health and safety law in the book,' she said lightly.

'Screw the health and safety laws,' he said softly, 'and take off your clothes.'

Her lips parted in shock. Her stomach clenched. Her inner muscles tightened. 'What?'

'I said, strip.'

'Right here? I can't do that.'

His mouth set in a hard line. 'Can't or won't?'

'Even if I wanted to do this, someone might come along.'

'No, they won't. There's no one up here but the two of us.'

A frisson of desire and fear rippled through her body. The floor was solid under her feet, but she was sure it shifted a little. Maybe the whole island or her world had just tilted, a millimetre, on its axis. She lifted her chin. 'I don't want to.'

As his eyes raked over her, her skin felt like he'd rubbed a hot chilli over it. Taking a step nearer to her, he raised the cutlass and pointed it at her breasts. It was just a foot away from her. Her nipples jutted against the cotton of her flimsy blouse.

He laughed unpleasantly. 'I can see how much you don't want to. Get on with it.'

She thought about making a joke, or simply leaving the armoury. It was game, a sexy, silly game that she could end right now. Instead, she found herself toeing off her ballet pumps, one by one. The flagstones were cold and hard under the soles of her feet. She felt the tiny grains of grit and sand left there by the visitors that day.

He held the sword steady. 'Now, take off your blouse.'

'Really, this —'

'Just do as I say.'

She reached for the hem of the blouse, gripped the cotton and pulled it upwards towards her neck. As she tugged it over her head, she couldn't see Jago for a few seconds. She was blinded and helpless and all he had to do was step forwards with the sword and ... The blouse came over her head. Miranda clutched it to her breasts, hiding them from him.

He smiled briefly then the cutlass tip wavered in the direction of her skirt. 'Now that.'

To take off her skirt, she had no choice but to let go of the blouse and reveal herself to him. Part of her ached to let him to see how turned on she was, and part wanted to keep her desire secret. It was just a game but ...she crushed the cotton fabric tighter to her chest.

'I'm waiting. Surely, you can't have gone shy?'

His voice was raw, his eyes glittering with desire. It was just fantasy, she told herself, they were playing roles, there was no actual danger or threat, but her pulse raced and her limbs were heavy, as if it was very real. She forced herself to lower the blouse from her breasts, knowing she would expose taut nipples and flushed skin. She hardly dared raise her eyes to his, afraid of what she might see in his face. She knew he was aroused, she could see him, hear his quickened breathing, and smell him.

She dropped the blouse on the flagstones and straightened up, her arms hanging loosely at her side.

'Carry on.'

His coldness threw her. Did he feel so little at having her half-naked in front of him. Was it a game for him? Or was he genuinely enjoying humiliating her? Except she didn't feel humiliated. She felt powerful and free. She reached for the hook and eye at the side. Her fingers fumbled with the fastening but it loosened. She pulled down the zip and the skirt dropped to the flagstones.

She stood in her panties, the skirt pooled around her feet, soft and warm in contrast to the floor and to Jago. He circled her slowly, never taking his eyes from her. His knuckles were white around the hilt of the cutlass. It was a game, just a game, but her knees felt like water and it took every ounce of self-control not to let him see she was shaking like a leaf, inside and out. She was already slick inside.

He stopped and raised the sword. 'Now those.' He pointed to her knickers with the tip of the blade.

'You have to be joking,' she said, trying to laugh.

'I'm not joking.'

'Jago, this is going too far.'

'No one ever said there would be a limit to this. Now, take off your knickers.'

He was blowing her mind. She lifted her chin defiantly. 'No. I will not.'

Silence hung in the air between them. Jago stepped forwards, raised the cutlass until the tip of the blade was inches from her stomach. She pressed her legs together, her heart rate rocketing, her stomach turning over and over.

'One last chance. Take them off now or I'll do it for you.'

She shook her head. 'Go to hell.'

The shining tip of the blade glistened in the moonlight, like a white-hot brand.

'I'll count to three,' he said. 'One.'

She closed her eyes as the cutlass tip brushed the damp silk of her panties. What if his hand slipped? What if she fell? Her body shook. She might pass out with lust and tension at any moment. The blade was so close.

'Two.'

She clenched her fists and tightened every muscle in her body as she waited for the count.

His voice was a silky whisper. 'Three.'

She opened her eyes. He moved to her side and, swiftly, pulled the ribbon of her panties away from her thigh. In a flash, he cut it with the tip of the blade and pulled her knickers off.

Her hands flew to cover her nakedness, in a pointless attempt to shield herself. Pointless because he could see every inch of her, and because being forced to strip by him had been her deepest, darkest fantasy. And yet, she couldn't stop shaking. She waited to see the smile of triumph or pleasure at seeing her stripped bare but Jago simply surveyed her with satisfaction.

'Don't move,' he said. 'I haven't finished with you.'

Leaving her naked on the flagstones, he laid the cutlass on the trestle table and arranged her shredded panties across the blade with care, almost like a trophy. Miranda gasped. Then he turned and looked at her again. His gaze was no longer cold, but hot and greedy and tender. 'You're beautiful.' A smile curved his lips as stepped forwards. 'Very chilly but very lovely and I think your nipples are about to go pop. If I don't explode first.'

In seconds, he'd taken her in his arms, his linen shirt rough and warm against her bare skin. 'It's freezing in this armoury,' she said, still unable to believe she was naked in such a public place.

He rubbed her arms and back and bottom vigorously, trying to bring the circulation back. Then he touched her gently in a place that was warm and she let out a tiny gasp of shock and pleasure. 'Come on, wench. I think it's time we went back to my room.'

He gathered up her clothes and they dashed up the stone staircase to his room. They almost fell through the door to the tower room, and Jago locked it behind them. He pushed her against the oak door; the ridged planks were rough against her back and bottom. Then his mouth came down on hers and she knew there was no going back.

Chapter Thirty

'Are you OK?' Jago asked as he led her to his bed. 'Not getting cold feet?' He smiled and glanced at her bare toes.

They were icy, in fact, but that's not why she was hesitating.

Miranda realised that in all her time at the Mount, she had never been in Jago's bedroom. She'd been in most of the private family rooms but not this one. There had been no reason, Jago had been persona non grata and, as far as she knew, only the cleaners had even been in here and Lady St Merryn instructed them personally. Her first thought was that it was at once grand in scale and yet very simple.

Moonlight filtered through the leaded panes of the window, casting lacy shadows on the floor and across the bed. It wasn't one of the heavy oak four posters that graced the public bedrooms but a large white-painted iron-framed double, draped in a patchwork coverlet that had obviously been handmade by some long-dead Victorian lady of the house. Not a man's room, nor even a boy's room, almost an innocent room.

'Yes. It's just . . . this is my first time.'

He deposited her clothes on a Lloyd Loom chair and turned. 'Now, I know that's not true.'

'In here, in your bedroom, I meant.'

'Good, because, despite appearances, I don't actually want to go around deflowering virgins, give me a wicked slut any day.'

Gently, he lowered Miranda back onto the coverlet. He parted her legs and licked her intimately from top to bottom, in smooth firm strokes, making her whimper. She gripped the metal bed rail and tried not to cry out louder, hoping that no one could hear her. Jago paused to strip his shirt over his head. She wanted to die at the sight of him, at the dark hair that arrowed down to disappear into the waistband of his jeans. He flicked open the buttons, sat on the edge of the bed to pull his jeans over his feet. Then he climbed back onto the bed beside her, naked, his cock jutting. 'I'll get a condom. We have to be safe.'

'Safe?' She held his gaze and there was no need to say more. Stripping in the armoury, making love with Jago, falling for him, and betraying her friends . . .

He smiled and kissed her forehead, reading her thoughts. 'I know, it's ridiculous, considering what we're doing, but we ought to do one responsible thing amongst all the mad ones.'

He opened the wardrobe and reached up to the top shelf. The moonlight threw flickering shadows across his bare backside. Miranda closed her eyes. Would he be gone when she opened them, just like the man in her fantasies? Was this all a dream conjured up by her desire for him?

'Do you want to help with this part or can't you bear to look?'

She opened her eyes to find him kneeling on the bed next to her, holding out a silver packet.

'I hope you like mint. I only have these Minty Tinglers.'

Miranda giggled. 'Mint's my favourite flavour.' She pushed herself up as he tore off the top of the packet. Her fingers shook as she helped him roll on the condom, wondering at the hot, silky feel of him, like she'd never touched a man before.

'I can see you've done this before,' he said, teasing her gently.

'It's been a while since I ... held a bloke's ... thing.'

He glanced down at his erection and gave a wicked grin. 'Me too, apart from my own. Always while thinking about you, of course. About the way you are now, naked and wet and ready to let me inside you. I can't wait to make love to you, Miranda.'

She couldn't wait either, so when he nudged her thighs apart and stroked her with his fingers again, she had to fist the coverlet in her hands to stop herself from coming. She heard herself whispering, 'Now, now, please.'

'Do you need to touch yourself?'

Touch herself? Oh God. She shook her head. He was already bursting and the intimacy of his question was about to send her over the edge. She let out a gasp as he nudged his way into her, marvelling at how tight he felt. He whispered tender obscenities to her as he moved inside her, faster and harder. She gripped his shoulders and waves of the purest, most intense pleasure rolled through her. He thrust into her again, and fell with her over the edge.

When she opened her eyes, her tiny but cosy bedroom with its pretty wallpaper and angled nooks and crannies had vanished. It had been replaced by the curved stone walls of the tower. The room was far bigger in the bright morning sun than it had seemed in the dark and the patchwork quilt lay in a wanton heap on the floor. She lifted her head but there was no sign of Jago, either next to her or anywhere in the tower. Had he gone out, leaving her alone? Was he regretting their night? She lay back against the pillows. From below the tower, she heard the clang of metal against stone, frantic shouts and, laughably, the hum of a vacuum cleaner somewhere in the castle.

They were normal sounds of people going about their business but she knew that nothing would ever be as normal again.

A draught of sea breeze rattled the window. Miranda pulled the tangled sheet up to her neck and heard a loo flush from behind a low arched door on the rim of the room. A minute later, the door opened and Jago ducked under the arch from what she guessed to have been a garderobe at one time. He wiped his hands on a towel then dropped it on a stool, revealing himself in all his glory.

His eyes lit with pleasure when he saw she was awake. 'Morning. How are you?'

She could have offered him a choice of answers: ecstatic, full of dread, desperately turned on at seeing his nudity revealed in the morning sunlight.

'I could do with a shower,' she said, fisting the sheets in her hands, aching to leap on him again.

He grimaced, but even his frown seemed sexy now that she knew him, now that he'd been inside her and she'd tasted him and dug her heels into his back.

'There's a washbasin and loo in the tower but no shower, I'm afraid. I have to use the one out in the main bathroom in the corridor.' He hesitated. 'But perhaps I can offer you an alternative.'

A few minutes later, he carried a porcelain washbowl of water from the washroom into the bedroom. Drops splashed over the rim of the bowl and onto the rug as he negotiated the uneven floorboards. He replaced it in the washstand and gave a little bow.

'Your shower, madam.'

Miranda slid out of bed, momentarily embarrassed at her own nakedness.

'This water couldn't be called hot,' he said apologetically. 'But it's warm and wet.'

She trailed her hand over the surface, rippling it. 'It's fine. Thank you.'

'The pleasure will be all mine, I can assure you.'

Her fingertips hovered above the bowl of water before taking the flannel and wringing it out. Jago rested against the bed stand with his hands behind his head, his eyes fixed on her. Miranda was unable to touch herself at first. Washing herself was the most intimate act, more intimate somehow than sex itself because it was normally so private to her. Taking a breath, she started with her arms, rubbing the dripping cloth from her wrists to her shoulder and then under her arm and back over her elbow to her hand. The casement window creaked and the breeze licked her damp skin, prickling her flesh. She dipped the flannel into the bowl again and squeezed it, her fingers hardly able to wring out the water because they were so unsteady.

Jago kept his eyes on her as she wiped her arms and neck, just as if he saw her wash every day. She paused, knowing what was expected of her but suddenly shy.

'Please carry on,' he said.

She applied the flannel to her right breast, rubbing it gently over her skin. Water trickled over her nipples, following the curve of her skin. She soaked the flannel again, squeezed it and pressed it to her other breast. Tiny rivulets of lukewarm water raced down her chest and belly, and trickled between her thighs.

'Christ, you're beautiful.' Jago climbed off the bed. 'May I?' He pointed to the cloth in her hand. She nodded, so he took the flannel from her hand and dipped it in the bowl of water. He wrung it out as droplets cascaded into the bowl with a musical sound.

'Turn around.'

After he'd rubbed the cloth over her shoulder blades, he eased it over the ridges of her spine. She tilted her face upwards, lost in languorous pleasure. Water tinkled again as he wrung out the cloth and then he turned his attention to the back of her thighs and calves. Her inhibitions melted away and she just enjoyed the sensation.

'Oh!'

Her cry was a mix of shock and pleasure as he washed her buttocks, rubbing the soft skin between her cheeks with firm, brisk strokes.

'Relax, I love doing this for you.'

She closed her eyes, drowsed with desire. He moved to face her and knelt on the floor. 'Your feet,' he said, running a finger down the blade of her foot until she giggled. She lifted her foot into his lap and held on to his shoulder with one hand as he washed the soles of her feet, rubbing between her toes and over the blade of each foot. She arched her back and tried not to tense as hot wetness pooled between her legs. He would feel her in a moment, if he touched her there. He would know.

Still kneeling, he dropped the flannel into the basin but didn't take it out. 'I don't need this now.' Miranda knew what he was going to do and invited it by pushing her hips towards his face. He groaned with desire then parted her legs and touched her sex with his tongue. She cried out as he used his tongue on her, and then pushed him away.

'Can't. Wait. Any. Longer,' she said and dragged him back to bed.

After they'd made love, the sun was brighter and the sound of hammering from below seemed to resonate through the stone walls. The maintenance team were dismantling the stage. There was also more vacuuming and this time the hum was a lot louder and a lot nearer. She nudged Jago, lying face down beside her. 'Hey.'

He grunted but stayed where he was.

'Jago. Wake up!'

Miranda slapped his bottom more sharply than she'd meant to but he simply propped himself up on one elbow and grinned. 'So it's like that is it, Miss Whiplash?'

'Can't you hear that noise?'

He rubbed his knuckles over his eyes. 'What noise? The banging or the hammering?'

'The hoovering. It must be Mrs Arblaster, the cleaner. She's coming.'

'I hope not. That wouldn't be a pretty sight.'

Miranda pulled the sheet up to her neck. 'But she'll catch us together!'

'Stop worrying; she won't come in here when she knows I'm in bed. Besides I locked the door last night and it would keep out an army.'

His eyes sparkled wickedly but Miranda's bubble had burst and she felt herself crashing down to earth. It was most definitely time to get back to reality, one in which she and Jago were going, literally, to the other ends of the Earth.

'I need the bathroom, but don't go anywhere.'

While he was in the washroom, Miranda gathered up her clothes from the floor and slipped into her blouse and skirt. Soon she would have to slink out of his room as countless other mistresses had slunk out of the lord's room at dawn. Her clothes felt sweaty and dirty but she could hardly do the walk of shame back to her cottage in the nude.

Wearing nothing but a Mount St Merryn apron, Jago emerged from the washroom with a kettle, two mugs and sachets of tea and coffee. He turned round, the apron ties dangling down and neatly bisecting his hairy bottom. He grinned back over his shoulder. 'Tea or coffee, milady?'

Miranda burst out laughing, her fears momentarily forgotten at the sight of him. 'Where on earth did you get that?'

'In the cupboard. This stuff must be a courtesy pack from a conference or when we had guests to stay. I have no idea where the apron came from. Perhaps Mrs Arblaster left it here.'

He made tea and coffee in a two plastic tooth mugs and held up a carton. 'There's only one milk. I'll wrestle you for it if you like.'

'You have it. I surrender,' said Miranda, her dread subsiding a little. The moment hadn't ended yet. There was still a little time left to enjoy the fantasy.

'That's the kind of word I like to hear. Because sooner or later, we need a truce and, for that to happen, one or both of us are going to have to back down.'

His words were so not what she had expected and her hopes lifted a little. In fact, they started to take flight and threatened to soar over the castle walls. Maybe there wasn't going to be a walk of shame. Maybe last night had been the start of many nights to come. The traitorous whisper of hope grew louder in her head. Maybe Jago had changed his mind and was about to tell her he would stay.

The drinks abandoned on the bedside table, he touched her cheek. 'You know you have to come with me, Miranda. Come back to Oz. Or anywhere. We can't carry on like this.'

'Come with you?'

'Leave here. Leave the Mount. It doesn't have to be Oz, you know. We can go anywhere we like: Hawaii, South America, round the world if you want to. Just come with me.'

Realisation slammed into her. Jago had just given her the world.

It wasn't enough.

It wasn't enough to have half a Jago, a man who was still living in the past and trying to run away – and the woman that went with him, wouldn't be the real Miranda. She'd be aimlessly travelling, always wondering what had happened to the Mount, her friends and the colleagues who had become her family.

'You know I can't do that. You have to understand. I can't abandon everyone.'

He threw up his hands in frustration. 'Unlike me? Christ, Miranda, don't say you still want me to stay and do my duty?'

'Not your duty. It's not that simple but I can't see this place end up in Southcastle's hands – in Jumeau's hands. I've thought about it so long and I won't be able to stay here when you're gone, Jago. He made me an offer, a very good one.' She thought Jago would explode with fury at that revelation, but he stayed silent.

'You *knew* he'd offered me a job, didn't you?'

'He hinted as much.'

'And you didn't care?'

'I do care. Of course I bloody care, but it's your future. I can't force you to do anything.'

'Well, I won't take it. I can't work for him but I don't know if I can stay and see what he'll do to the place.'

'So it's fine for you to run away from the Mount when it suits you? You'll be leaving here anyway so why not leave with me? What's the difference?'

'Betrayal. Guilt. My conscience,' she shot back.

'Oh for God's sake. Those values went out of fashion in Victorian times, if they ever really existed. There is no honour or duty any more, Miranda, just the here and now. We only have a duty to live for today. I know that and I want you to realise it too.'

He jerked upright and strode off, raking his hands viciously through his hair. When he turned round, his face was dark with bitter disappointment. 'You know what your trouble is? Your trouble is that you fear being disappointed so much that you don't dare risk anything at all. I don't blame you after what happened with your family, but you've run away here and shut yourself up. You've played it safe ever since so you can never be disappointed again and I'm afraid you're going to be disappointed in me too.'

She knew he was bitter and hurt at her rejection but she was in agony too. 'Like you disappointed Rhianna? Because you wouldn't help her when she needed you most?'

She held her breath as he opened his mouth as if to shout, teetering on the threshold of anger. Instead he lowered his hands from his head and dropped them by his side, defeated. 'Go your own way. Take Southcastle's offer if you want to, or don't. Either way, I'm never going to live up to your ideal of the noble lord of the manor. I'm not the man you think I am, Miranda, or, at least, I'm not the man you want me to be.'

She thought he could be anyone if he just forgave himself. She'd seen him tender and gentle, willing to risk himself to save a little boy he cared about. She'd seen what it had cost him to do what he thought was right for Rhianna. She'd seen him passionate, angry and outrageously unreasonable and now she felt the hurt he was causing her and yet she still loved him.

'You may be right about me in some ways but not this: if I'd always played things safe, I'd never have got involved with you.'

He sat down beside her on the bed, reached out a hand and stroked her hair gently. 'True, and I'm so sorry you have got involved with me, in every way, but for your sake, not mine.'

Miranda felt like someone had taken wire wool to her emotions and rubbed them raw. 'Jago, there's another thing I need from you.'

'That's two things.'

'I'm allowed a last request. If you care about me even a little a bit, do something for me.'

'I care about you more than a little bit. You know that.' He paused, as if he was wrestling with a great decision. She allowed herself one last tiny spark of hope. He covered her hand with his fingers and she couldn't bear the soft pressure. 'What's your last request?'

'Face them. Tell the staff the truth about the sale to Southcastle. If you're resolved on it and decision is final, don't keep them wondering any more. I haven't told anyone about the plans but I know they suspect something is up and they're very worried. Be honest with them. Even though it's not the news they want to hear, you owe them that.'

He heaved a sigh then nodded. 'You're right. I've hidden the truth for far too long. I'll call a meeting for tonight and ask everyone to come to the Great Hall. And then I'll tell them.'

Chapter Thirty-One

'My God, have you seen *this*?' Ronnie blocked the way to Miranda's desk and held a letter aloft. It was printed but had a bold signature at the bottom.

Miranda homed in on the crest and the name.

He'd done it, then.

Jago had kept his promise. In one respect, at least, he hadn't disappointed her and, while he'd granted her last request, it tasted as bitter as acid.

'No, I haven't seen it. I've been busy since this morning.' The truth was she'd been avoiding the office and Ronnie as much as possible since she'd crept back to her cottage from Jago's bedroom. She'd found things to do in obscure corners of the island, minor clearing-up jobs that could have been left to the rest of the staff but, by afternoon, she'd had no choice but to go back to the office and face the music.

'I wondered where you'd got to this morning. I guessed you were having a lie-in after the Festival.' Ronnie passed the letter to her. 'This won't help your mood.'

She took the letter and read it as Ronnie carried on ranting. Miranda didn't blame her or the rest of the staff. No matter how many rumours had been flying about the island, seeing their fears confirmed must have come as a hell of a shock to the staff.

'Jago sent this round to everyone. I've been on the phone since one of the office assistants brought it ten minutes ago. She says everyone who works or lives here has got one. Miranda, this can't be anything good. You must know something about it?'

Miranda replaced the sheet on the desk, almost paralysed with shock. The letter asked everyone to attend a meeting that evening in the Great Hall where Jago had something 'important to tell them'. It said it was 'vital' that they attend, if at all possible, and it was signed in fountain pen ink, in Jago's own hand and formal style.

St Merryn

Ronnie picked it up gingerly as if it was a hand grenade. 'Looks like a bloody death warrant, doesn't it?'

Privately, Miranda agreed the signature was very like Henry VIII might have issued when ordering a haircut for one of his wives, but she didn't need to reply because Ronnie did all the talking for her. 'What's Jago doing, calling us all to the Hall tonight? I call it bloody inconsiderate and typical of his lordship. It's my night off and I'm supposed to be meeting Neem at the Pilchard for dinner. What the hell is going on?'

Miranda answered truthfully, if not completely. 'I wish I knew.'

'You know what I think?' Miranda could guess but let Ronnie continue, clutching at any chance to avoid telling more lies. 'I think he's flogging the place to that French bloke. Creepy git, I never liked him!' She turned a laser stare on Miranda. 'You've shown them round; you must know what's going on. You would tell me, wouldn't you?'

Miranda traced Jago's signature on the paper with her finger. Outside, she could hear the insistent beep of a van as it reversed along the quay, and shouts as the workmen packed away the stalls and equipment for another year. Next Festival, if there *was* a next Festival, she wouldn't be here. Perhaps, Ronnie wouldn't be here either. Miranda certainly couldn't imagine her working for Jumeau and Devlin for five minutes without throwing one or both of them off the battlements. Lady St Merryn would be in San Francisco, threading flowers in her silver hair like a hippy and Jago would be in the middle of the ocean, drifting again.

They'd come so near to being together, and yet so far. Oh God, she had to tell Ronnie what was happening now, or she'd burst into tears.

'Miranda. What's the matter? You look like shit again.'

There could not be many occasions when being told you looked like shit made you want to hug someone, but this was one of them. She would miss her friends so much. Would they have a Ronnie and a Reggie or even a Fred in the Scottish castle she'd applied to? She doubted it and, as for a Jago, he was a one-off.

The phone rang out, making the desk vibrate and the dust motes shimmer in the thick warm air. Ronnie cursed but picked it up, barking into the mouthpiece. 'Yeah? Sorry? Who did you say? Right . . . I'll see if she's available.' She covered the mouthpiece with her hand. 'It's for you, Miranda.'

'Who is it?' she mouthed.

'Some woman. Says she's called Teresa Taylor. Shall I tell her that you're in a meeting?'

Miranda stood quite still. She felt astonishingly calm all of a sudden. It must be shock, she thought, marvelling at her ability to stand outside herself while everything fell apart around her.

'Miranda? Are you OK? Shall I ask this woman to call back later?'

'No. No. I'll take it.'

After a few seconds' hesitation, Ronnie laid the handset on the desktop. 'I'll give you some privacy,' she whispered and slipped out of the room.

Chapter Thirty-Two

The sun was slipping towards the horizon behind him as Jago hung back from the door of the Great Hall. There was no one else outside with him as he hesitated, but through the twin oak doors he could hear the buzz inside. He felt it too, as a sickening ache inside, as if he'd banged a bone on metal.

He lifted his wrist to look at his watch and knew he couldn't put off the moment any longer. He'd called the meeting for 7 pm and the minute hand on the dial had already crept five beyond the hour. All the Mount's staff had made an effort to be here, even those who were normally off duty; each one had been summoned by his letter, including Miranda.

He scanned the terrace, half expecting her to be waiting for him outside but there was no sign of her. That morning, after they'd parted, she'd said she'd be there at his side when he broke the news and he was desperate for her to be there even though it was a selfish request.

He stepped under the shadowy archway and emerged at the back of the hall. Someone had arranged rows of chairs like in a chapel, with an aisle between them, as if he was about to run the gauntlet at an ancient tournament. Any moment now, he expected wooden clubs and studded balls to swing down and wallop him on the head and knock him to the ground. He wouldn't blame the people if they did.

As he walked up the aisle, the voices died away. Every head turned to stare at him and his breath caught in his throat at the shock of remembering: the last time he'd been in this situation was when he'd followed the coffin into his father's funeral in the village church. He'd been on show then, with everyone waiting and watching his reaction, looking to him for clues to his grief.

This evening was worse. The faces were even more sombre than they'd been back then, the emotions born not of sympathy but in fear. The loss of the Mount, as they surely must suspect by now, would feel like a far bigger blow than the loss of one of its owners.

A baby let out a howl and its father shushed it and it was then Jago noticed just how many small faces peered at him, from wooden chairs or their parents' arms. Why were so many children here on an occasion like this? Then he realised that people wouldn't have been able to get babysitters at such short notice or maybe they wanted to bring their kids while they could. Perhaps their parents wanted to remind him of just what rested on the decision he had made and was about to tell them.

Jago wanted to shout out that no one need remind him of his responsibilities. The decision had borne him down for months now, as if he were carrying the castle and the rocky island it was built on.

His footsteps rang out on the stone floor as he walked towards the dais at the end of the hall, a thousand hopes and fears and expectations burning into his back. The door clanged shut behind him. He climbed onto the dais and he faced the people, who had all fallen silent. Their faces gazed up at him, as he scanned the crowd, in vain, for Miranda.

Miranda stopped the Land Rover at the crossroads. There it was.

The Song of the Sea Caravan Park. Half a mile.

Song of the Sea. Just the name of the place had made Miranda want to go there when she was little. Her gran had taken her one summer to stay in a static caravan. They'd walked on the beach every day and waded in the tidal pool between the great split rock that dominated the coast. Gran had told her that an ancient earthquake and the sea had split the rocks, but Miranda had always known that Neptune had splintered the two cliffs in two with his trident. She'd read in a book that mermaids once gathered in the pool, which was why it was called Song of the Sea. She'd even written stories about the place, little booklets illustrated with drawings, curled up in a corner of the caravan.

She steered the Land Rover down the narrow lane that led to the caravan park and indicated to turn into the site. As she drove into the car park, children swung on the swings and clambered over the climbing frame and reminded her, with a sickening jolt, of what must be happening at the Mount even as she sat here, alone. She pictured the children of the Mount in the Great Hall, waiting with their families, while Jago told them that their lives were about to change forever.

And she wasn't there to see it, hear it, feel it.

She'd told herself she needed to see her mother but when the phone call had come, she'd grabbed at the excuse like a drowning person clings to their rescuer. The truth was she just couldn't bear to see Jago crush the hopes of all those people. In the end, she'd run away again and abandoned him when he needed her most.

Chapter Thirty-Three

Jago looked out over the people crammed into the Great Hall. His throat was swollen and tight and the realisation of why made it close up a little more. Shit. He would fucking cry if he stayed here a second longer. He would disgrace himself in front of all these people and bawl like Braden. They were growing restless, he could hear them shuffling in their seats, hear the odd whisper of concern, of mounting anger, feel the tension like a taut wire stretched to breaking point.

And still, he couldn't see Miranda, but it was too late. Too late to wait a second longer.

'I think you know why I'm here.' He heard and felt the inward drawing of breath as he spoke. He swallowed, trying to force some moisture into his mouth. 'And I apologise for calling you all here like this when I know you have work to do and families to care for and lives to live beyond the St

Merryns and this island. But I felt that I had to gather everyone connected with the Mount and everyone it matters to.'

Everyone except one person, the one person who mattered most to him. Where was she? Where was Miranda?

'I know there have been a lot of rumours about the future of the Mount. You may have seen and heard things yourselves over the past few months and I'll admit that I haven't helped by not being straight with you, so now I *am* going to be straight with you.'

There were mutters and grumbles and an angry voice hissing 'Shut up!' In the front row, a toddler pointed at him and let out a giggle.

'Despite anything you might have heard, I want to scotch all the rumours now. I'm not selling the Mount and I never will.'

Never. That word, spoken with such passion, surprised even him with its force. He'd decided before the meeting that he was going to stay, a decision he'd thought he'd come to through hours of soul searching since Miranda had left him that morning. But now he realised that his change of heart had taken days and weeks and months. Perhaps he had always intended to stay but refused to acknowledge or recognise it. He might never know what had happened inside him since Rhianna had died and he'd met Miranda but saying his piece out loud in the Hall in front of everyone had convinced him he was doing the right thing.

Now he'd made the leap, on the side of staying, he felt wildly at peace if wildness and peace could co-exist at the same time. Not until his bones lay in the crypt in the castle church would the Mount leave St Merryn hands and not then, if he could help it. He would bring up his heirs at the castle – he could see his children now, darting around the Hall, splashing in the rock pools and dancing around their mother – he could see a future here at last.

He suddenly felt intoxicated with certainty, but clear in mind enough to know that these emotions would pass too. He was riding the wave of relief at having done something, having clung on to something solid and certain in his life. In the days and months to come, he knew that there would be moments when he might regret taking on the Mount but, for now, he'd fight tooth and nail to keep the place and the livelihood of all these people. He'd do it, not out of guilt but out of passion and love for the place – and he'd fight tooth and nail to keep Miranda by his side too.

A few of the people were crying now, and not just the women. He recognised a former boatman who must have retired even before Jago had left for university. The guy must be nearly ninety but he still lived in one of the cottages and he was weeping. A few rows back he spotted Daisy from the ice-cream kiosk, sniffing into her handkerchief. Even Reggie, dreadlocked and huge, looked dangerously close to cracking.

It was all Jago's doing. He'd held the power to reduce these people to tears and that had terrified him. Even now, when the deed had been done, the responsibility scared him and he knew he had to get out of the Hall. He was no saint, no hero, just a very flawed human being.

The crowd wouldn't let him be human and flawed. That's not what they wanted; they wanted him to be Lord St

Merryn, whatever that represented, however much it really was just a title – a figurehead, a name.

'Three cheers for his lordship!' shouted the old man.

What? Jago wanted to die of shame.

'Hip hip hurrah!'

No. Christ, no. He felt sick. He didn't deserve thanks for what he'd done, let alone applause.

'No, please!' He wanted the flagstones to open up so he could sink through them, out of sight and forgotten.

'Hip, hip, hurrah!'

He held up his hands. 'Really, please.'

'Hip, hip, hurrah!'

He jumped off the dais and stumbled slightly as people slapped him on the back. They shouted down his ears and the final hurrah shook the hall to its timber rafters. He scanned the crowd, frantically searching in every corner, behind every pillar for her, but she wasn't there. She should have been here, listening to him do what he should have done a long time ago.

'Thank you,' he called, voice breaking as he raised his hands in the hope of some quiet and space so he could speak again. The hubbub died and the room fell silent. A baby wailed and laughter rippled through the people as the tension was replaced with relief and joy. They were all smiling back at him. 'Thank you all for your patience. I'll speak to you all individually over the next few days. There will be changes here, but for the better. But now, I have to go. Please, go home and have a good evening and thank you. Thank you for supporting me and my family. Goodnight.'

'Bugger me but we all thought you were going to flog the

place to some big corporation.' Reggie pumped his hand up and down as he made his way through the crowd.

At least Jago managed a truthful answer. 'I couldn't do that,' he said. 'Have you seen Miranda?'

Reggie shook his head. 'Come to think of it, no. Funny thing, I thought she'd be up there with you but I haven't seen her for a couple of hours.'

'Thanks,' said Jago, meaning the opposite. He strode off down the aisle, managed to get out of the door and ran over to his mother, leaning on her stick by the wall.

'I have to find Miranda. Have you seen her?'

'No. Jago, wait!' She clamped her fingers around his arm. 'I was at the back watching you. Why did you change your mind?' she asked, as people flowed out from the hall, laughing and joking.

'*Dum spiro spero*. While I breathe, I hope. The St Merryns don't give up.'

She smiled at him and he felt like a little boy again, offering her a starfish he'd found in the bay.

'Well done. I carried on hoping too that you would change your mind and realise that you belong here but is there another reason for you to stay besides living up to the family motto?'

'I've asked myself that. I've been unhappy for a long time. Yesterday I finally realised that casting off this burden is not the way. You can't just sell something that's ingrained in your bones as this place is. It's not that simple. I know. I can see a future for me now. Here more than anywhere.'

She kissed him on the cheek. 'I'm very proud of you,

darling, but you do like taking things to the wire. I thought I was going to have a heart attack in there and you must have been responsible for more than a few grey hairs among the staff.'

'I've been stupid. Unforgivably stupid.'

'Not stupid. Just in the dark for a while.'

'Call it what you want but I'll make up for it now. This place is in my blood. I admit it. I couldn't let it go, not to some faceless corporation with no interest in it, no passion for it beyond profit. I always knew that was wrong, but I kidded myself I didn't care. It's more than a place, it's a living thing. I don't want to surrender it, I want to fight for it, and even if it kills me I want to carry it on.'

Realising what he'd said, he thought of Rhianna and asked her to forgive him one final time, for waiting to do the things he had left undone and for keeping the people he cared about waiting and suffering so long now.

'Have you phoned Southcastle to tell them?' asked Lady St Merryn.

He gave a rueful smile. 'Oh yes. I spoke to Jumeau just before I came up here.'

'And?'

'He told me I'd regret my decision for the rest of my life.'

His mother sighed. 'That sounds rather ominous. And very predictable.'

'I think he may try to sue me but, to be honest, I don't give a toss.'

She patted his arm. 'I can't stand the man myself. He reminds me of your father. I should have told you how I felt before but I didn't want to add to the pressure you were under. I simply hoped you would come to your own decision. I'll support you. I'll stay if you want me to.'

'No, Mother. You must go and do what you have to. I haven't signed anything yet and I have some very good lawyers. If Southcastle do try to sue, I'm prepared for the consequences.'

She squeezed his arm, her grip surprising him with its strength.

'Have to go,' he said gruffly, before he lost his composure again. 'I have to find Miranda. I offered to go away with her, it wasn't enough, and she knew me better than I know myself. She knew what I needed, more than I did. Now she thinks I've sold. I tried to find her before the meeting and I thought she'd be here but now I think she may have left.'

He took the steps to the harbour two at a time and reached Miranda's cottage in double quick time. As he'd suspected, it was empty so he ran to the security office. Inside, Ronnie was wiping her nose with a tissue.

'Summer cold,' she said roughly as he walked in then glared at him.

He smiled. 'You all knew I planned to sell, didn't you?'

'We'd guessed.'

'So Miranda didn't say anything?'

'Not in so many words but I knew she knew. We're in security, you idiot. We have eyes and ears and Miranda is just about the worst liar I've ever come across. I could have forced her to tell me what was going on, but I care too much for her to put her on the spot like that. She's gone through a lot to keep your secret, you know.'

He groaned. 'I'm sorry. I put her in an impossible position. I was wrong and I regret it. I will always regret doing this to all the people who live here.'

'I suppose you were entitled to do it,' said Ronnie, 'even if it was the worst thing you'd ever done, but you might have guessed we'd all find out. This is a tiny community, close-knit doesn't even describe it. What did you expect?'

'I was naive. Don't forget I'm actually the new boy here, Ronnie.'

She folded her arms and he knew exactly why his mother had appointed her head of security. 'You'll learn. You know, I never thought I'd say this but I'm proud of you.'

'Yeah. Yeah.'

'But if you ever think of selling it again, the natives will turn very nasty indeed.'

He laughed dutifully then shook his head, remembering that while he'd started to rebuild one important foundation of his life, the other had disintegrated. 'Where the hell is Miranda?'

'I don't know.'

'You must do!' He shoved both hands through his hair. Christ, he was going to burst with frustration.

'Just sit down,' she said.

He wanted to scream. If Ronnie didn't know where Miranda had gone, who would? But Ronnie must know and Ronnie wasn't telling him. 'I won't sit down. Please tell me where she is.'

'I can't.'

'Can't or won't?'

'I don't *know* where she's gone. I haven't seen her since

afternoon. I expected her to be in the Hall tonight. In fact I came down here to phone her and see where she was.'

Jago was in despair. 'I've been into her cottage, she never locks the door and she's not there. The place is a bit of a mess. The wardrobe door had been left open, shoes lay on the carpet, papers scattered about.'

Ronnie's pocket beeped and she pulled her phone out. 'It's a text from her.'

'Tell me!'

She scanned it and heaved a sigh of relief. 'Phew.'

He snatched the phone and read the message: 'Ronnie. I'm OK. Need some space.'

'Where is she?'

Ronnie's face twisted in indecision. Jago went for broke. 'I love her, Ronnie.'

'Love? Miranda?'

'Yes.'

'Well, bugger me. I missed that one. I thought she had a bit of a crush on you and I wound her up about it, but as for the Big "L". If I'd known how serious it was, I'd have warned her what a bastard you are. Does she feel the same way about you?'

Jago dragged his hand over his mouth in despair. 'I don't know. I hope she does. I need to see her right now and tell her everything.'

'If I knew, I'd tell you but I really don't.' She hesitated and the doubt in her voice scared him. 'You could try to find out from the mobile company, but I don't think you want to do that, do you? She isn't in danger, is she?'

'No. Not danger but I must find her. Are you sure you've

330

no idea at all where she might have been headed? Did she take the Land Rover?'

'I'm not sure, but we could check if it's gone.'

It took barely a few minutes to discover that the Land Rover was gone. In fact, Fred had seen Miranda drive off in it a few hours before at low tide. Pathetically grateful for some concrete information, Jago shook Fred's hand and barely escaped without Fred tugging his forelock.

Jago paced about the staff car park, ranting. 'Now we know she's left the island, we need to find out where.'

Ronnie shook her head at him. 'No shit, Sherlock.'

'Ronnie, you may be Miranda's best mate but I also may have to kill you. Did Miranda say anything at all that might be a clue to where she's gone?'

Ronnie rubbed her mouth thoughtfully. 'Well. There was one funny thing.'

He tried to avoid shouting in frustration. 'What?'

'Miranda did take a phone call this afternoon from a woman called Teresa Taylor. She seemed a bit upset afterwards but I didn't want to pester her about it. I wonder if that has something to do with where she's gone? It must be serious if she missed the meeting tonight.'

'Teresa Taylor?' It didn't ring a bell with him. 'Was she local?'

'No. Not as far as I could tell. In fact, if anything, I'd say she sounded like she was from my neck of the woods in Essex, but she asked for Miranda Taylor. I thought I'd misheard or she'd made a mistake, because she changed it and asked for Miranda Marshall. I know this sounds crazy, but I got the feeling she and Miranda knew each other very well.'

Jago caught his breath. 'It was her mother.'

Ronnie frowned. 'But I thought they were estranged.'

'They are. They were. She's never had a father and she ran away from her mother and stepfather when she was a teenager.'

'And you know all this and she never told me?' Ronnie looked terribly hurt.

'Don't be too hard on her. She had good reason. She needs to tell you herself but first I need to find her. Is there anywhere you can think of?'

'There was a place she mentioned. A caravan site that her gran used to take her to. She talks a lot about her grandma.'

'Where is this site?'

'I don't know, but the way she described it sounded like it was near Land's End. She spoke about some pink granite cliffs and an old engine house overlooking the bay. There is a small caravan park tucked away down there.'

'The site at the far end of the bay above the Song of the Sea rocks?'

'Yes. That's the one.'

'I know it,' said Jago. 'Can I take your car?'

'Sure, but . . .' Ronnie's face was pale. 'If she's upset about you selling the Mount and has decided to meet up with her mother after all these years, you don't think she'd do anything . . . stupid, do you?'

Jago snatched up Ronnie's car keys. 'Not in the way you're thinking.'

But as for leaving him and never coming back, Jago was very much afraid that that was exactly what Miranda had done.

Chapter Thirty-Four

Miranda walked across the beach. The woman she'd known as her mother pulled her cigarette from her mouth and ground it under her boot into the sand. Miranda squashed down a gasp of shock. Her mum could only be described as haggard, much thinner than she'd remembered and with a face that seemed to have fallen in on itself.

Teresa Taylor surveyed her from head to toe. 'If I hadn't seen you on the telly I wouldn't have recognised you,' she said. 'You're so thin.'

Miranda was too shocked to say her mother looked far worse. 'It's running up and down the steps at the castle all day.'

'You were a chubby teenager and I was always on at you to lose a bit of weight, but now I think you'd do better with a bit of flesh on you.'

Miranda bit back a retort. So was this it? After fourteen

years? The same critical tone of voice, the same pointless conversations? Why had she come here? Why had she sacrificed supporting Jago and her friends to see this woman?

'You said you needed me, Mum,' she snapped.

That was why. That word. *Need*. Her mother had said she needed her when she'd called the office a few hours before Jago's meeting. Miranda could never recall her mum using 'need' before and the glow of hope it had started had drawn her here like a moth to a flame. Miranda glanced at her mum's ring finger where a gold band glinted in the evening sun. 'You got married,' she said as if that was more shocking than her mum's appearance.

Teresa held out her hand to show the ring. 'Yeah, a couple of years ago. He's called Kev and he's a security guard in Exeter.'

Exeter? So her mother hadn't been so very far away from the Mount after all; but it may as well have been the moon. Miranda wanted to ask if she had any more children, who would be her half-brothers and sisters – her family.

Teresa must have read the question in her face. 'Kev's got two kids of his own but they're grown up too. I didn't want any more. Not that you ... well, you know I'm not the maternal type, eh?'

Miranda shrugged. She felt like a sullen teenager again, unable to frame with words all the hurt and loss that had been and, still was, bottled up inside her.

'What do you want, Mum?'

Teresa's expression was pained, seeming genuinely hurt. 'Why should I want something? I just thought maybe I could come and see you sometimes. Maybe bring Kev and the kids? You wouldn't mind that, would you, after all this time?'

Would she mind? Miranda's emotions were jumbled like pieces of a jigsaw thrown on the floor, impossible to put together into a meaningful whole. Not yet, maybe not ever? She felt fear, anxiety, hope, expectation and disappointment in her mother and her own madness in coming here to this place. The hope was the most confusing, the creeping sense that after all this time her mother really wanted to take an interest in her. The possibility that they might be able to move forwards again was so alluring and that made it scary and dangerous. What if all those hopes crashed down on her? What if they both ended up running away again?

'I know I was never good enough for you, Miranda.'

'That's ridiculous, Mum!' Yet it might be true, thought Miranda, so what kind of person did that make her?

'Maybe it is mad, but if you knew how I met your father, you might understand. He was clever you know, a lecturer at the local college. Older than me, good-looking –' she smiled ruefully '– he was lovely, with a gorgeous voice. He chatted me up when I was working in a pub and I was impressed and flattered that he'd taken an interest. He seemed . . . sophisticated. That's the word. What a bloody joke that was. When he found out about you, he wanted me to have an abortion and, yeah, it would have been the sensible thing to do but I didn't want one, even though he said he'd give me the money.'

Miranda wanted to howl with shock.

'I wanted you and when he found out I was going ahead, he left. Just pissed off to some other university in the States and I was on my own, apart from your gran, of course. She stood by me, typical of her.' Teresa sounded almost disappointed as if she was comparing herself to her own mother. 'After you were born, I was lonely, I needed someone, looked for someone else but they all turned out to be disappointments too, as you kept reminding me.'

'I never said that, Mum!'

'You didn't have to, I could feel it every day, but I suppose you were right. I was a mess and I resented knowing it. How would you feel if you knew your own child felt let down every day? Oh, I know you didn't mean to judge me, but it felt that you were. But —' she heaved a sigh '— Kevin's different. He's . . . What's the word your gran would have used? He's solid and steady and, perhaps in the end, I might just turn out to be that way too. We've been together over five years now so there must be something going right.'

'I'm happy for you,' said Miranda, not sure whether she was or not. 'Mum, why didn't you try harder to get me back?'

There. She'd said it. There was the rub. Miranda had wanted to be pestered and pursued when she'd run away. Even though she'd vowed she would never go back, she knew now that she'd wanted her mother to care enough not to give up trying to get her back. That admission was dangerous. The dam that held back so many years of raw-edged, confused emotion had cracked a little more until it was close to bursting.

'I should have tried more. I could have tried harder to make you come home, but when I knew you were OK and you were going to university, I knew you'd changed forever.

I thought you were better off without us. And, love, I'm sorry about the money.'

'The money? It wasn't just about the money!' Miranda was horrified at her shriek but too upset now to restrain herself. The dam had burst. 'It wasn't the money. It was the stamping on Gran's memory and the ripping apart of *her* hopes and dreams for me, as well as my own. You lied, Mum! I thought you were keeping the money safe for my future. It hurt so much.' The pain tore through her again now as the tears ran down her cheeks.

'I was young and, like you, I was disappointed with what life had thrown my way. I'd believed in your father. I thought I'd get a fairy tale ending and I got slammed down hard. I had a lot of growing up to do too and even though I was supposed to be the adult, I didn't feel like being one. I'm sorry I spent the money. I know now what it meant to you and what it would have meant to Gran. I'll admit, it was wrong of me.'

Miranda groaned. *Wrong?* She turned away and started to walk across the sand.

'Very wrong, but not as wrong as taking out my disappointment in your dad on you.'

She stopped. Turned.

'I didn't want it to be like this when I saw you again. I saw you on telly and that was it. You looked so much as if you belonged there and I told myself I had no right to interfere in your life – not now, especially, but I need my daughter now more than ever. Don't walk away. I promise I don't want anything but there's something you should know.'

*

Jago found the caravan site on autopilot; long-forgotten memories from his childhood must have carried him there, because now he'd reached the place, he had no recollection of how he'd found it. His every thought had been focused on Miranda and what she must be going through and how he could make her believe in him again.

He parked his car outside the reception and threaded his way between the static caravans arranged in rows on the field. There were a few younger children playing on the slides and swings, while older couples and pensioners sat outside their caravans and motorhomes, talking, drinking wine and poking at barbecues. It was a picture of normality and one that he now yearned to experience again.

He jogged towards the sign that showed the clifftop path, rounded a final caravan and saw Miranda down on the beach. She wasn't alone but with a woman and he guessed immediately who that woman was and knew what Miranda needed most from him now.

He stood at the top of the cliff and he waited.

Chapter Thirty-Five

'Miranda. Hear me out. I don't want anything, love.'

Love? What kind of a word was that? A word her mum had never used. Not since a time so long ago she couldn't know whether she'd ever heard it or just imagined it. Her guts twisted. For her mum to use that word, something awful must be about to happen. The axe was about to fall, the bomb about to drop on her and blow her world to smithereens.

Yet her mother carried on speaking, matter-of-factly, as if she was telling Miranda she'd just bought a new washing machine from Tesco. 'I wanted to see you now before it was too late. I'm hoping it's not too late because I'm not done for yet, but I need to see you just in case.'

'No.' She shook her head. She wanted to run away again and avoid hearing what was coming.

'I had a lump. Here in my breast,' said Teresa, touching her chest. 'It was a while ago now and I found it early and had it removed. No one made any promises and I've been shit scared, I can tell you. I'm not out of the woods for good but it's been five years now since I went into remission and I finally got the all-clear a few weeks ago.'

Cancer? Remission? All-clear? In just a few words, her mother had run through the most momentous events in her life. Miranda felt as if she'd been shown the most important film of her life, but it had flashed by so fast she couldn't make out a single image. All she knew was that the story had been so shocking that she'd been left spinning out of control.

'You went through all that. All of that worry and pain and you didn't tell me? Oh, Mum!'

'Why would I tell you? After all this time, why would I contact you with that weighing on me? Why would I want to lay it on you? That would really have been cruel.'

Miranda's answer emerged as a howl of pain. She'd devoted herself to a place, a thing, a thing owned by stranger and abandoned her own mother, let her own flesh and blood go through that fear and worry.

'Don't cry like this, for God's sake. It's not the end of the world. They say I've got a good chance of a complete recovery.'

'Mum. Mum. I'm so sorry I never knew!'

'No, don't be sorry. That's a waste of time for both of us now. I'm here now and I plan on being here as long as I can bloody cling to life. But I decided when I got the all-clear from the doc, and when I saw you on the telly yesterday, that now was as good a time as any to make my peace with you, if you'll take it. I thought long and hard about it last night. You looked happy and well and I felt like I shouldn't come crashing into your world, but, in the end, you know I'm a selfish cow so here I am, but I'll understand if you don't want to see me again.'

Miranda shook her head over and over and wiped her nose with the back of her hand like Braden. 'I don't want to ... run away or send ... you ... away,' she said between her sobs. 'I don't want to be without you. Not now.'

Teresa held out her arms. They'd never hugged much, if ever, and the body that had given birth to Miranda felt like a stranger's now, or maybe not totally alien. Something was familiar and sweet to her. 'That's Youth Dew, I remember it.'

Her mother patted her back tentatively. 'I still use it. Your dad once told me he liked it. I'd stolen some off your gran when I went on a date with him. I thought it was soph-isticated.' She laughed but Miranda sobbed her heart out. 'There's snot down my top, Miranda, and this is my best one.'

'Sorry, Mum.'

Her mother shook her head. 'You know I don't think I've seen you cry since I spent Gran's money.'

Miranda wanted to wipe her hand across her nose.

'Here.' Teresa pulled a tissue from her pocket and handed it to her. 'I always have them these days. I've got into enough states lately so I'm never without one.'

Miranda blew her nose noisily.

'I know this has been a shock and you need time to

take it in. We both do and I don't want to outstay my welcome, no matter how long we've been apart. So I'm going to phone Kev and ask him to take me home, but you have my number now and I'll wait for you to be in touch.'

'I will be. I promise.'

'So I can come and see you again and bring Kev?'

'Yes. I'd like to meet him. Have you got an address?'

Teresa smiled. 'I'll text it to you.'

'I'll put it in my phone,' said Miranda, reaching in her pocket. The mobile was switched off and, when she saw the blank screen, she remembered why. She'd wanted to escape. She turned it on and it beeped like crazy.

'You're popular,' said Teresa.

'Yes. I mean no, I'm not. Not any more. Oh shit, I don't seem to be able to make much sense.'

'That makes a change. You always had an answer for me when you were little.'

Her mobile showed nine missed calls and messages from Ronnie and Jago.

Teresa raised her eyebrows. 'Boyfriend?'

'No. Work.'

Teresa halted, her attention caught by something behind Miranda. 'There's a man at the bottom of the cliff. He looks like the bloke that owns your place. I should have known you'd go far.'

Miranda turned round. So, Jago had found her. She wasn't surprised but didn't know why. She felt numb. Maybe she just didn't have the capacity for any more emotions or maybe she didn't want to face what she knew he'd come to tell her. 'I haven't gone anywhere with Jago. He's my boss,' she said.

'Are you sure? If he's only your boss, he's come a long way to find you. Don't go running away from him too.'

'I can't,' said Miranda, finally accepting there was nowhere left to run and no point in trying.

Chapter Thirty-Six

Jago stopped as Teresa passed him. She smiled briefly but carried on walking. Miranda lingered on the sands, like a piece of driftwood, stranded on the vast beach and dwarfed by the great twin rocks. He waited, aching to run to her but waiting for her to move. Just when he thought he might split apart with tension, she started walking back towards him, dragging her feet through the shingle. As she drew closer, he started to walk faster and then to run.

Miranda ran too, tripping over stones, stumbling, tears streaming down her face. She slammed into his chest so hard it took his breath away, and buried her face in his shirt. He covered her hair with his hand, stroking it over and over. 'Miranda, what's wrong? Has she hurt you again? My lovely girl, what is the matter?'

'It's too late. I found Mum and she's been ill and it's almost too late.'

'Almost? Almost too late?'

'She had cancer but she got the all-clear a few weeks ago and she saw my interview on telly.' She glanced up at him. 'Oh God, my boobs were hanging out.'

He chuckled softly. 'No wonder she remembered you.'

'She did remember me and she came for me and I don't want to lose her again.'

'You won't. I'll make sure of that.'

How could he? she thought. He wouldn't be around. But she was too deep in the pleasure and comfort of his embrace to break the moment. She didn't ever want to let him go but she knew she had to. For now she let him hold her, as he breathed into her hair and pressed her to him as if he was another half of the same person.

Finally, her sobs grew quieter and she became aware of the wind on her face, the waves on the beach and the voices of other people on the sands. And Jago.

'How did you find me?' she whispered.

'Ronnie told me you might be here.'

She glanced up at him in surprise. 'She couldn't have known about this place.'

'Ronnie said you talked of a caravan site your gran brought you to a few times and we narrowed it down to this place. I saw the Land Rover in the car park and walked down here.'

'You've been before?'

'Once or twice when I was young. I'm a Cornishman, as you're only too keen to remind me. It's the sort of place I'd choose too, if I wanted to escape and think.'

'I wasn't there at the meeting,' she said. 'I saw your

announcement to the staff. I promised I'd be there to support them and you. I let everyone down and ran away.'

'It doesn't matter. I survived you see, without being lynched. Ronnie hasn't clapped me in irons yet either.'

'It is too late. It's over.'

'You just worry about your mother. There's no need to worry about the Mount.'

'But I do. I have to.'

'Let me do that.'

Her eyes sought his. 'You? You don't want to worry about the place. That's why you're getting rid of it. You said you don't want the burden any more and you just want to be free.'

'Read my lips. I love you and I'm not selling.'

Love. That word again. 'You love me?'

'Yes.' He shook his head trying to look annoyed but his eyes gave everything away. They were full of a light she'd never seen before.

'Yes, I do. But did you not hear the other thing I said?'

'Which one?'

'The thing about not selling the Mount.'

'What? But you wanted to sell. You called the meeting in the Hall to tell everyone about the sale to Southcastle. You've just come from there, haven't you?'

'I have, but I didn't tell them I was selling, I told them I was staying. I couldn't do it in the end. It meant too much to me.'

'I don't understand! Wild horses wouldn't have stopped you from selling. I couldn't stop you . . . ' A horrible thought struck her. 'You haven't decided to stay for my sake? I don't want that. I don't want to force you to take that place on against your will.'

He laughed. 'You could have fooled me. Time was when you'd have chained me to the bloody place like Prometheus and watched the eagles peck my heart out.'

'I wouldn't have done that!'

'Yes, you would.'

'OK. I would, but that was then and this is now. All I wanted was for you to do what gives you peace and happiness.'

'And that's exactly what I have done. Staying at the Mount, making a success of it – an even bigger success – is what I want. Facing the music will make me feel I'm alive, not handing my responsibilities over to some faceless corporation who don't give a shit about anything.'

As she listened, her face ached with smiling and astonishment. 'And you won't regret it?'

'On the contrary, I'm sure I will regret taking on the place, many times, but not now. Not today.'

'And you're not just saying that?'

He threw up his hands in frustration. 'Miranda Marshall, if you tell me what I want one more time, I won't be responsible for my actions, and they won't be noble, I can tell you that.'

The evening sun shone through the great cleft in the rock, the late rays dappling the green pool with sun sparkles. Her heart was so full, she thought it might burst.

'I want stability, I want a heritage, heirs, kids.' He stopped, suddenly embarrassed. 'But maybe you don't want to stay any longer. I'm sorry, but I've been in your house and I've seen the application packs. You really were leaving, weren't you? I didn't think you'd actually go.'

'I couldn't stay and work with Southcastle, Jago. I'm a coward too, in a way. I was ready to leave the people. I needed to make my own way, not stay and be at their rule, doing what I know I believe in. I . . . ' She shook her head, not knowing whether to laugh or cry.

'And now?' he asked. 'Are you staying or going?'

Epilogue

Three months later – Heathrow Airport

Miranda sipped her champagne cocktail and sank back into her seat in the business class lounge at Heathrow Airport. It was her second cocktail of the day and it was barely lunchtime. What was it they said about avoiding alcohol when you were flying?

Sod that, she thought with a smile. She wasn't the one who was about to jet off to San Francisco. She and Jago had travelled to the airport with Lady St Merryn to see her off on her trip to the States and she had now found herself, briefly, alone.

Lady St Merryn had gone to powder her nose and Jago had disappeared off to take a phone call from his lawyers. Southcastle had threatened legal proceedings but nothing had happened yet and his solicitor had assured Jago that they had no grounds to pursue any kind of claim. Nonetheless, Miranda had seen the light burning in his study until the small hours many nights and many times she'd been in there with him, sharing the burden.

If she'd hoped for a quiet life at the Mount, the past months since Jago had arrived there had proved her spectacularly and wonderfully wrong. When they'd returned from meeting her mother, she and Jago had come clean about their relationship and if a few people had raised eyebrows and mentioned the words 'gold' and 'digger', Miranda didn't care. Most of the staff just wanted to get on with their own lives, and once the initial gossip had died down, they'd accepted that she and Jago were an item.

Theo wasn't one them, of course. She'd known he'd take it badly and he did. She'd met him in person to tell him she was seeing Jago and he'd left her in no doubt that he thought she was a fool to get involved. She'd stung at the memory of his bitter words, but bit her tongue and wished him well. Miranda had half hoped Theo would get together with Louise Dixon but knew that was way too much to expect. Instead, Louise was dating one of the paramedics from the ambulance service and Theo had been seeing a crew member of the Porth Ivo lifeboat. Miranda doubted that he would ever reconcile himself to the St Merryns' existence but she had to look after her own relationships.

At least, things were going better with her mother, considering how long they'd been estranged. Jago had met Teresa twice and Miranda had seen her half a dozen times, both in Exeter and at the Mount. Teresa was still healthy and, although their meetings were awkward, they were gradually coming to something like an understanding.

Miranda liked Kev just as her mum had promised; in fact, she got on far better with him than her mother, not that she would ever let on.

She glanced up to see Lady St Merryn making her way back from the ladies' washroom, a colourful galleon sailing through the travellers in the minimalist business lounge. Now that Jago was staying, she was free and happy to continue with her plans to 'see the world' as scheduled.

Jago followed his mother into the lounge and headed straight for the bar. He wore a dark-blue suit and looked heart-stoppingly gorgeous and the bar staff almost fell over themselves to serve him.

'Ah. That's better. One should never get on a flight looking less than glamorous, though God knows what state I'll be in after twelve hours in transit,' said Lady St Merryn, settling down into the leather club chair. Clad in a new kaftan in a leopard-skin print, her hair loose and silvery, she looked years younger and happier than Miranda could ever remember seeing her. Miranda decided to take the plunge.

'Tell me to mind my own business, if you want to, but can I ask a very personal question?'

'Personal? Of course. I'm sure there can be few things you can ask me that I would want to hide from you.'

There was little that Miranda had to hide from Lady St Merryn too. She knew about Miranda's mother. Miranda caught sight of Jago leaning on the bar, his suit trousers tightening over his backside and almost blushed. On the other hand, maybe there was quite a bit she couldn't share with his mother.

'I've wanted to ask you this for a long time but felt it was intruding. Why are you going to the US now? I know your arthritis is painful but you're not ill in any other way, are you?'

Lady St Merryn regarded her with a steely eye and Miranda was afraid she'd said the wrong thing. 'Do I look it?'

'Oh no. Quite the opposite, in fact, you look really well, but I have been worried about you and, when I first found out you were going to San Francisco, I'll admit it wasn't what I expected.'

'It wasn't what *I* expected until last Christmas but you needn't be worried about me. I'm going to see a very old and very dear friend.' She smiled. 'I think you know that my marriage to Patrick was not a happy one. Oh, don't try to deny, you knew. Everyone at the Mount is well aware he had mistresses all over the place. In fact, he dropped dead outside the flat of one of them, poor girl. He left her without a penny, you know, but that's the way it went with Patrick. I'm not sure he ever loved anyone, except himself and possibly his son, though he made it his mission never to show it. Even before I produced Jago, we'd certainly ceased to love each other.'

It was upsetting to hear; mostly, Miranda thought, for the misery and unhappiness Lady St Merryn must have endured. But there was no point pretending she hadn't heard the rumours. She wouldn't patronise Lady St Merryn like that. 'I'm sorry you weren't happy,' she said.

'Don't be too sorry for me, because I'm not blameless in the whole debacle, either. After the initial euphoria of the wedding, I quickly realised that Patrick had other women and always would. I put up with it because that's what wives did back then.'

The loud pop of a cork drew their eyes to the bar. Jago laughed with the bar staff as they popped the cork of a bottle of champagne. Lady St Merryn's hand flew to her mouth and, for a horrible moment, Miranda thought she might be about to burst into tears.

'Please go on, Jago can't hear,' said Miranda gently.

'A few years after we'd been married I still hadn't produced an heir, let alone a spare and Patrick made it clear that I wasn't doing my duty and had no function in our marriage. He went to the Far East – "on business" – he said and told me to get myself sorted out, whatever that meant. I needed a break so I decided to visit an old school friend in San Francisco. She was married to a professor at the university there and I stayed with them for a few weeks. The professor had a research student, an Italian-American boy called David Minnelli. He was so beautiful.'

Miranda was transfixed by Jago's rear view, at the dark, almost black, hair brushing his suit collar, at the olive-skinned hand holding out notes to the barman. He was a beautiful boy too.

'You're not saying?'

St Merryn gave a small secretive smile. 'I'm not saying anything. I was only in SF for a few weeks. When I got home, Patrick was back at the Mount and insisting on his conjugal rights again. In those days, he was legally entitled to take them so I lay back, gritted my teeth and thought of England. Nine months later, I obliged by producing Jago. You have to admit, I went beyond the call of duty.'

'Does Jago know about David?'

'He knows that I met a man on holiday years ago and that we've been in touch, but what conclusions he's come to, I don't know. It's of no relevance in the long run. Jago might be David's or he might be Patrick's. I have no desire to know and it doesn't matter. He's my flesh and blood and he's the rightful person – with you, my dear – to take over the Mount. I tell myself this: over the centuries, how many of the St Merryn heirs have truly known their parentage with any certainty?'

And, Miranda thought, how many St Merryn heirs had actually been fathered by the owners of the Mount, all unrecognised because they'd been born out of wedlock? Being a parent had very little to do with blood or birth, but what you did and felt.

'I won't say anything to him.'

'Jago probably worked out long ago that things aren't quite what they seem. I think it's been the least of his concerns in the past few years and the least of them now.'

'But he knows you're going to meet this man again?'

'Oh, yes. I've been perfectly open about that and he's happy for me. David is a professor now and he's been a widower for the past two years. My friend emailed to tell me at Christmas and said he wanted to get in touch. As soon as Jago agreed to come home, I didn't hesitate. I'd hoped he would take over at the Mount and I must admit I was horrified that he wanted to sell, but I just kept on crossing my fingers and trusting that the place would work its magic on him.'

Thank goodness it did, thought Miranda, shuddering to

think how close she'd come to losing everything. 'So have you seen David since your . . . holiday?'

'My affair, dear. Call a spade a spade. You don't have to be coy. We were at it like rabbits for the whole three weeks and I have seen him, if not in the flesh. I'm not as inept on the computer as I let Jago believe. We've talked on Skype and he's still a beautiful man. I feel the same about him as I always did, and he says he feels the same about me. I don't have forever at my time of life but I hope I have long enough. I'm not prepared to waste a single moment from now on.'

Lady St Merryn's face was luminous, her eyes a young woman of twenty-one, full of hope and excitement and passion. Miranda did something she'd never done before. She put her arms around her hugged her. 'I'm so happy for you, Lady St Merryn.'

Lady St Merryn patted her back warmly. 'My dear, if you're going to marry Jago, you'll really have to stop calling me Lady St Merryn. Hilary will be perfectly acceptable.'

Hilary? Miranda didn't think she could and as for marrying Jago . . . 'He hasn't actually asked me yet,' she said.

'Oh he will, I know him. He's not like his father. He's a serial monogamist, which is his downfall. He cares too much about people and that's why he will get hurt and already has been. It's also why he's ten times the man his father was, or perhaps . . . that's why he is the good man he is.'

She took Miranda's hand in hers and, touched, Miranda didn't know how to reply.

'Will you come back and see us at the Mount, um, Hilary?' she asked, the name feeling very strange on her lips.

'Of course, and you will come and see David and me?'

'Try to stop us.'

Moments later, Jago stood in front of their table, with a tray of glasses, looking at them with amusement and a definite trace of suspicion.

'What am I missing?' he asked.

'Nothing,' said Miranda.

Hilary took a flute from the tray and toasted them both. 'Champagne, excellent. To all our futures, the Mount included.'

A few hours later, with Hilary soaring somewhere over the Atlantic, Jago stowed Miranda's overnight bag in the rack of their couchette on the night train back to Penzance. Miranda watched the lights of London slip by as the train pulled out of Paddington. She thought she might go pop with happiness. 'It's going to be a long journey back to Cornwall,' she said as Jago took off his jacket and hung it on the door.

He slipped his arms around her waist and buried his face in her hair. 'And this is a very small cabin. So you can't get away from me.'

'I don't want to,' she whispered. 'Not ever.'

'In that case, Miss Whiplash, there's something I've been meaning to ask you.'

Do you love contemporary romance?

Want the chance to hear news about your favourite authors (and the chance to win free books)?

Kristen Ashley
Ashley Herring Blake
Meg Cabot
Olivia Dade
Rosie Danan
J. Daniels
Farah Heron
Talia Hibbert
Sarah Hogle
Helena Hunting
Abby Jimenez
Elle Kennedy
Christina Lauren
Alisha Rai
Sally Thorne
Lacie Waldon
Denise Williams
Meryl Wilsner
Samantha Young

Then visit the Piatkus website
www.yourswithlove.co.uk

And follow us on Facebook and Instagram
www.facebook.com/yourswithlovex | @yourswithlovex

PIATKUS